Wrapped In a Ribbon of Glass

a novel

Katherine L. Phelps

Wrapped In a Ribbon of Glass
ISBN: Softcover 978-1-960326-51-5
Copyright © 2024 by Katherine L. Phelps

Parson's Porch Books is an imprint of Parson's Porch *&* Company (PP*&*C) in Cleveland, Tennessee. PP*&*C is a self-funded charity which earns money by publishing books of noted authors, representing all genres. Its face and voice is **David Russell Tullock** who you can contact at: dtullock@parsonsporch.com.

Parson's Porch *&* Company *turns books into bread & milk* by sharing its profits with the poor.

www.parsonsporch.com

Wrapped In a Ribbon of Glass

Dedications

My husband, Keith: You've seen me kick this book around for years. Thank you for hanging with me from beginning to end. Your love is truly my anchor. You have jumped on the proverbial bandwagon of every idiotic idea I have ever had. Those who know me will attest to this as they shake their heads. Thank you for believing in me when those idiotic ideas panned out (ha, ha, ha) and especially when they did not (oh no). Because of this and so much else my love for you has never diminished.

My Daughter Sarah: I never wanted to be anything but your mom. I was lucky to have such a sensitive daughter who has cared for me and who has always tried to look out for me. I love you until the day after forever.

My brothers Greg and Rick: Greg, you gave me the encouragement I needed to push this to completion. Rick, your efforts to be the glue that was Mom have kept us all grounded and in touch regularly. I love you both.

To all the dogs we were lucky enough to have in our lives. Each one brought immeasurable love and joy to us. These include Duchess (Beagle), Natasha (Beagle), Taylor (Rotty), Kendall (Rotty), Gallo (Rotty), Nikki (Rotty), Kharma (Rotty), Bear (Rotty), Carly (Rotty), Pinto (Bogle), and Sadie (Coonhound).

To all the foster dogs who have passed through our doors. We loved you all and are so glad you found your forever homes.

To Katie Fine: Katie runs Field of Dreams, our local animal rescue. For more than ten years she has worked tirelessly and selflessly to help hundreds of dogs and cats find their forever homes. There is no one I admire more.

Dear Reader: Consider being a foster home for a displaced, abused, or abandoned animal. Most rescuers rely on foster homes to help these animals. Without foster homes, these animals are left alone with no one to stop the pain of abuse or starvation. They need your love. There are enough of us out there to make a difference.

CHAPTER ONE

(1994)

My mother is dead, and I am plagued by two conflicting feelings. One is the abject grief of knowing I will never see or speak to her again. Two is the freedom I feel now that all my decisions will not be put under a microscope and critically picked apart. Death's finality haunts me.

I lean against the rental car and admire the acres of dense marsh grass that stretches out before me. The relentless heat and humidity of the South grips the air. The swaying greenery lulls me, as a welcomed breeze gently sweeps the long grasses, and whispers escape from their depths. The smell of salty air mixed with a faint paper-mill stench recalls youthful summers spent along the canals and inlets of the Carolina coast. Fifteen years ago, I fled north to the land of corn and dairy cows. I have rarely been back before this. My list of excuses got longer as time went on and the death of my mother was catalyst enough to make me return.

We buried my mother in early March when the trees were still barren, and winter's gloom seemed endless. When they lowered her coffin, the moan of the machinery shattered the ceremony and made the finality of her death too crisp. Nearby, two black men casually leaned on their shovels and waited for their call to work. The hollow sound as clods of earth hit the top of her coffin felt like a slap to my face. With each splatter of dirt, more of my questions went unanswered. So much blame was left to heap upon her shoulders and so much guilt for the pile I'd already put there. Now she would never be able to help me unlock my tormented dreams. Maybe I was a secretly pleased to lose the key. The truth can be a nightmare to those left awake. This is my first time back since the funeral.

My siblings and I agreed to return in the summer to put her affairs in order and pack up the house. I get back in my car. I quickly start the engine and shove the air conditioning up to maximum, letting out a sigh of relief when the cool air blasts over my body. Reluctantly I pull back onto the small two-lane blacktop that shimmers with the midday heat and head toward my mother's house.

Her house is a low-slung, sprawling, plantation-like structure on the canal side of Pilot's Island. Profuse vegetation along the road nearly hides the entrance. The yard, however, consists primarily of gray sand covered with pine needles. Ancient tree roots shove their way menacingly into the ruts of the driveway, poking through like the shiny dark elbows of a large underground troll. The house is palatial and breathtaking at first glance. I had almost forgotten the grandeur of southern architecture. But now I notice the roof is in desperate need of new shingles and ribbons of white paint have peeled loose under the harsh island elements. The wraparound porch gives a panoramic view of the lush lowlands. The porch was the main reason Mom purchased this house twenty-three years ago. She used the insurance money after my father's truck missed a sharp turn on a muddy logging road, ran off a cliff, and exploded into flames when it landed in the ravine below.

When I pull into the sandy drive, the smell of pine straw hangs heavily in the air. My brother, Wilkes Randolph Wheeler, the fourth, has strategically parked his rented Lexus in the shade, the front windows cracked an equal number of inches on both sides.

Wilkes sits on the porch with a glass of iced tea pressed against his forehead. He barely opens his eyes as I climb the wooden steps. He smiles weakly and mutters an unintelligible greeting.

The porch floorboards are wide strips of pine bowed a bit in the middle with age. The original gray paint is barely visible, confining itself to the edges and corners. I remember going to my mother's side for advice or confession as she sat on this porch in her favorite rocking chair. However, she either couldn't or wouldn't empathize with the anguish of my many teenage dilemmas. When I left home, I quit asking for her love and acceptance, although silently I continued the quest. As I stand here on the porch staring at the wooden rocker where she spent much of her time, I must accept that I failed to secure either.

Wilkes and I watch a boat full of noisy tourists float back from the ocean on the Intracoastal Waterway with the late afternoon tide. As the wind picks up, the marsh grass along the waterway makes a soothing taffeta rustling sound. I smell an approaching storm in the humid air.

"So how are you, dear sister?" Wilkes doesn't wait for an answer. "Dang, it's hot! Don't you think it's hot?" He runs the iced tea glass across his cheek. "It's just too dang hot!"

I laugh, remembering what a wimp he always was about the heat. "You're right, Wilkes; it is too dang hot!" I take in the magnificent view of the Intracoastal Waterway from the porch. I walk down to the perimeter and look down at the surrounding ground. With the tide starting to move out, the small fiddler crabs scamper from one muddy crater to the next, their single large claw making them appear cartoonish. The suddenness and swiftness of their movement are mesmerizing.

I remember, in the barbarism of children, how my brothers and sister and I would equip these poor one-armed creatures with small firecrackers. They would innocently grab the colorful sticks and swish hurriedly down their holes, only to be blown to smithereens a second later. I feel criminal now; the guilt of childhood visited upon the adult.

With an effort, Wilkes noisily pushes himself out of his rocking chair and sets his glass on the windowsill behind him. He is tall with a thick head of dark hair, kept long, and brushed neatly back from his face. He is still lean and handsome even at forty-three. I notice though that he's developed a hint of middle-aged flab on his waistline, and there are deep lines around his eyes as if he'd spent a lifetime squinting into the sun instead of stuck behind a desk. He is still dressed in his suit but has neatly folded his jacket over the back of the mom's rocker. As he stands, he adjusts his loosened tie and then fingers the undone buttons at the top of his shirt as though he feels uncomfortable being so casual. His hands drop to his sides as he studies me closely for the first time. "Well, Ms. Hannah Hoskins, you don't look too bad for a thirty-eight-year-old, recently divorced woman."

"That's Dr. Hannah Wheeler to you, dear brother. Besides I'm only thirty-five."

Wilkes raises one well-groomed eyebrow and says nothing.

"All right, thirty-six. But that's as far as I'm willing to go."

"So, you've decided to take back your maiden name. But, Dr. Wheeler, aren't you afraid everyone will think you're a real doctor?"

"I am a real doctor."

"I don't think your Ph.D. is going to save anyone's life, dear sister. Oh, excuse me, that's Dr. Sister." Wilkes bows formally clicking his heels together. The smirk on his face tells me how genuinely he relishes the role of an older brother. "What if someone comes to you with a broken arm? What are you going to do, think them into getting better?"

I try to suppress a grin. "There has to be a smart aleck in every family, counselor," I say. Exasperated with his teasing I put my hands on my hips and say with mock indignation: "Why don't you shut up, esquire boy, and mind your own business?"

He smiles and then winks at me. "Oh, that's a snappy comeback. Is that what you say to your students at the University when they ask you a question?"

"My students know better than to make fun of their professor," I reply evenly.

Wilkes wisely changes the subject. "Where's my beautiful niece?"

"Carly's with her father."

"You left old Jack in charge? That should be interesting."

"Carly's nearly seven and besides, Jack's not so bad," I begin defensively. I'm surprised at how smoothly old family patterns ease back into place. I stop myself from defending my cheating ex-husband. "It's good to see you too, Wilkes."

He hugs me and then sits back down. "Speaking of family, Dr. Hannah Wheeler, your sister Madeline was out here earlier, and she made some tea. It's sweetened with that artificial junk, but it doesn't taste too bad."

I sit in the rocking chair next to him. "When is Maddie coming back?"

He gently pushes his rocker back and forth. "She's staying at her place in town tonight. Tomorrow morning, she said she'd pick up Kyle at the airport and then meet us at the lawyer's office."

"Do you want to start sorting through Mom's things tonight or wait for Maddie and Kyle?"

"Let's wait," he says in a subdued tone.

I look at him. "This is hard for you, isn't it?"

"Yeah, especially now with the merger about to take place and then all this to deal with." Wilkes crosses his arms which are neatly encased in a custom-made long-sleeved shirt, undoubtedly the culprit of his discomfort.

I successfully resist giving clothing advice. "To tell you the truth, I'm surprised you came."

He leans the chair back on its rockers. "You know, I almost didn't, but felt I owed you and the others a duty to at least show-up. Besides," he brightens, "there may be some stuff of Mom's I'd like to have." He suddenly lets the chair loose and it rocks forward and he excitedly swivels around to face me. "Hannah, do you remember that Japanese sword Dad brought home from World War Two? It had all the places his destroyer went engraved on the scabbard. If that's still around, I'd like to have it."

Before I can answer he's already gone on. "Mom had a couple of nice jewelry pieces I want to have appraised. I also contacted a real estate agent about selling the house. Beach property, even canal-side property, is going for a hefty price these days. They'll probably have to bulldoze the house, but the land is worth quite a bit."

My stomach churns as my worst fears teeter on the brink of reality. I knew Wilkes was going to want to do everything his way. I make a silent prayer that we all come out of this speaking to one another.

He stands and stretches. "What time are we meeting with Mom's lawyer tomorrow to go over the will?"

I detect an edge to his voice. "One o'clock."

"What's his name, anyway?" He struggles to recall this piece of trivia. "You know that old geezer. Calumet or something like that, I know it starts with a C."

"Bartholomew," I interject.

He turns to face me. "Yeah, Mr. Bartholomew. Is he still alive?"

"Yes, and he's still Mom's lawyer. We're to meet with him at his office downtown."

"Good God, how old is that guy?" Wilkes muses. "I know this is silly, but as a kid, I thought he looked like a lizard who'd scarfed down a big fat bug and I was afraid I'd be next."

I slip off my shoes and wiggle my toes. "He is sort of creepy," I agree, "but harmless. He's semi-retired now but keeps seeing long-time clients a few days a week. I talked with him on the phone. He sounds the same, like he just ran up a flight of stairs, always out of breath. You remember?"

"Yeah," Wilkes answers distractedly. "Hannah, do you think there are any surprises in Mom's will?" He watches my face closely.

I shrug my shoulders and steer the conversation back to safer ground. "What's going on with the merger?"

"Well, you know how we lawyers can be." He sits back down. "Take any of us as individuals, and we're great people, but as a group, we're pond scum. Now you put a whole pack of us together and, well, we're talking about heavy-duty, professional pompousness a regular bunch of contemptible butt heads, if you'll excuse my French."

"Where does that leave you?"

He grins at me. "That would make me the sediment in the pond full of scum." Then he leans back, grabs his tea glass off the windowsill, and swallows the rest of its contents.

My curiosity gets the better of me. "Is the merger going to go through?"

"I think so, and I suppose we'll be glad in the end." He gets out of the rocker and looks out at the threatening clouds moving in from the ocean.

"But you're worried anyway."

"Of course, I am," he laughs. He gets quiet, then turns to face me. "You know, Sis, at first, I was all for this merger. For Christ's sake, I was the one who drafted the initial proposal." He swirls the melting ice cubes in his glass. "But I got to tell you, Hannah, I'm having second thoughts."

"What do you mean? Why?"

"I'm not sure what I mean. I guess I'm worried about the details of the merger contract." He shrugs his shoulders, then bends down, kisses the top of my head, and says, "I'm glad you're here."

Wilkes then dumps the last of his melted ice over the porch railing, opens the screen door to the kitchen, and heads into the dark confines of the house.

CHAPTER TWO

She hears the creak of someone moving down the hallway. The floorboard on the right by the linen closet groans as the weight of a footstep pushes the loose floorboard into place. The sound puts her on immediate alert. Instead of running, her eyes stay fixated on the knob as it turns, and the door clicks open. The hall light floods the doorway. He steps into the opening. His bulk fills the entrance and blocks the light like an eclipse, making it impossible to see his face. She clutches her quilt in both hands and bites her lip before her scream becomes her enemy. She holds her breath, wishing herself invisible. He waits motionless. Finally, her body takes over and she nearly gulps the air down as it rushes involuntarily into her oxygen-starved lungs. His head turns toward the noise. Her fear floods the room. She mentally searches the room for an escape. There is none.

He doesn't speak, but closes the door tightly behind him, plunging the room back into total darkness. He doesn't seem to be in any hurry, as if he knows she has nowhere to go. She hears his feet on the floor, the whisper of his shoes against the carpet. She scrunches up in the corner against the wall as she tries to make herself smaller. He stops as he hears her scramble for a safe place. She can almost feel him smile in the dark. The suspense is unbearable. Like when playing a game of hide and seek, she has an impulse to scream out 'here I am!' if only to have the waiting be over. His arm snakes out and grabs her shoulder in an iron grip.

The scream awakens me. I open my eyes in a panic. I look around the room, unfamiliar with the surroundings. My heart beats wildly, sweat covers my face. I realize the scream is mine. I remember I'm at my mother's house. No one can hurt me; I'm safe here. I catch my breath and listen for Wilkes. I hear no movement from his room next door. I mentally thank him for being a sound sleeper. I know I can't go back to sleep, or the nightmare will pick up where it left off, or worse, start over from the beginning; familiarity never lessens the terror. The only cure is to get up. I slip out of bed and turn on every light in the room. After I wash my face and hands, I read quietly for a few hours and try not to think about anything but the contents of my novel. The light of day and the need for coffee finally send me to the kitchen.

Wilkes isn't up and about yet. Not too surprising, when I find nearly all the beer in the refrigerator is gone. The coffee is wonderful, heavily laced with chicory, a unique Southern custom I had forgotten and covet more with each sip. I take a large mug out onto the porch to watch the incoming tide. The sun has already brushed off its early morning blush. I will have to move fast if I want to work in my side trip before going to the lawyer's office. For the moment, however, I plan to sit quietly on the porch swing with my legs curled underneath me, my white cotton robe wrapped loosely around my shoulders, and think of nothing but the wonderful sounds and smells of the Carolina coast.

After a few minutes, Wilkes interrupts my peace, noiselessly appearing on the porch. He is barefoot, wearing only a colorful pair of boxer shorts, his upper body the product of a good health spa. I had expected hand-woven silk pajamas and custom-crafted slippers.

Wilkes catches me staring. "Hey, it's too hot to wear pajamas on this God-forsaken Island," he says as though he heard me criticize his selection in sleep wear. "How did Mom stand it here without air conditioning? I don't know how anyone could get any sleep when it's so hot. Oh good, you made coffee. Is there any left?" His voice has a desperate quality only a hangover can evoke.

"It's on the counter in the kitchen."
He hesitates, assuming I will fetch him some. When I turn my attention back to the waterway, he grunts and reluctantly goes inside. He lets the kitchen screen door bang shut behind him and then cusses the same door as it amplifies the throbbing in his head. I hear rummaging and cursing inside. "Where's the cream?"

I try to suppress the beginnings of a smile. "I don't think there is any," I holler back, "but you might try the refrigerator, or maybe there's some instant in the pantry."

After nearly five minutes, Wilkes reappears with a cup of coffee cradled almost reverently in his well-manicured hands. He tries not to spill it as he lowers himself into one of the rocking chairs near the center of the porch.

I feel sorry for him and his obvious discomfort. "Did you find any cream?"

"If that's what you call that white powdery crap." He slowly lowers his lips to his coffee mug.

"OOOOHH, damn that's hot!" He jumps and spills some into his lap. "ARGH!" He leaps from the rocker and then shoots me a venomous look that quickly douses my amusement.

"Jesus, I burned my tongue." He holds the wounded appendage between his fingers and sounds like Elmer Fudd. "I thon't belwieve ththis," he lets go of his tongue and wipes the coffee spill from his boxer shorts. When he looks over at me again, I quickly avert my gaze and bite the inside of my cheek to keep from smirking. "You better hope your face doesn't freeze like that," he warns.

I grin. He winks at me as he lowers himself back into the rocker without further incident. For a few moments, we sip our coffee in silence and listen to the sounds of the late morning. I had forgotten how peaceful it is here.

Wilkes sets his near-empty coffee cup on the floorboards next to his rocker. "Why is Maddie going all the way out to the airport to pick up Kyle when it would be much easier if he took a taxi?"

"It's called Southern Hospitality," I answer.

Growing up, Maddie and I had not been very close. She was the only relative living close by and must have witnessed firsthand Mom's decline and eventual death, which meant she had to make the funeral arrangements. I could only imagine Maddie's pain as she looked at coffins and compared prices, alternating between the crisp professional bank officer and the grieving daughter. I probably hadn't thanked Maddie enough for all she'd done or for all she went through emotionally to get it accomplished.

While I saw the freedom of no longer having Mom hold my dreams and desires hostage or having her limit my life with endless worries and misgivings, I also knew how much I would miss the patter of her life. While I rarely came back to visit her, she made frequent trips to visit me and Carly.

To take care of Mom's belongings, we return, one by one, like criminals tiptoeing back to the scene of the crime.

"I'm going in to get dressed," I tell Wilkes as I move past him and into the house.

"We don't have to be there for another two hours."

"I have a small errand to run before I head into town. I'll meet you there." I hurry inside before he starts to ask me questions.

"Well, at least tell me where you hid the damn aspirin," he yells after me.

I want to visit Mom's grave alone before I go to the lawyer's office and dissect her life on water-marked bond paper. The cemetery is behind a small chapel appropriately named Island Methodist. The church has only fifty or so members, but the graveyard dates to the mid-1800s. Mom always admired the quaintness of the church and the beauty of the overhanging trees with their elegant Spanish moss. I haven't been here since the funeral. Her grave is along the back, bordering an ancient brick wall that keeps the surrounding acres of pine forest at bay. The headstone is now in place; pink granite polished to a high gloss with her name and proper dates engraved in block letters and an angel etched at the top. Mom had always liked angels and used to tell us kids about how everybody had a guardian angel looking out for them.

When I was seven years old, I told Mom I had seen my guardian angel, and she was a Negro. I got a hell of a beating and was locked in my room with no supper. I never saw my guardian angel again.

Next to my mother's tombstone, my father's looks worn, the marble sun-bleached. But the name and dates are still chisel-sharp. The inscription has no embellishments; nothing to say what happened, or what didn't.

I still harbor a child-like panic of being grabbed by the ankle, so I sidestep his grave. I hate that I'm so easily spooked.

I lower myself onto the soft grass, ignoring the slight dampness from yesterday's rainstorm. "How ya doin' Mom?" I ask out loud. A lump begins to form in the middle of my throat. "I miss having you around, you know that?" I start to feel little chinks in my composure. I absently pull a few weeds and toss them over the wall into the overgrowth. I sit quietly and absorb how much I miss her, even though nothing was ever easy between us. One month we would be the best of friends and the next, estranged. I couldn't decide if it was better, she'd died during one of our friendlier periods. I would miss her more, but at least we left less unsaid. I lay my cheek on the soft mound and close my eyes. I hear the first sound of thunder faintly rage in the distance. "I love you, Mom," I whisper to her. I lie still, not waiting for an answer, but for the crushing heartache to dissipate before I must go about the business of putting her legally to rest.

Bartholomew's law office is in a squat three-story brick building in downtown Georgetown. The building was constructed in the 1950s and refurbished in the mid-seventies; not much has been done since. The smell of stale cigarettes permeates the halls, and the worn and tattered carpeting desperately needs replacing. The walls have pine paneling wainscot. Sea-green paint shines dimly from above the wainscoting. Under the flicker of fluorescent lights, the effect is ghastly. To make the imagery complete, sections of the paneling bulge slightly from the wall as though something hideous from the other side is trying to escape. I rein in my imagination and take the elevator to the third floor.

The carpet on this floor is newer, and the frightful paneling is nowhere in sight. A nondescript beige wallpaper covers the walls. The doors are wood with opaque glass inset in the top half; the names of each resident are stenciled in gold letters. I passed the offices of a dentist, an ophthalmologist, and an accountant before coming to the law offices of Bartholomew, Hughes & Radcliff. I open the door and go into the reception area. Wilkes and Maddie are seated next to each other, deep in conversation.

Wilkes looks relieved to see me. "What took you so long? You left before I did and still, I beat you here." He has on a light blue summer suit, the pants crease neat and crisp. He's combed and moussed his hair just so. You'd never know that a few short hours ago he was cradling his head from the aftermath of too many beers. I admire his powers of reclaim.

"I told you that I had a little errand to run. I didn't mean to worry you." I bend to kiss my sister on the cheek and effectively cut off Wilkes's questions. "How are you, Maddie?" She stands to hug and kiss me in return. She has on a daffodil yellow pantsuit. She's pulled her honey-colored hair back into a taut ponytail accentuated with a yellow bow. Her bangs hang loosely in the front. She is the picture of a quintessential southern working woman.

I stand back and hold her at arm's length "You look wonderful, Maddie." The only other person in the room is a well-dressed, middle-aged woman reading a magazine in the far corner. "Where's Kyle?"

Maddie retakes her seat next to Wilkes, "Kyle will be back in a minute."

As if on cue, Kyle walks into the reception area from somewhere beyond the inner sanctum and past the well-groomed receptionist who has, until now, ignored us. His hair is a darker blonde than I remember, now cropped close to his head. He has two small gold-hoop earrings sticking through his right ear. He looks awkward in his dress shirt with his tie askew. I love him for making the gesture, for trying to dress appropriately for our sakes, and out of respect for Mom. He looks at me sheepishly as he awkwardly fingers his earrings, a crooked smile on his face.

For the funeral, Kyle had borrowed a suit from Wilkes, who couldn't believe that Kyle didn't own a single suit. By the end of the weekend, the thought had turned into a mantra with Wilkes shaking his head and saying, "I just can't believe. . ." and whoever was in earshot would chime in with ". . . that Kyle doesn't own a suit."

The earrings are new. I hug him and kiss him lightly on the cheek. He's eight years younger than me, the baby of the family. He looks tanned and healthy. His life as a musician-wannabe in California agrees with him. I feel a pang of jealousy at his carefree existence. He seems genuinely happy to see me and gives me an unexpected second hug that makes me spill my purse.

We nearly bump heads as we both stoop to rescue my scattered belongings. I stand and straighten my skirt. "Do they know we're here?"

The woman behind the counter answers: "Yes ma'am, I've notified Mr. Bartholomew that all of you are here. It won't be but a few more minutes."

As promised, a few moments later the outer door opens and a young woman in an expensive suit comes out into the foyer and introduces herself as Ms. Logan, Mr. Bartholomew's assistant.

She has a crisp New England accent. "Would you follow me, please?"

We all follow her silently into a small meeting room with a bank of windows on one side. Dingy white Venetian blinds cover the windows, but they are slanted open, allowing a view of the downtown business district. From a three-story height, the view is not overly impressive. Well-padded armchairs surround an rectangular walnut table. On the south side of the room under the windows is a matching walnut credenza with coffee and other beverages.

"Can I get you anything?" Ms. Logan asks.

Wilkes starts to speak up, but Maddie cuts him off. "We'll be fine. I'm sure we can help ourselves."

"Very well," Ms. Logan hesitates, "if there's nothing else, Mr. Bartholomew will be in shortly." She quietly backs out of the room and shuts the door behind her.

"That was nice," Wilkes declares as he seats himself in the chair close to the door. "Maybe I wanted some coffee, did you ever think of that?" He petulantly straightens his suit, then runs his fingers down the pants crease of his crossed leg.

"Well, then get it yourself, crippled boy," Maddie shoots back.

"Oooh, getting a bit snippy, aren't we?"

She takes a seat on the other side of the table, her body language dismissing him. "Hey, I just call 'em like I see 'em."

"Party pooper," he taunts.

I'm not sure if they're angry at each other or not. "Come on, everyone, we shouldn't squabble. We don't get many chances to all be together."

Maddie looks annoyed. "Hannah, we're here to read Mom's will. You don't always have to play the peacekeeper?"

"OK, OK, I get the idea." I take a seat two chairs down from Wilkes.

Kyle takes a chair along the wall behind me. "What do you think that was all about?" Kyle whispers to me over my shoulder as though the others are deaf.

"I'm sure I don't know," I whisper back loudly.

We all wait in strained silence.

Suddenly Wilkes swivels around to face me. "Where did you go before you came here?"

His gaze is steady and demanding.

"I went to visit Mom and Dad's graves."

"Why?" he asks.

His question puts me on the defensive. "Well, since I only come here every decade or so, it seems I should make the effort. What's your excuse?" I deflect and parry my old nemesis guilt.

Maddie smells a fight in the air and is moody enough to want to fan the flames. "When was the last time you visited Mom and Dad's graves, Wilkes?"

He's suddenly speechless.

I lean forward and place my hand softly on his arm. "What is it?" I whisper. This is an old question. Wilkes has always been at odds over the death of our father. For years I thought being the oldest son and cut adrift when he needed the most guidance explained his behavior. But it's more than that. It's something he's avoided talking about for nearly a quarter of a century. But a mystery lies buried not only with the remains of my father but in the depths of Wilkes's soul.

Before he can answer me, the door opens and Mr. Bartholomew steps in, followed by Ms. Logan. Mr. Bartholomew takes the chair at the head of the conference table and places a briefcase in front of him. Ms. Logan moves a chair a discreet distance behind him and takes a seat.

Bartholomew speaks in his characteristic breathless voice. "May I presume you've all met my assistant, Ms. Logan? Ms. Logan is from Connecticut and is a second-year law student at Carolina. Her grandfather is an old friend of mine. I hope none of you object, but I've asked Ms. Logan to accompany me today to help take some notes." He doesn't wait for a response.

"My, how all of you have grown," he observes. "Why, I remember. . .. Well, I won't get started down that path, we're here to discuss your mother's estate. I'm sure you're all eager to get this over with as quickly as possible."

Mr. Bartholomew has hardly changed from what I remember. Less hair perhaps, his hands are more gnarled and shake a little as he opens his briefcase, takes out a stack of papers, and places them on the desk. Ms. Logan removes the briefcase, resumes her seat, and waits quietly with her pen hovering over a yellow legal pad.

"Your mother was a very thorough lady." Mr. Bartholomew says as he sorts through his papers in search of the right document. "To tell you the truth, I never thought I'd see the day when I'd outlive Elizabeth Wheeler. She was always so healthy and vibrant. I can't believe she died of a heart attack. Why, the last time I saw her, which I believe was right after Christmas, it was about three months before she passed on, God rest her soul. She was shopping in town, taking advantage of the various after-Christmas specials. She stopped for lunch at Ruby's Cafe, where I was wining and dining a potential client, my principal duty since semi-retiring."

Wilkes impatiently uncrosses his legs and lets out an exasperated sigh.

Bartholomew continues, unaware of Wilkes's impatience. "She dropped by our table weighted down with packages. I asked her to join us, but she said she was meeting someone. When I got ready to leave, she was still sitting alone. I offered to keep her company, but she wouldn't hear of it. She said her friend would be along soon enough, and that she didn't mind waiting alone. I believed her. Elizabeth always could entertain herself." He muses, as he recalls the incident and forgets the immediate task at hand.

Wilkes anxiously gets him back on track. "Mr. Bartholomew, while we all appreciate your long-time friendship with our mother, we still must go through and empty her house. Could we please dispense with the various pleasantries and get on with the business at hand?"

"Of course, Wilkes, please excuse a sentimental old fool. My wife, God rest her soul, always said I could make stubbing my toe into a half day of storytelling." Bartholomew clears his throat and runs his tongue slowly over his parched lips. "The will is straightforward. It details how she wanted the property divided and who gets what. There are some specific bequests that your mother made that I will also read aloud." Bartholomew puts on his reading glasses and begins. "The house, land, and all the possessions, except the few named herein or others that individual family members may wish to keep, are to be sold and the proceeds to be split evenly among the four children with the following exceptions: I want Kyle to have the grandfather clock in the main hallway, the mahogany dining room set and first pick of any of the antique furniture in the house. Maddie is to have my jewelry and Hannah is to have Grandma Wheeler's jewelry and silver. Wilkes is not to have any items from inside the house; he knows the reason." Bartholomew reads without emotion.

There is silence around the table.

Wilkes slaps the tabletop with his hand. "What the hell is that supposed to mean?"

"I believe your mother thought you would know the reason for her actions as she states in the will," Bartholomew says, unruffled by the outburst.

Ms. Logan, who has dropped her pen, is nearly on her hands and knees as she tries to retrieve it from under her chair.

"Well, I don't know!" Wilkes barks at Bartholomew. He turns to all of us, a dog on the attack. "Do you know what the hell she means?"

We all shake our heads, and none of us dares to speak.

Wilkes flops back in his seat. "Well, for God's sake, Bartholomew, you drew up the damn will, what was on her mind?"

Bartholomew takes off his reading glasses. "I would never presume to guess what a client means," he says. "As a lawyer yourself, Wilkes, you must understand how these things work."

Wilkes leans forward in his chair; his voice drops to a growl. "Well, I don't do wills and estates, so why don't you tell me what she was up to, or you're going to find yourself in court."

"Wilkes," Bartholomew says in a tone a father would use to address an errant child, "even if I knew what your mother was, as you put it, up to, and I'm not saying I do, I would not be able to share that information. You of all people should know that."

There was absolute quiet all around the table.

I break the agonizing silence. "Would you finish reading the will, Mr. Bartholomew?"

Bartholomew puts his reading glasses back on. "Your mother left several additional bequests. First, to Martha O'Donnell who took such loving care of me for so many years, I leave the sum of fifty thousand dollars. Second, to Fred McFarland, who faithfully did his best to take care of the house and grounds until his retirement, I leave thirty thousand dollars." Bartholomew reads in a monotone voice from the document before him.

Wilkes's voice is low, his words almost too precisely spoken. "Excuse me, but could I cut into this little tribute fest for just a minute? Who is Martha O'Donnell?"

"That's Bird," I tell him.

"Are we talking about leaving fifty thousand dollars to the damn maid and another thirty thousand dollars to the friggin' gardener?" Wilkes's voice rises in volume as he progresses.

"Mr. Wheeler," Bartholomew breaks in, "I beg you to watch your language in this office. I might point out that this is your mother's estate, and she is free to dispose of her assets in any way she feels is appropriate." He adjusts his glasses, picks up the document, and continues. "The Pilot Island Methodist Church is to receive five thousand dollars; the Georgetown public library, three thousand dollars; the Cawkins Home for unwed mothers is to get two thousand dollars."

Bartholomew sets the document back on the polished table, smoothes the top page with his right hand, removes his reading glass, and places it gently on top. He looks at each of us, letting the silence hang heavily in the air. Wilkes inspects the wood grain on the table. Bartholomew finally speaks to all of us. "I assume you're going to go through your mother's things while you're here. I can give you the names of several worthy charities to which you might consider donating her clothes and any other affects you do not wish to sell or keep for yourselves. Are there any questions?" Bartholomew starts to arrange his stack of papers before he places them back into his briefcase.

Wilkes pushes himself roughly from the table, nearly toppling his chair, and hurriedly leaves the room before any of us can make a move or think of what to say. The rest of us file out slowly murmuring to Bartholomew our thanks and make our way out the door.

"I'll meet you downstairs in a minute," I call after Kyle and Maddie.

I take the lawyer's hand to say good-bye. "Mr. Bartholomew, I'm sorry about Wilkes's outburst, but I know he acted out of hurt and not with any malice towards you." He gently squeezes my hand in both of his. "But I have to ask you," I continue, "do you know why my mother would want to hurt him this way?"

Mr. Bartholomew smiles, his eyes are kind and understanding. "No, I don't. But I think Wilkes does, don't you?"

I nod, shake hands with Ms. Logan, and make my way to the elevators.

CHAPTER THREE

On the way back from Georgetown I find myself poking along on the freeway as truckers blare their annoyance. For a while I speed up, forcing myself to concentrate, then slowly my mind drifts back to the scene at Bartholomew's office and my foot floats off the gas pedal undetected.

A station wagon passes full of adults in the front, kids in the back, and a mountain of possessions casually piled on top. When they're safely in front, a towheaded boy mashes his face against the rear window. As I consider whether to stick out my tongue at this tiny rogue, a grownup in the back seat swivels around, reaches back, and swats him on the behind.

The station wagon slowly moves ahead and out of sight. I don't know why I'm letting mom's will upset me so much. Mom didn't cut me out, and she must have had some reason for what she did. Yet, I can't think of anything, not anything, that would be so unforgivable that Mom would cut Wilkes out in such a trivial yet significant way and do so in such a public forum. This wasn't a case of a few choice words being spoken in anger; this was revenge, plotted, planned, and executed.

When I pull up to mom's house, Wilkes's car isn't there yet. I feel relieved. I'm not up to mending this rip in the family fabric. My mother's housekeeper and cook, Bird, is in the kitchen humming. She's peeling potatoes and already has several pots simmering on the stove that fill the house with tantalizing smells. I find myself transported back to when I would beg to help. Bird always had the time to show me how the blend of herbs and spices was as important as the selection. Bird claimed that cooking wasn't a duty or a chore, but an expression of love.

She is a petite woman; her body is still lean from years of hard work. I find it hard to believe that she is in her sixties. Yet gray strands pepper her wiry hair and the lines on her charcoal face are especially deep around her large dark-brown eyes.

She turns when the screen door knocks closed behind me. She smiles and wipes her wet hands on the front of her apron as I have seen her do countless times when something interrupts her cooking: the phone ringing, the doorbell buzzing or some child demanding attention. She holds out her arms to me. "Miss Hannah, it's so good to see you. Why, you ain't changed one spec."

"You always say that, Bird." I gladly walk into her open arms. "Besides, you just saw me a few months ago. How fast do you think I'm going to age anyway?" She holds me tight. I take in the aroma of cooked pies, fried okra, crab cakes, and a hundred other smells all mixed in a welcoming scent that could only be Bird O'Donnell.

Bird got her nickname when she was growing up in the off-road shacks that litter rural South Carolina. She possessed a special talent for saving small animals, especially baby birds. If they were sick, she nursed them back to health; if they were hurt, she helped them recover from their injuries; and if they were abandoned, she saw them through until they could make it on their own. Her mother told her she had a God-given gift and nicknamed her Bird.

I squeeze her tighter. "God, I've missed you, Bird."

"My Lord, child, you ain't nothin' but breath and britches." She puts her hands on my shoulders and gently puts me at arm's length. "You not gonna cry on ol' Bird is ya, sweetie?" Her eyes grow misty. "Cause if ya do, you sure gonna open ol' Bird's flood gates, and you know once I get goin', why, we'll have to move to higher ground." We both smile and the moment for tears passes.

I sit at the kitchen table, slip off my good shoes, and wiggle my grateful toes. "Has Wilkes been here this afternoon?"

"No, Hon, I ain't seen him today." She pauses, trying to read my face. "Is somethin' wrong?"

"No, nothing, Bird, I was just wondering where he was, that's all." I go to the stove and take the lid off one of the simmering pots. "Watcha making?"

Bird gently swats the top of my hand. "You put that back."

"Ouch!" I squeal in mock horror, as I quickly replace the lid. "My, aren't we getting testy in our old age."

With her hands on her hips, she throws her thin chest out in a defiant stance. "Whom you callin' old, child?"

"Why I'd never call you old, Bird," I sweet talk her. "Cause if I did, you'd quit cooking, and there I'd be with an empty stomach and no one to blame but myself."

Bird lifts a lid and sticks in her wooden spoon for a good stir. "That's right, missy, and don't you be forgettin' it, either." Steam washes over her dark face as she closes her eyes and leans forward to taste.

"Mmmm, that's good." She picks up a barrel-shaped saltshaker and scarcely lets it hover over the open pot. She stirs the contents a bit and then takes one more taste. Content with the results, she replaces the lid and turns her attention back to me. "Who's gonna be here for dinner? I got to know, or there might not be enough corn bread to go around."

"Maddie and Kyle are coming around seven o'clock."

"What about Wilkes?"

"I don't know. Things didn't go too well at the lawyer's office." I start to explain. "I really shouldn't talk about it, Bird, that would be violating Wilkes's privacy."

"Go ahead, violate Wilkes' privacy," he calls from outside the screen door, the sun behind him causing us to see nothing but the outline of his body. He leans against the door frame making no move come in.

I get out of my chair and head towards him. "I was getting worried about you."

He holds up his hand to stop me. "No need to worry Sis, I'm just fine." He turns toward Bird. "So, Hannah hasn't told you about our little visit to the infamous Mr. Bartholomew's office today?" He yanks open the screen door. "Well, allow me." He enters the kitchen with his hair mussed, his tie askew and his suit jacket slung carelessly over his arm. His expression is inscrutable. "You see, dear Bird, it seems Mom doesn't want her oldest son's hands on any of her stuff." He watches Bird's face. "That's right, I'm good enough to take her money, mind you; why, hell, Bird, even you're good enough to take her money. I'm just not good enough to touch her personal belongings." He holds his hands out before him as though the offending appendages might reveal the secret of his agony. He drops his hands limply to his sides. "Well, no big loss really, it's not like she's got anything I want." He tries to smile but only manages a harmless snarl.

"Don't worry, little sister. I know you're surprised that I look, shall we say, unkempt?" He stands back and throws both arms out. "But I had all the windows in my car rolled down. You know, as Mom would say, use nature's air conditioner. She's right, you know. Why fool around with advanced technology, when I can simply slough off my jacket, roll down the windows and go ninety miles an hour?" He points a finger accusingly at Bird. "I know that look. You don't approve, do you, Bird? What is it exactly that you disapprove of? Is it the state of my attire, the fact that I was perhaps driving a tad too fast, or maybe it's my existence that has your apron in a bunch?" He leans towards Bird and gently pokes his index finger at her chest.

Bird doesn't give an inch of ground. From the look on her face, I can see she's going to dig in her heels. Wilkes shouldn't challenge her; it only makes her ornery and stubborn. Bird leans forward and sticks her face towards his. "I think you look hurt and that the fiddler crabs don't care."

Bird always could give as good as she got.

I try to interrupt. "Wilkes?"

He waves me off. "Keep out of this, Sis." He turns a wicked grin on Bird. "This is between me and Bird. Isn't it, Bird?"

"You got that right, *Master* Wheeler."

"Stop that." He looks as offended as she surely predicted he would be. A slight whine slips into his voice "I am not your master."

"Is that so, Master Wheeler? I thought you bein' the master an all you sho' be tellin' ol' Bird what to do. Does you wants me to fetch you some supper 'fore I scrub da floors or do you want me to shine up dem dar shoes fo' you 'fore I's takes up ya supper?"

Wilkes's discomfort is obvious, Bird's pleasure, equally so. "Come on, Bird, that's not fair." He gives up, sits on one of the kitchen chairs, and fingers the stack of napkins in the middle of the table.

Bird softens immediately, her motherly tone meant to soothe. "You shouldn't take it so hard, honey."

Wilkes looks like a small boy who's lost his favorite GI Joe to the brute next door. "You mean that Mom doesn't want me to touch her precious things?" He finally looks at Bird and then takes a deep breath to regain his composure. "Bird, do you know Mom left you and Mr. McFarland some money?"

"Yes, Sir. I got a letter from Mr. Bartholomew. That was so nice of your Ma to remember us both. She was a very special lady, and I'm most grateful for her bein' so generous." Bird suddenly looks uncomfortable, not sure how to read Wilkes.

"You deserve it, Bird. You took really good care of Mom for a long time, and you've been kind enough to look after everything here for the past few months. We're all very grateful for everything you've done for all of us over the years." He gets up, puts his hands on Bird's shoulders, and kisses her tenderly on the forehead.

I'm proud of Wilkes, I knew he didn't mean what he'd said at Bartholomew's office.

He silently turns and makes his way down the hall. "I'm going to go take a shower," he calls over his shoulder, "I'll see you both later."

"Is what he said true?" Bird asks after Wilkes is out of earshot.

"Yes. Mom specifically stated that while he gets an equal share from the sale of her assets, he's not to have any of her personal belongings. Bird, do you know why she'd do such a thing?" I watch her face closely. Bird can be extremely tight-lipped, but she's an abhorrent liar.

She turns back to her pots and pans and begins to stir. "No, Sweetie, I don't,"

We both hear the shower turn on. I open the refrigerator to make a quick pre-dinner reconnaissance run for any goodies that might lurk on the shelves.

"No no, Miss Hannah," Bird chortles. "You'll ruin your supper."

The front doorbell echoes loudly throughout the house. Bird silently waves for me to sit down, wipes her hands on her apron, and heads to the front of the house. A few minutes later she returns with a long white floral box under her arm.

"Who's sending you flowers, Bird?"

Her embarrassment makes her flustered, a rare sight with Bird. She hurriedly places the box in my unsuspecting lap. "These ain't for me, silly, they for you."

I stupidly look at the box as though it might move. "For me?"

"Ain't you going to open 'em up?"

I set the box on the kitchen table and slid the top off. Inside are the most beautiful tiger lilies I've ever seen. There is at least a dozen or more. I lightly finger the exquisite orange blossoms. "Wow! These are my favorites."

"I'll go see if I can find somethin' to put those in," Bird says. "Lord, I hope I can find a vase big enough for all them flowers."

I rifle through the box looking for a card, sure there's been some mistake. Hardly anyone knows where I am, let alone that these are my favorite flowers. Jack, my cheating ex-husband, must be missing me. Having to take care of our daughter Carly all alone can be an eye-opening peek into the thrills of single parenthood. Perhaps this is his foray into trying to patch things up between us. God knows he always needs a motive to do something nice for me, but flowers, and so many, are extravagant, even when Jack is in the best of moods.

After rummaging in the potting shed, Bird returns holding a large dirty white vase above her head in triumph. "Here, this ought to do it. I'll clean it up and it'll be good as new," she promises, the determined look of a serious cleaner on her face.

I finally locate the envelope at the bottom of the box as Bird hands me the vase. Bird puts the flowers in water and with a few flourishes makes the flowers beautiful in their new home. I step back to admire as I still hold the small envelope in my hand.

Bird asks, "you not gonna look and see who they from?"

"What if they're from Jack?"

"Well, we ain't never gonna know at this rate, are we?" She reaches for the card herself.

"Hey, these are *my* flowers," I playfully snatch the card out of her reach and open the small envelope.

"Well, you gonna read it out loud, or you wanna watch me drop dead from the suspense?"

"They're from Sam," I whisper, stunned by the blow of the unexpected.

Even Bird looks surprised. "You're old beau? Sam Lancaster?"

"Yes."

Bird is clearly irked by my dawdling. "What does he say?"

I read the card aloud. "For all the old times." I look at Bird in hopes she'll be able to sort it out for me. I feel like pea soup has filled my brain. "Sam," I repeat aloud, as though the actual sound of his name will illuminate my path to understanding.

Bird is unable to contain herself. "Well, did he sign it just 'Sam' or did he say 'love, Sam'?"

In a daze, I hand over the card to her eager hands.

She holds the card at arm's length, so she doesn't have to retrieve her glasses. She gives up, fishes in her apron, and stuffs her glasses onto her face, eager to answer her questions. "Do you think he wrote the card or did the lady at the flower shop do it for him, you suppose?"

"What?"

"Get with it girl, it could be important." Bird hands me back the card, removes her glasses, and drops them back into one of her many apron pockets. "Do you think he wrote this card, or do you think he called in the order and the lady at the flower shop wrote it?"

I wonder why she's harping on this. "Why does it matter?"

She lightly stomps one tiny foot. "Well, answer me, child,"

"It looks like his handwriting, but it's been a long time, Bird."

"Well, if he took the time to fill out this card hisself, you could be in trouble."

I'm truly lost now. "Bird, what the devil are you talking about?"

"Well come on darlin', anyone can call in an order of flowers. But to go down to the shop, special order your favorite flowers and fill out a card takes a bit more plannin'." Her smile gets broader as she sees me catch on at last. "You understandin' me now, ain't ya, child?"

"OK, OK, so he put some thought into it. That doesn't mean anything other than he's a nice guy, which I already knew." I fuss with the flower arrangement to hide my growing confusion and unease.

"Here, let me do that." She picks the vase up off the table and moves it to the counter by the sink. She takes all the flowers out of the vase, lays them gently on the counter, cuts the flowers down, fills the vase with water, and goes about arranging the flowers with true artistry. She stands back to admire. I can tell she's not satisfied.

"Come outside with me a minute, I want to get some ferns to liven up these flowers." She grabs a pair of floral shears from the kitchen drawer, deposits them in an apron pocket, and heads out the screen door. We go around the back of the house. She kneels to clip various fern leaves and other greenery. Still, on her knees, she looks at me over her shoulder. "You still don't get it, do ya Miss Hannah?"

I take the ferns from her outstretched hand. "You're not going to start that again, are you?"

"OK, darlin', I'll leave it to lie for now, but I'm tellin' ya, you ain't heard the last from that boy."

When we go back inside, the shower has quit running. I sit at the kitchen table and watch Bird arrange the tiger lilies and greenery.

A few minutes later, Wilkes emerges dressed in blue jeans and a polo shirt.

He picks up an apple from the counter and takes a bite. We both watch Bird put the finishing touches on her arrangement. She has a true artistic flare. I am saddened for a moment to think of what talents she has wasted cleaning homes to help keep her family fed.

He points at the vase of flowers. "Who are those from?"

I try not to sound defensive. "No one."

Wilkes leans against the counter and takes another bite from his apple. "Are those from Jack?"

"No." I'm desperate to change the subject. "And where are you headed so dressed down?"

"Won't work, Hannah. You still haven't told me who the flowers are from. You know, the more evasive you get, the more interesting this becomes, and the more I'm going to persist until you tell me. So, you might as well spill the beans and let the rest of us live vicariously through you, my dear." He swings a chair around until the back is facing me, straddles it, and places his arms and chin on the top, looking at me like a puppy. "So come on, tell me, already."

"Well, aren't you in a better mood?"

"Bird, do you hear this? She thinks if she evades me long enough, I'll just go away. Now Bird, in all honesty, do you think that tactic's gonna work?" He doesn't take his eyes off me.

I see Bird shake her head and smile to herself. "Now, Master Wheeler, don't you be draggin' me into none of ya'lls squabbles, I got too much to do to be messin' with the two of you." She leaves her pots to simmer and heads for parts of the house unknown.

"I hate it when she calls me Master."

I get up to inspect the simmering pots. "That's why she does it." As I lift a lid to check the progress of whatever smells so delicious, I hear Wilkes shove his kitchen chair back under the table. Its legs noisily scrape the linoleum. He comes up behind me. "You going to fess up here, or am I going to have to tickle you?"

"No, I give up," I turn around with my hands up in the air in mock surrender. I still have the wooden spoon clutched in my hand and the contents begin to drip down my arm. "The flowers are from Sam."

He raises both eyebrows. "Sam Lancaster?"

I nod.

"The Sam?"

"Yes."

He takes another bite of his apple and with his mouth full he murmurs. "Your Sam?"

I lower my arms. "Yes!"

He leans against the end of the counter. "Wow."

"Wow? What does that mean?"

"I'm just surprised, that's all. Isn't he still married to his second wife?"

I wipe off my arm. "As far as I know, he is."

He looks at the vase full of flowers as though they are now the enemy. "Then what's he sending *you* flowers for?"

I cross my arms in exasperation. "Well, once upon a time, we were very close."

"But that was what, ten, twelve years ago?" He looks to me for confirmation of his estimate.

I concede. "Fifteen."

"I don't get it. You were, as you say, 'very close', fifteen years ago, he's married to someone else and, until recently, so were you, and now he's sending you flowers. You don't think that's the least bit peculiar?"

I started to feel defensive. "Shut up, Wilkes, and mind your own business."

"OK, but it sure seems weird to me that after all this time and, given his circumstances, he's sending you flowers."

"Don't you have somewhere you have to be?"

"As a matter of fact, I do." He tosses his apple core halfway across the room and it lands neatly in the garbage pail. "Tell Bird I won't be back for supper; I'm meeting a couple of friends up in Myrtle Beach for a few beers."

"Have a good time." I call after him, "Wilkes?" He turns around to face me. "I'm sorry about this afternoon at Bartholomew's office, I really don't know what Mom was thinking."

"It's not your fault, Hannah." I see a cloud pass over his face. "I'm just going to forget it for now. Would you tell Bird I'm sorry if I was a bit rough on her?"

I assure him I will. He heads out the door. I listen as he starts his car and pulls away.

Evening approaches and Maddie and Kyle will arrive soon. I go to my room to get a few minutes to call Carly and see how she's doing before the mantle of family responsibilities falls onto my shoulders.

Carly is distracted by friends who are over playing, and we don't talk for long. I lie down on my bed and think of Sam. Has it really been fifteen years since we were together? I wonder what he's like now. I wonder if he's still married. I chide myself on my naiveté and turn my attention to the awful heat. With almost no breeze, it's going to be difficult to sleep tonight. Despite the warmth, I fall into a troubled sleep and when I wake up it's almost dark out. I hear voices coming from the kitchen. The clock says it's after eight. When I get to the kitchen, Maddie, Kyle, and Bird are all laughing and talking.

Maddie is the first to notice me standing in the doorway. "Hey, sleepyhead. How are you feeling?"

"Why didn't someone get me up?"

"We didn't have the heart; you were sleeping so soundly."

I head for the stove to make a pot of coffee. "Please don't stop on my account. It's nice to hear all of your happy noises enjoying yourselves."

"Is Wilkes coming back for dinner?" Maddie looks suddenly nervous.

"No, he's meeting some friends at Myrtle Beach."

They all look markedly relieved.

"Oh, come on, you're not being fair." When they look at me in disbelief I plunge ahead. "He's had an extraordinarily bad day, don't you think? What if it had been you Mom cut out of her will? How would you feel? This isn't easy for anybody." I realize I'm starting to sound like Mom - a fate worse than death.

"Well, he didn't exactly get cut out of the will," Kyle gently corrects. "He's still getting his share of the proceeds from selling the house and all the other stuff."

"Yes, I know, Kyle, but that doesn't mean his feelings aren't hurt. Why would she make a comment in her will like that? I don't understand. Poor Wilkes. He even told me before all this happened that he wanted the scabbard from Dad's World War Two sword."

"Hey, I wanted that," Maddie pouts.

"Well, I guess you're going to get to keep it now, aren't you, thanks to Mom."

She sounds hurt. "I didn't mean it that way."

"Look, it doesn't matter, anyway." I pat her shoulder. She flinches when I touch her.

Kyle chimes in with his own idea: "Why can't we just give him the stuff he wants? She didn't say we couldn't do that."

"We could," I tell him. "But I don't think Wilkes would accept our generosity." I changed the subject, "Bird, when are we going to eat? I'm starved."

"As soon as someone sets that table so that I got somewhere to put all this food."

"I'll do it, Bird." Kyle gets the place mats out of the kitchen buffet and spreads them around the table.

I stand behind Maddie. "I'm sorry if I was too harsh. This thing between Mom and Wilkes has really upset me, and I guess I'm taking it out on you. Can we forget it?"

She nods, watching Kyle set the table.

"Thanks." I softly touch her arm. This time she doesn't shrink back.

Kyle starts to fold the napkins. "I was admiring your beautiful flowers. Bird tells me they're from Sam Lancaster."

"How nice of Bird to fill you in," I say through gritted teeth turning a scorching glare towards Bird.

Bird smiles sheepishly then innocently shrugs her shoulders as she goes back to taking up dinner.

I sit down next to Maddie. "Yes, they're from Sam, but I wonder how he knew I was here."

Maddie lowers her voice to a guilty whisper. "I'm afraid I told him you would be here."

My attention goes on full alert. "You've seen him?"

"Just a few weeks ago at Lombardi's"

"The bar?"

She nods. "I was out with a friend celebrating her divorce when he came over and talked with me."

I interrupt. "Who?"

"Sam," she says, incredulously.

I wave my arms at her. "No. No. Who got divorced?"

"Oh, Marsha Ellis. Can you believe it?"

"It's about time. She should have gotten rid of that chump a long time ago. I don't know why she married him."

"Me either but get this; she didn't leave him."

"Get outta here."

"No, it's true. He left her."

"Really?"

"And," she adds dramatically, "he left her for another woman."

"You mean there are two idiots out there who want Tom Ellis? Hard to believe." I shake my head. "All right now, let's get back to Sam. You said you saw him at Lombardi's. Go on."

Maddie warms up to the story. "He said he'd heard about Mom's passing and wondered how you were. He sent flowers to the funeral, you know."

"No, I didn't know," I tell her, disappointed I hadn't known at the time.

"Anyway, he asked all about you. I told him you were divorced. He asked if you would be down for a visit any time soon. I may have mentioned you were coming in a few weeks to sort through Mom's stuff."

I stop her. "What do you mean, you may have mentioned it?"

She looks nervously at Kyle. "Oh, all right, I told him when you were coming."

"It's OK, Maddie. I'm not sorry you told him; I don't know what to make of all this."

She looks at me. "Are you going to see him while you're here?"

I shrug my shoulders. "Oh, I don't expect to hear from him. I think he just wanted to extend his sympathies about Mom."

She leans toward me and lowers her voice. "I don't know, you didn't see how happy he was when I told him you were single again."

"Yes, but isn't he still married?" I fear her response.

"Yeah, I checked. He had on a wedding band."

I lean back in my chair. "Well, in that case, I doubt Sam will be calling to talk to me."

"Hannah, I wouldn't underestimate his feelings for you, he had a look on his face."

She's piqued my interest again. "What do you mean he had a look? What kind of look?"

She reels me in the rest of the way. "I guess you had to be there, but I think he's still carrying a torch for you."

Before I could ask Maddie any more questions, Bird interrupts.

"Come on, you two, quit puttin' your heads together like a couple of ol' Billy goats and come eat. Ya'll better hurry up 'lessin you want me to throw this food to the dogs."

Maddie winks at me. "Bird, we don't have any dogs."

"You want me to go and find some?" Bird threatens.

We all shut up and await the coming feast.

CHAPTER FOUR

The night is unbearably muggy. I close my eyes and try to invoke a fantasy revolving around air conditioners. All I accomplish is making myself more aware of my discomfort as I turn the pillow over in search of a cool spot for my face. In the end, I lie awake and think about Sam. The first time I met Sam, I was twenty-two years old, and he was twenty-nine. When it was over, I had lost more than the time we had spent together, I had lost the years ahead of me without him to fill them up.

I hear Wilkes come home. His getting-ready-for-bed noises soon give way to silence. I abandon my attempts to sleep and leave my sweat-soaked sheets to dry. I go to the kitchen and get myself a tall glass of iced tea. I take my tea out on the porch hoping for at least a breath of air. The moon is nearly full as cumulus clouds whisper over its light. There is a hint of a breeze and I covet every moving particle. I make myself comfortable on the porch glider. As I push the swing into motion with my toes, my memories slowly begin to travel down their rutted path, wounds, and scars forgotten.

Sixteen years ago, we met at a minor league baseball game where friends gathered on Sunday afternoons for the time-honored tradition of watching our valiant home team get resoundingly stomped. But we were a loyal crowd, always hopeful; there is always hope in baseball - possible redemption lurks at the bottom of every inning.

* * *

My thoughts are on the ball game with an occasional interlude devoted to the decision of whether to eat a hot dog or a bag of peanuts. I opt for the hot dog. I notice him right away in my peripheral vision. It wasn't his looks that drew me; although the shock of reddish-blonde hair and beard were hard to ignore, it was the way he looked at me. I had my hot-dog piled high with chopped onions and mustard leaking out the side, exactly the way I like it. My mouth is suspended open like an airplane hangar in anticipation of this delicious, pork-part delight. When I look up and there he is, watching me. I bite into the hot dog, mustard spurting out, followed by a small cascade of onion bits.

I turn my attention back to the game. I cheer my favorite players and boo the blunders and errors that only a single-A team could produce with such gusto; being a fan was a full-time job. Later, I sneak a glance over to see what my red-headed voyeur is up to. He had leaned over to talk with some friends seated on the row in front of him. I no sooner locate him in the crowd than, he looks up and catches me staring at him. I didn't look away but merely raised an eyebrow. He doesn't retreat like a gentleman and look away, instead, he winks at me. I blush. I have lost the hand of poker without even the bluff of a pair of deuces to save me. I tried to turn my attention back to my friends and the game, but it was useless. I finally decided to head to the lady's room. Once I get back to the main aisle, I begin to walk up a dozen concrete stairs, his row only a few steps up from mine. I didn't look up, but I kept my head down and hurried. Yet, when I pass his row, he is on the steps waiting for me.

"May I walk you to wherever you're going?" he asks, his voice husky and deep. I was speechless, so I merely nodded my head. He puts his hand on the small of my back and gently glides me up the steps to the concession stands.

At the top of the stairs, he hesitates, then smiles. "Do you want something else to eat?"

I imagine I have mustard perched somewhere on my face like a beauty mark gone sour. "No, I need to visit the lady's room," I hastily explain as I make a beeline for the marked door on my right.

I look at my reflection in the bathroom mirror. "Gee, what are you gonna do for an encore?" I ask my reflection in the mirror. I rub mustard off my face with a dampened paper towel. The mirror was irritatingly quiet and the people around me began to stare. "OK," I say to my reflection, "take a deep breath, fix your hair and makeup, and be yourself." I take my advice, throw my shoulders back, and march out as though he was lucky, I returned at all.

He is waiting for me when I come out. When I approach him, I stick out my hand and introduce myself. "I'm Hannah Wheeler," I say in a crisp business-like tone.

Without missing a beat, he took my outstretched hand. "Hannah, it's a pleasure to meet you. I'm Sam Lancaster." He shook my hand firmly but gently. "Now that we've been properly introduced Miss Wheeler, would you care to take a stroll with me before we return to the game?" He held out his arm for me to take. There was a twinkle in his eye.

I place my arm through his. "I'd love to Mr. Lancaster." I follow his lead to the stadium exit. The garden down the walkway from the ballpark was in full bloom, the scent of lilacs wafts lazily through the air as we walk silently past the meticulously tended flower beds. When we came to a bench, he suggests we sit for a while.

"So, Hannah Wheeler, what do you do with your time when you're not cheering on our version of the 1962 Mets?"

Oh, a fellow with a sense of humor. I silently thank the powers that be and swear that if this guy was a good kisser, I was going marry him. I wondered what he would do if I kissed him right then and there. While I consider my smooch fantasy, I belatedly realize he is looking at me, amused, as he waits for me to answer his question.

He watches me force myself back to the topic at hand and then he asks. "Where were you?"

"I was thinking about what you asked me, about what I do with my time." I lied. "Right now, I'm taking a couple of college courses trying to decide whether to go back to school full time."

He casually takes my left hand in both of his. "What will make you decide one way or the other?"

He slowly begins to massage my hand. His touch is soft, and the stroke of his fingers makes me forget my end of the conversation. He draws me in with the sensual feel of his caress. I slowly look up at his face, his eyes look directly into mine. There was no hint of amusement, no teasing, but an intensity that made my breath catch in my throat. With difficulty I pry my eyes away and try to concentrate on the shrubbery behind him, then the birdbath across the path from us; anywhere but at those burning green eyes. He saw my discomfort and gently put my hand down. I feel foolish but at the same time grateful when he stops.

When I face him again, he smiles warmly as if to apologize for making me feel awkward. I clear my throat, cross my legs, and stupidly repeat the question.

"I guess I've already decided. I attended college but dropped out after a few semesters. And now, after working dead-end jobs the last couple of years, I've decided that going back to complete my degree isn't such a bad idea," I explain and then ask where he went to school.

"I'm a self-taught man, Hannah. My parents didn't have the money to send me to school. But to tell you the truth, I'm not sure I'd have had the patience anyway. I've worked mostly in lumber and construction. I'm good at what I do and maybe more importantly, I like what I do," he answers me not the least bit defensive or embarrassed.

I like the breathless feeling I have when I am near him, I love the way his touch makes me forget everything else, and perhaps most of all, I admire his attitude. A man with confidence in himself, a man who was comfortable in his own skin was a rarity. I knew I'd found someone special.

* * *

I remember that day sixteen years ago with such painful clarity, but incredibly I almost need to remind myself that I had a life before I met Sam Lancaster. My energies were tied up with college and friends. In the beginning, after suffocating the confines of high school and the stifling restrictions of living at home, college life was an exhilarating freedom.

* * *

I pose for pictures at my high school graduation in my ankle-length acetate gown as sweat runs down my back. My four-cornered hat constantly sprung loose from the bobby pins I'd jammed around the edge to hold it in place. Mom dithers endlessly with her camera as my brothers and sister look on, barely able to contain their yawns of boredom. I send Mom a murderous glare, but it doesn't help.

"I should've brought more film," she says yet again as the camera begins to merge into her face. The four of us kept imagining what we were going to do to the traitor who came up with putting thirty-six pictures on a single roll of film. "Damn, only twelve more exposures on this roll!" she exclaims. Our smiles are genuine when she clicks the next picture.

Then there were presents to unwrap. Luggage, clothes, and money from relatives. By mid-August, I had written all thank you cards, recovered from every graduation party, and had money in my pocket from a part-time job at Dairy Queen. Then like magic, poof, it was off to college with only negligible preparation, pointless guidance, and no interference; just 125 pounds of sheer anticipation.

Earlier that fall, when Mom and I first visited the campus at the College of Charleston on the coast of South Carolina, we were part of the official parent-selling tour. The campus was located downtown but was walled off from the city. Once you were inside the gates you forgot you were ensconced in the middle of a thriving metropolis. Open space was at a premium in a crowded city. Every patch of dirt surrounding the college buildings was filled with blooming Azaleas. The cistern, located at the center of the campus, was the only sizable space of greenery. It was littered with students reading on blankets or lounging on wrought-iron benches. The walkways were made of century-old brick and the original buildings were painted in ox-blood pink. As was the custom in this soft-soiled coastal city, none of the buildings were more than three stories high.

The liberal arts buildings were ancient and imposing. The newer construction housed the sciences. Science labs abounded with black slab tabletops. There were mountains of beakers and test tubes while periodic charts dangled from painted cinder-block walls. Our guide assured us that all the lab equipment was top-notch, and state-of-the-art. During his luncheon speech, the university president confirmed the tour guide's assertions; nothing but the best for their young men and women. Too bad a stomach-churning dissection in high-school biology had squashed my scientific ambitions.

The newer dorms were spacious and well-appointed. I was sold the minute I saw an air conditioner protrude out the window of each room. If only I hadn't caught a brief glimpse of the cafeteria.

During our two-day weekend, Mom and I were guaranteed I would receive mind-enriching lectures and experience an abundance of culturally stunning events. The administration assured us that each student got a virtual bombardment of brain-cell-filling ideas from the best scholars that an over-budget, public institution could buy. Although he didn't put it in quite those terms.

At the beginning of school, the rush of autumn days was filled with the freshmen's promise of sorority secrets and fraternity parties while the upperclassmen gravitated towards the bars and coffee houses. We were still young and naive enough to think that what we did or thought mattered to anyone outside our circle of friends. A few years later I was sick of them all and tired of explaining to my family what I was going to do with a degree in English literature. A job, any job with a paycheck, seemed more appealing. I was smart and I didn't need a piece of paper to prove it to anyone I was wrong.

* * *

Sam and I sat in the park and talked that first day for quite a while. I was overly aware of everything I said and mindful of my growing attachment. When the sun had arched its way overhead and left us with the certainty that the ball game was long over and our friends were probably on their way home, we headed back.

He asked me if I would like to go out with him the following weekend, and I nodded my head. He said he'd call me. I knew he would. Before we get up to leave, he takes both my hands in his and looks at me. Silence.

"What is it?" I whisper. I want to turn away, worried he will tell me something I don't want to hear, yet captivated by the depth of his gaze. He reaches up with his right hand and runs the back of his fingers lightly over my cheek and then cups my chin in his hand. I am mesmerized by the motion. His fingers send electrical currents down my spine that cause my heart to beat dangerously fast. Before I can recover, he is already standing, holding his hands out for mine. I feel trapped in a time warp. I don't remember him removing his hands from my face or him getting up; yet there he stands, time ticking at a normal speed for him. Wordlessly I stand, take his hands and we head to the parking lot.

My best friend Marie sits perched on a concrete retaining wall outside the park. She swings her feet impatiently as the last light of the day drags her shadow out across the sidewalk.

"Marie," I call out as I let go of Sam's hand. "I didn't think you'd still be waiting for me."

She sounds irritated. "Where have you been?" She hops down from her cement perch. "Did that sound exactly like my mother or what?" She laughs. "Hi Sam," she acknowledges his presence before going on. "Hannah, did you really think I'd leave you stranded?"

I was unable to hide the note of genuine surprise in my voice. "You know each other?"

Sam explained "We've seen each other around from time to time, but we've never been formally introduced," Sam turned to Marie. "Sorry if we worried you, but we lost track of the time."

Marie looked back and forth between us, picking up the nuances of our body language. "Yeah, I bet you did."

Nothing ever got past Marie.

Sam fishes in his pocket for his keys. "I gotta go." He put his hand on my shoulder and said softly; "I'll talk with you soon." He apologizes again to Marie before heading off towards his car; after a few steps, he lapses into an easy jog. I couldn't take my eyes off him.

Marie lightly pinches my arm, "Hello? What am I, chopped liver?"

I smile sheepishly. "Sorry."

Marie expertly navigated her car towards my house. "Well, are you going to keep me in suspense, or do you want to walk home?"

Marie's threats were seldom idle ones. I confess everything. Truthfully, I was grateful to have someone in which to confide. I try to explain my feelings to her, but I sound stupid and trite even to myself. She looked at me like I'd lost my mind. Finally, I say, "Marie, do you believe in love at first sight?"

"Oh God, please tell me you're kidding."

I immediately get on the defensive. "Come on Marie, it happens."

She looked at me like I was a puppy about to be run over by a bus. "I think you meant to ask me if I believe in lust at first sight."

"OK, I admit, I have the hots for this guy but . . ."

"That's right, the hots, and that's a lot different from being in love," she interrupts as she points her finger at me.

"But it's more than that!"

In a patronizing tone of voice, she said, "Hey, if you say so."

"Now you are starting to sound like your mother," I told her, angry that she didn't understand.

We looked at each other as the heat of our disagreement rose.

"You take that back," she teases, easing the tension between us.

"I will not," I taunt. We both laugh and the awkward moment passes.

I remember how scared and excited I was about seeing him again and wondered if he felt the same. It's funny how I can recall all these feelings, yet what I couldn't or wouldn't see at the time would soon break my heart. Whether I suffered from deliberate blindness, inexperience, or both, I suppose I will never know. But with the precision of hindsight, the messengers of my impending heartache were on the horizon. I was filled with the zest that youth brings to the game of love, ran them over, didn't hear them flop under my wheels, and never looked back to see what I'd hit.

Marie drops me off in front of my small apartment building. For the most part, my neighborhood contains an assortment of low-budget architecture with many of the older homes transformed into apartments. Each home was built in isolation from its surroundings. There co-existed a conglomeration of two-story clapboards, brick ranches, and colonials. There was an occasional small English Tudor and a peppering of salt-box houses stashed onto half lots. The overall effect looked as though a group of architects had thrown their arms up in desperation. The sizes and styles were random. The lawns ranged from the perfection of the bored and retired to the haphazard upkeep of the rental crowd.

The Calhoun's were a retired couple who lived across the street. Their constant bickering was loud enough for all to hear. When the cable was on the fritz, they often were the evening's only entertainment.

To the right of my apartment lives a man of about fifty who mostly keeps to himself but plays a beautiful piano. He rarely had any visitors although I knew he had a grown son living in Colorado whom he visited from time to time. I take in his paper and look after his cat when he is gone. He works as a foreman at the textile mill in town. He comes across as mournfully alone. He rarely talks about himself. I don't think I'd have found out about the son; except he asked me to watch the cat. I decided he must have had a wife who had tragically died, and he had never recovered from his broken heart. It probably wasn't true, but it did lend him a certain mystique I thought he needed.

On the other side of my building lives a young couple. She is pregnant with their first child, and they are exasperating to the point of avoidance. If I was unfortunate enough to run across them on the sidewalk, they came verbally armed with their baby expertise; how to deliver a baby, how to raise a baby, and the unintended how to be obnoxious parents before your baby's born. I hoped the daily grind of dirty diapers and cleaning spit off their clothes would tone down their enthusiasm.

Across the street and two houses down lives my close friend Albert Vanelli. When we first met, he couldn't believe I wouldn't fawn over him, and I couldn't believe that anyone would. A natural foundation for a long and lasting friendship. He makes incredible Italian dinners, and I was often the thankful recipient of his largess. He usually starts the evening with some unusual music he'd found at the radio station where he worked as an afternoon Deejay. Then he'd pop open some esoteric wine for us to try. He imagined himself a wine connoisseur and I classified him as a courageous experimenter. I was willing to listen and drink anything he came up with because his stuffed pasta shells as well as lasagna were extraordinary delights. I was grateful for his friendship and for the protectiveness provided by his Italian culture. He felt compelled to look out for me whenever he thought I was faced with any sort of threat whether real or imagined.

"Hey, you want me to take care of it for you?" He would ask in his stereotypically Italian accent, which he didn't possess, but longed to.

"Thanks, Al, but I better handle it this time."

My only real nemesis was the woman who lived upstairs. She was loud, and rude and had a small son she ignored except as a tool to extract money from her ex-husband. If her child hadn't been almost as annoying as she was, I could probably have worked up some sympathy for him. But the truth was, he terrorized my dogs and woke me up early on the weekends; both punishable-by-death offenses.

Overall things were pretty good on Queen's Row, a neighborhood nickname. With the help of my mother and a savings account from working the last few years I was able to make ends meet. I had friends, my two black labs and the only thing absent was love. I thought Sam Lancaster might be the answer.

The next day, Sam called before I had finished my first cup of coffee. I hadn't even had time to wonder about what I might say. Anticipation was usually as much fun as the event.

His voice was husky and sexy even over the phone. "What are you doing this morning?"

"To be honest, I'm still in my nightgown drinking a cup of coffee on my porch, trying to wake up," I said as I enjoyed the perfect moment of coffee, summer's waning breeze, and the anticipation of love around the corner.

"I hope I didn't call too soon, but this was the only chance I thought I might have this morning to get in touch with you."

I was chagrined that I had forgotten he had to work on Monday while I lazed around without a duty beckoning until my one o'clock class in the afternoon.

"I'm glad you did. I hoped I would hear from you today," I said honestly, excitement beating at my chest's door.

"Will you still be free this weekend to go with me?"

Visions about what to wear, makeup, and shoe choices danced deliciously in my head. "Where are we going?"

"I sing in a band on the weekends and we're going to be at the Country Club. Will you be able to come?" The note of hopefulness in his voice gave me the edge of power I needed to feel in control of my chest again.

"I wouldn't miss it, Sam," I say, grateful for the delectable feeling of getting to know someone new. The chance to switch from: 'You already told me that,' to 'tell me more.'

We meet at the Country Club at five o'clock, to give the band time to set up and put together a song list before the guests arrive at seven. The feeling of being in on the before-party preparations was exciting. Girlfriends of the other band members were also there, and I fell into their clique easily enough. I was surprised they were so interested in me and figured any new face was a welcome diversion.

Sitting through the next two hours was a mixture of intense anticipation, shyness and excitement occasionally catching Sam's eye, his smile or touch as he passed by the table to see how I was getting along. The band starts promptly. I was amazed at how good they were. While I hadn't any preconceived ideas about what they would sound like, I was surprised at the professional quality of their performance and the positive reaction of the crowd. Sam was a phenomenal singer and performer; he sang not only with genuine talent but with flair. It was obvious that his speaking voice was an offshoot of his expansive singing voice. Hearing him sing was to be caressed by low tones, nuzzled by subtle notes and musical nuances that only a talented song interpreter could reveal. The breaks were spent with the two of us huddled together as we held hands and got to know each other better. The evening was over so quickly, then the long wait while the band dismantled and packed up their equipment. I waited until he was through, and I could have his undivided attention.

By the time they finished, it was very late, and we were only able to spend a few moments together before I had to leave for home. The parking lot shines from an early evening rain shower. The moon's reflection on the blacktop cast shadows on his face. He looks both mysterious and seductive, a heady combination. He walks me through the parking lot, and neither of us says a word. I lean against my car and feel the residue of rain making the back of my dress damp. I wait in anticipation for a kiss. I hope he won't disappoint in delivering or in delivery. He reaches up and silently smooths my hair back from my brow and then takes my face in both his hands. Never taking his eyes off mine, he bends and kisses me softly on the lips. A fire ignites in my chest and moves down my body as a soft groan escapes me. He then wraps both his arms gently around me and pulls me closer. His kiss is more insistent this time. I swear I feel faint.

I turn and jam my key into the door lock. "I had a lovely time Sam," I say as I practically leap into my car. I start the engine and wave, not saying another word, still trying to catch my breath. I know I am doomed. I am in love.

The next few weeks are nearly a blur. He phones nearly every morning. I began to time my day around his calls. My desire for him grew nearly as passionate as his kisses, almost beyond endurance. My resistance was nearly a joke. Yet I still wait. Everything happened so fast; I hadn't seen my friends in weeks. I spend most weekends on the road with Sam as the band travels around the county going from one gig to the next. My friend and neighbor, Al, looks after my dogs while I am gone. I find it hard to concentrate on my schoolwork. Sam was always too tired after work to spend much time with me, but I didn't object because it gave me a chance to get some studying done. Besides we had nearly every weekend together and that was enough.

On the seventh week of our courtship, after the band played on Saturday for the local Quality Inn, Sam seemed especially quiet. I wondered what was wrong; naturally, I speculated on what I might have done. On Sunday afternoon Sam knocks on my door. I feel apprehensive.

Sam looks at me with intent and says, "I know I should have called, but may I come in?"

"Maybe for a little while," I say standing back so he can get by the door.

I was fidgety as I chatted about nothing. I go around the room and straighten things that didn't need straightening. He sits on the sofa and watches me.

"Hannah, what's wrong?"

"Nothing," I say too quickly and then let out a nervous laugh.

"What are you doing?"

"Nothing." I sound silly even to me.

"Why don't you come sit down next to me for a few minutes."

I sit rigidly on the couch beside him. He puts his arm around my shoulder and uses his other hand to turn my face towards him. He kisses me lightly on the forehead, then on the cheek, then my neck. My body responds despite any intentions I might have had to the contrary. I put my arms around him, and we kiss deeply as he pulls me tight against his body. I felt his desire and it matches my own. He pulls away for a moment and looks into my eyes, his passion is evident on his face, and he holds me spellbound.

"I love you, Hannah."

It was so simple a phrase, as it slid between us electrifying the air. I know he loves me, I saw it in his eyes, even if he hadn't said it aloud before. But to hear the words spoken, makes my heart catch in my chest as tears come unbidden to my eyes, tears of true joy. He bends to kiss me again and I match his ardor with every cell of my being. He pulls away, stands up, and reaches out for my hand. I put my hand in his as I get to my feet. He kisses me softly again and then almost effortlessly picks me up in his arms and carries me the short distance to the bedroom. His lovemaking was soft and sure. Never had I felt such love, such hunger, and longing for a man. Every touch made me sigh with pleasure every kiss felt like a warm balm.

As we lay next to each other, the morning dust of light settles upon us, I turn to him and prop myself up on one elbow so I can see his eyes. His face is nearly glowing. I could feel his love for me in my soul. I stroked his cheek with my hand and kissed him gently on the lips. The afterglow of love makes me content and lazy.

"I love you, Sam Lancaster," I whisper.

A tear comes to his eye, rolls down his face, and falls on the pillow. As the moisture spread across the fresh white cotton, I realized that something was dreadfully wrong.

A thousand questions run through my mind. "What is it, Sam?"

"Hannah. . ." he stops, his voice chokes with emotion.

I hear fate's unmistakable footfall.

"I'm married."

CHAPTER FIVE

The inconsistencies were there all along, so I suppose I chose to ignore them. He only called me from work and never from home. He didn't give me his home number and had some flimsy excuses when I asked him for it. He was always too tired to spend time with me after work. In the telescopic lens of hindsight, these were not mere warning signs, but giant red flags whipping conspicuously in the wind. Lord knows any advice columnist could have predicted the outcome. But I was young, naive, and in love. My heart was broken.

After the telling, he pleads for my understanding as words of love fall from his lips; those same lips that had kissed me so lovingly only moments before. My shouts of 'How could you?' countered by his shouts of 'Give me a chance to explain,' filled the room.

His excuses were sickeningly predictable; he didn't love his wife, they no longer slept in the same room, and he had a young son to think about. 'Oh my God, a child!'

How could I have been so in love and so stupid? We fuss and fume for another hour; my voice is hoarse, and my head pounds.

I finally overwhelmed his unwillingness to leave with my fierce determination to have him gone. He reluctantly steps over the threshold, and I firmly close the door behind him and click the lock into place.

I call Marie. When she arrives, I tell her the whole story. Everything seems so ridiculously melodramatic. For a while, I get lost in the telling leaving Sam's obvious flaw for last. She waits patiently and does nothing to hurry me along. She understands my need to retell the tale from beginning to end.

I sit on the bed, my back against the wall. Marie is ensconced in the stuffed chair. I told her about the band and my love for their music. I am in love with a singer, but the rhythm and sensual beat offer more than the singer could tell alone. Songs aren't poured out in a dramatic heat but are the collective vibrations within which the words exist that were what made a song enter your soul.

I try to explain this to Marie: "Remember how certain songs don't just remind you of someone you loved, but also of the time? You know, you hear the song, and it makes you remember the backdrop to your life the mood of your life at the time."

Marie says nothing.

"I'm not a raving romantic," I tell her, although even I hear the near-frantic tone in my voice. I stop speaking engulfed with the weight of it all.

"Go on Hannah, I'm listening," she assures me.

I knew I was being indulged, but I plowed on anyway. "OK, suppose you fall in love. On the radio, you hear a song, and the words seem to speak to your heart. You're even grateful to the songwriter who stepped in and said what you could not. It even becomes 'your song.'" I sit up taller in bed and cross my legs. "Now let's say that things don't work out and a while later you meet someone new, and you fall in love again. The words from this song now fit your new lover even better than the first guy. So do you give guy number two this same song?"

Marie shakes her head.

"Of course not. And not only because fella number two wouldn't appreciate a retread, but because the song doesn't fit for you anymore; the essence of the song is attached to other feelings and emotions in your life." I curl my legs up under me. "Do you understand? It wasn't only Sam I was in love with, but the backdrop of his music he brought to my life." I felt silly and exhausted, but I could see in her eyes that she was grasping what I had tried to explain.

She stands up, walks over to the bed, and squeezes my hand. "You're trying to describe the almost physical connection a song can have when you feel yourself spiritually summoned by the music."

I sigh and slump down on the pillows. We were still sympatico. She not only understands what I mean but appreciates its importance. I am also sure she'd now be able to comprehend the magnitude of my loss. Marie drops back down into the chair she had vacated a few moments ago giving me some space.

"Hannah, why don't you tell me what happened? You were so upset when you called. Did you and Sam fight? Did you two break up? What? You need to tell me what's going on, OK?"

At the mention of his name, I closed my eyes and put my hands over my face, it was hard to breathe.

"Hannah is Sam dead?" she prods, her voice nearly a whisper.

This sent me into a spasm of sobs. "Oh my, God," she says as she assumes the worst. She starts to exit the chair.

I hold out my hand in a stopping motion. "No. Not dead," I tell her between hiccupping sobs. "Wish," sob, "he was," I finally manage to say.

"Oh," she says a bit incredulously.

I could almost hear her go through a mental list of what Sam might have done that would have made me this upset. It was a pitiful short list.

"Another woman," Marie says as a matter of fact. Her pronouncement renewed my tears her diagnosis was verified.

"That bastard!" She says to no one in particular. "Who could he find better than you?"

My words of gratitude for her staunch support of me are caught in my throat, my sad self weighs me down as I shake my head.

"No!!" She whispers in shock, "he's married."

I let out a heart-rending moan. I roll to my side and turn my back to Marie, too embarrassed and ashamed to face her.

"How did you find out?"

After a few minutes, I force myself to sit up. I am surprised at how worn out I am. I hadn't done anything but cry most of the day and yet I could hardly move; each gesture was an effort. Marie plopped a large box of tissues on the bed. I grab a handful, wipe my eyes, and blow my nose. "I look terrible, don't I?"

Being the good friend that she was, she says; "Yeah, you do sort of look like something my cat dragged in last week."

"Is that supposed to cheer me up?"

She walks over to the bed, the sight of my afternoon pity party, and pats me on the arm. "Hey, you asked."

I gave her a dirty look.

"Well?" She waited for me to answer. "How'd you find out?"

I couldn't look her in the eye. "He told me."

"Why'd he wait so long to tell you? Or better yet, why'd he tell you at all?"

I begin to shred the tissues in my hand. "When he came over this afternoon, he told me he loved me and then we made love," Tears threaten renewal, but I fiercely stave them off. I take a deep breath. "Afterwards, I told him I was in love with him too and he started to cry. At first, believe it or not, I was flattered. But then I realized something was wrong and that's when he told me." I drop the tattered wad of tissue in the waste basket beside the bed and grab another handful.

"Just like a man. Waits until he gets the girl into bed and then confesses," she nearly spits out. "He was probably just feeling guilty."

"No. I know what I saw on his face." I explain feebly, "I'm not trying to defend him,"

Marie gives me a disapproving stare and gets ready to launch into a lecture.

"I'm not. But I saw his eyes, Marie, he loves me whether he wants to or not."

She looks at me squarely. "And you *love* him?"

I could tell she was worried about my answer. "Yes," I whisper.

She shakes her head in disbelief. "Are you going to keep seeing him?"

"I can't. He's someone's husband, someone's father; what kind of guilt would that be."

"Wait, he's got a kid?" she asks, aghast.

I get off the bed and tell her, "Yes, he has a son. But he says he and his wife sleep in separate rooms, that he doesn't love her," I explain parroting back what Sam said to me.

Marie stands up and takes me firmly by the shoulders. "Do you hear yourself? Don't fall for that bunk, Hannah. What did you think he was going to say? 'Oh, gee Hannah, sorry about that, but I was really only looking for a nice piece of ass and you happen to fit the bill,'"

"Stop it! I know it all looks bad." I blow my nose. "I'm not going to see him again, but I know he loves me," I tell her more whining than defiant.

She drops her arms, stands before me, and says, "I'm sorry, I'll drop it for now. But don't expect me to be a fan of Sam Lancaster's anymore."

We plotted and schemed my revenge for the rest of the afternoon. Bodily harm escalated to mutilation before we got tired and ran out of ideas. Then Marie went in search of the only proven remedies for a broken heart, a bottle of wine and a gallon of chocolate ice cream.

While Marie was out, I took a shower to clean up before I started to dwell on the cause of my pain. I stood in the shower and let the streams of hot water run over me until I felt dizzy. I find myself forcing thoughts of Sam out of my head. I think of school assignments, world hunger, John the Baptist, John Travolta even John Denver; anything to shove out thoughts and images of Sam; Sam singing, Sam laughing, Sam making love to me. . . Out! Out! Out!

The hot water finally runs out. I emerge from the shower a bright shade of pink and feel a little better. The phone rang as I dried my hair. My heart skipped a beat. Then I wondered if I should answer it. Maybe Marie had car trouble. I pick up the receiver and hold my breath. If Sam said anything, I'll hang up. I wait the seconds tick by in silence.

A man's voice on the other end tentatively says, "Hello?"

I wait.

"Hannah, are you there?"

It was my neighbor Al. "Al? Is that you?"

"What's going on?" His tone demands an explanation.

I went for innocent. "What do you mean?"

"I've hardly seen you for the last few weeks. You don't return my calls and now your car hasn't moved all day. Are you sick?"

"No, I'm fine." I don't even convince myself.

"Well, at least you're not dead."

"That's it, look on the bright side." He is right, at least I wasn't dead. Then I think of Sam. God, how could I have sucked up every deceitful word; I want to scream.

"Hannah, are you there?"

"Yeah Al, I'm still here," I say as though I wished I weren't.

"How about coming for dinner tomorrow, we can either talk all about what's wrong or we can pretend nothing's wrong and have a wonderful mind-numbing time." His voice gets more animated. "I have an interesting wine for you to try and the new guy at the station brought in some great tunes from a blues guitarist, Robert Cray, I haven't heard before."

A moment before I had briefly considered ending it all over Sam. How ironic that now I hesitate at the idea of laying my life on the line tasting one of Al's *interesting* wine selections I guess I want to live after all.

Al's insistent. "Come on, what do you say?"

I am touched by Al's invitation, his willingness not to pry and to save me from myself if only long enough to poison me with some maniac's homebrew.

"I'm going to take your silence as a yes. I'll come walk you over around six o'clock, OK?"

"Sure Al, I'd like that, thanks." I am grateful for his love and understanding. I was even more glad to have something to look forward to, to keep my mind off things. Getting through the next day or two had taken on a new level of difficulty.

The next weeks consist of bitter days and desperate nights, as one day melts into another. Sam calls me a few times and each time I hang up. He writes me a letter and I return it unopened. He left a note taped to my front door that says he loves me, that he's left his wife and moved in with one of the members of the band. He calls, calls again, and again. I change to an unlisted number; the torment of not answering the phone is more than I can bear.

Even though we were only together for a few months, the weight of his absence is a burden. A month passed and Sam stopped trying to contact me. My disappointment was palpable, but my relief was even greater. Life finally settles down to at least a form of a routine. I don't cry every day anymore score one for me!

The care of my two black labs, Quentin and Daisy, forces me to carry out at least some mundane tasks. I shop for dog food and some other essentials. I arrive home after dark, lock my car, and pile grocery bags into my arms. The landlord had cut the lawn that afternoon and the evening dampness made the clippings stick to my sandals. I set the groceries on my steps, wipe my grass-covered feet, and unlock the door. Then I heard Sam's voice call to me from the parking lot.

I freeze in mid-step as my heart nearly leaps out of my chest. He's been waiting for me. I turn and there he is leaning against a streetlamp, his hands shoved in his pockets, his awkwardness apparent. He doesn't move to approach me but keeps his distance as if he's worried, he'll scare me off. His tortured face makes me quickly forget my suffering. I smile at him. He walks over, puts his arms around me, and holds me close. He does all this with such temerity I cannot put up my guard. He doesn't speak a single word. I didn't move at first, wrestling with my conflicting emotions unsure of what to do or say. But his arms around my body felt so good, his embrace was so easy to fall into. I put my head down on his shoulder and breathed in his wonderful smell. I slowly, almost involuntarily, put my arms around him and held him close. We stay locked in our embrace for a long time, neither of us wanting the moment to end. Finally, he steps back and looks at me. He smooths my hair out of my face but doesn't move to kiss me. He knows instinctively it is too soon. We sit on the steps, my get-me-through-the-night pint of ice cream forgotten as it melts in the bottom of the bag. The evening turned late. I was drawn in by his charm, and for a while forgot the pain, but in the end, I went inside alone. I was more confused than ever; wracked with indecision. The only place to go in such a situation was home to the shore for the weekend.

Maybe if I lay around the beach at Mom's house for a few days and give myself a break from thinking about all this I'd feel better or at least have some idea of what to do. I pack up the dogs and we head off for the three-hour drive to Mom's house.

The Labs love to play on the beach as they fetch errant Frisbees, chase sandpipers, and bark at seagulls. Mom didn't like me to bring the dogs but was willing to tolerate them if I made them sleep out on the porch. I think she let them come so she'd instantly have something to complain about and didn't have to wait for me to do something she considered stupid. This was my way of giving her a jump on her weekend entertainment.

The desire to go back to Sam was strong; his touch struck down all my logical arguments, but I was determined to do what I thought was right. My change of mind, my decision to let Sam back into my life, came from the most unexpected place Bird.

I know better than to discuss this with Mom. I'd only get a lecture and then we'd end up in a fight. At least I had learned something in twenty-two years. But Bird listened patiently as I examined and reexamined my heartache until I had surveyed and noted every crevice. Finally, when my voice fell silent, when I was weary from my own words, Bird sat down next to me and took my hand. Her hands feel like supple leather, tough from years of dishwashing and floor scrubbing.

"Child," she wiped the last set of my tears from my cheeks as I smiled through bloodshot eyes. "It seems to me you're punishing this man because he made a mistake."

I listened and hoped she had an answer I could live with.

"Everyone makes mistakes, and so'd this man of yours. We can't be judgin' nobody. That's not within our boundary, that's the Lord's duty. Who are we to say what this fella's been through? You gonna punish him some more 'cause you think you're better when maybe all you really been is luckier?"

I feel naked in the face of her indictment.

Bird went on. "You bein' pretty harsh don't ya think? Can you look ol' Bird in the eye and say you never made a mistake?"

We both knew this was an understated rhetorical question.

She lets go of my hand, leans back in her chair, and crosses her arms. "So, he chose wrong the first time and now he's payin' for his mistakes. That mean he can never be forgiven, even by the almighty Miss Hannah?"

I look at her and see that sly smile on her face. "Gee, Bird, why don't you say what's really on your mind? Don't hold back on my account."

Her smile turns into a grin.

Then I ask her the hardest question of all. "What about his son?"

Bird uncrossed her arms, leaned forward, and put her elbows on her knees as she listened.

"If it wasn't for me, he'd still be married, still be a full-time daddy." I continue.

She looks up at me. "You really think that if you never speak to this boy again his marriage is gonna up and save itself, that he's gonna magically turn into a lovin' husband and father?"

I study her face. "No Bird, I don't."

"That's right," she said, the voice of experience. "This boy's problems were in full swing long 'fore you ever showed up. No one can force a man to leave his wife, that was his decision and his decision alone."

I hug Bird tightly she has shown me the yellow brick road.

I got home Sunday night barely past dusk. I unpack and get the dogs settled. They are so tuckered out they land with an oomph in the entranceway and are snoring before I get all our gear inside. There is a knock at the door. It's Al holding a large vase full of Tiger Lilies.

I pluck the vase out of his hands. "Oh, Al, you shouldn't have."

He shoves his hands into his pockets. "I didn't. They were sitting outside your door on Saturday. I knew you'd left to go to your mom's because the dogs were gone, and I didn't want these sitting outside as an advertisement you weren't home."

"What would I do without you, Al? Come on in." I put the vase in the center of my coffee table. I took out the card. They were from Sam. 'Being away from you has caused my sanity to waver, but never, ever, my love.'

Al was full of curiosity. "Are these from your mystery man?"

He still stood in the doorway. I wave him inside. "You mean you didn't read the card?"

"I was tempted, but rules are rules." He steps into the room and gently closes the door behind him. "It's a federal offense that, if convicted, results in a possible fine and maybe even a prison term."

I laugh out loud for the first time in weeks. "That's for opening other people's mail."

Al shrugged his shoulders, "Well, I didn't want to take any chances. You know curiosity killed the cat."

I grin, "Yes, but satisfaction brought him back."

He flops down on the sofa. "Oh, I know if you'd been holding flowers for me, you'd have read the card in an instant." He puts his feet on my coffee table. "Hell, Hannah, you'd have shown it to your friends, yielded it as a party favor. But that's the difference between you and me; you're a shallower person than I am."

I swat his feet off the table. "Oh, come on, Al. This has nothing to do with you possessing a greater ethical foundation. You're just a coward, that's all."

He slips off his shoes and gently puts his feet back on the coffee table. "True," Al admits, "but I like the ethical foundation stuff so much better, don't you?"

I ignore his feet and go to get water for my flowers.

I didn't know how to get in touch with Sam. I would have to wait until I could catch him at work. What I had to say could only be spoken in person. The next morning, I wait until Sam's lunch hour. He mentioned once that because the sawmill where he works was out in the country, there was only one place to eat; a small diner called Lula's located across the street from the mill. I arrived a half hour early. The waitress has a blue plastic name tag pinned to her neat white uniform that says her name is Betty. I told her I was waiting for someone and would order later. She stuffs her pad back into the front pocket of her red apron and shoves her pencil through her thick brunette hair until it perches on her ear. "Suit yourself, Hon," she says.

Betty was in her mid-forties, a slim build, but too much makeup caused her to look more worn than her years. But she had starched and pressed her uniform and neatly arranged her hair; the overall appearance was created with thought and care. I watch her as the lunch crowd starts to thicken. People swarm in and out and lunch orders are shouted at full volume. Waitresses whisk past tables as food magically sails from their hands to their intended recipients. Betty was brisk and efficient as she carried plates stacked on her arms like jets waiting to land at an airport. She deposits her culinary burdens as she swings her hips expertly to go around table corners on her way to and from the kitchen as well as to avoid friendly swats and pinches; all accomplished without dropping a single plate. She heard orders above a din. I couldn't hear myself think. She busily scratches them on her pad and then shouts them over customers' heads towards the kitchen. In the kitchen was a short burly man, whom I assume was not Lula. He grunts and mops his brow as he expertly wields various skillets and pans, food slides down onto Blue Willow plates. Periodically he pounds a small silver bell with his meaty hand and shouts, "Pick up!"

Then suddenly I notice Sam as he comes through the door. Instinctively I rise out of my chair and watch his face. He looks around the room expectantly until he meets my eyes. I forget the pain and the waiting, as he makes his way towards me sifting through a sea of humans. He never takes his eyes off mine. He gathers me in his arms and whispers my name. He knew my coming here meant only one thing that all was forgiven. People stared.

A moment later Betty was beside us clearing her throat impatiently as she licks her pencil and poises it over her pad. "What'll ya have?"

Sam let go of me neither embarrassed nor flustered and turned to her as though this was an everyday occurrence and said, "Betty, we'll start with two iced teas please."

Betty didn't bother to write this down; she looked a bit annoyed.

Sam turns to her and says loud enough for her to hear. "My girlfriend and I are gonna get married."

The woman smiled, all ordering aggravations forgiven and forgotten. She pats his arm. "That's nice Honey, you take good care of each other." She smiles at Sam as her gum snaps in her mouth. "I'll be back with your iced teas in a jiffy." With that she disappears, expertly navigating the snarl of warm bodies. In a few minutes, she is back with two iced teas and several plates of lunch orders nestled up along her arms. She dropped off the tea glasses without a word and winked at Sam.

I marvel at his ability to turn people in his favor; charm was indeed a powerful weapon. I felt a moment of jealousy, but it passed when he took my hand and smiled at me.

Sam moved in a few weeks later, and the fun of playing house consumed nearly all my energy. Marie was cool, but tolerant of Sam. Al, being Al, thought Sam was the best thing to happen to me since sliced bread. Of course, Al was unaware of our history; I didn't bother to enlighten him.

Sam, his wife, and I all agree on one thing a quick divorce. In the South, the only way was to file under charges of adultery. His wife named me as correspondent. Sam was sick about this. I wasn't thrilled, but the alternative was to wait. I felt like a kid playing grown-up games. Sam's four-year-old son, Cal, came over on an occasional weekend; his mother was stubbornly reluctant to grant more visitation, and Sam was unwilling to demand more for fear she wouldn't go along with the divorce; the kid became the weapon of choice. I knew nothing about kids and found Cal's presence a disturbing reminder of my acknowledged and public sin. Cal was also the cutest kid I'd ever seen. He was both funny and earnest as he tried to fit into his new world. I was smitten on the first visit.

For the most part, though, I found my life with Sam to be wonderful my time spent on carefree weekends following the band. While I freely admitted that Sam was no Adonis, he had an animal magnetism that attracted women like moths to a beacon of light. Being the singer in a band was a powerful aphrodisiac. After a few drinks, a man with a silver voice can be hard to resist. Fortunately, Sam only had eyes for me, and I made sure that whenever his eyes were open, I was standing down front.

My boring existence took on pizzazz. I had always been a loner of sorts. Now there was a party every Friday and Saturday night and I got to be with the man all the women wanted. How wonderful my pitiful life is. How terrific for my ego. Because I had a worry quota to fill, I got anxious that he'd get tired of me. What did he see in me I often asked myself my love was true, my desire unending and I didn't ask for too much; never too much.

Several months later, the divorce became final. A celebration was in order, but Sam was distracted. I often found him brooding at the kitchen table in the middle of the night smoking cigarettes, a habit he'd kicked years before. He started to get short-tempered, first with the band members, then with me. He told me he was overly tired, working all week and then playing with the band on the weekends, said he was getting too old for life on the road.

I steered clear of him during his increasingly long moments of despondency. I felt helpless, nothing I did would cheer him up. I feel like a Laker girl without her pom poms. A few weeks after the divorce was final, Sam's wife announced she was getting remarried. The news stunned Sam. He was sure she was seeing someone while they were still living together as man and wife. Not that his pot could call her kettle black, but he took the full brunt of the guilt when it was now evident, she was equally guilty. I was furious for Sam; he was dazed by the implications. A few months later, his wife finally put their house on the market, the sale being part of their negotiated divorce settlement. He had to go over a few evenings during the week to make cosmetic repairs before they could show the place. On one such evening, he didn't come back.

At first, I was concerned, then I worried, and then I became frantic. What could have happened? I couldn't call her house. We had never met or spoken and I certainly couldn't give her the satisfaction of knowing I didn't trust Sam. Besides, I worried that he might still be there, and the humiliation would be more than I could bear. The evening turned to night; the night dragged on interminably. I called the girlfriend of one of the other band members and asked her for the phone number of her boyfriend, the drummer. She was gracious enough not only to give me the number, but not to ask any questions. I called him, his name was Michael. I had woken him. I apologized and decided to be honest. He and Sam had been friends since high school. He promised to call her house and then took my number promising to call me back if he found out anything. My gratitude was enormous but hard to express over the phone. Now all I had to do was wait. I wondered if I added up all the time I have waited on men in my life and what the tally would be. What intellectual feat could I have accomplished instead? I calculated that I could have translated War and Peace into Spanish.

I couldn't stand it anymore and did the only sensible thing a woman could do in my situation I scrubbed floors. I scrub the bathroom floor, then the kitchen. I have an old toothbrush in my hand cleaning behind the refrigerator when the phone finally rings. The ring sounds ominous; I chide myself for being overly dramatic. It was Michael. I could tell from the sound of his voice he was going to tell me something I didn't want to hear. I sit down anticipating the worst. He doesn't disappoint. Michael tells me that Sam was all right, but he was still at his wife's house. I correct him and say, ex-wife. We both knew that was a hollow victory. I didn't ask and he didn't offer any details. I thanked him once again and hung up the phone.

Sam comes home at dawn. I pretend to be asleep, and he lets me go on pretending. He showers, changes his clothes, and heads off to work. I cry when the door clicks shut. We never talked about that night, but it was the beginning of the end. The magic was gone. I began to sound like a wife with too many years under her belt and he began to behave like a disinterested husband who didn't have the nerve or the heart to say goodbye.

A month later, in January, I graduated from college with a degree in business. A securities firm in Chicago offers me an entry-level position in their government bond division. I told Sam about the job, hoping he'd ask me to stay. Instead, he seems to think it would be 'good for me' to accept the offer. I take the job as much to punish Sam as to get away from the disintegration of our relationship. A fresh start was so enticing, but my main motive was to scare Sam with the threat of losing me, so he'd beg me not to go. He didn't beg. He didn't even ask. I was too proud not to go. There was no turning back.

How did I get into this situation of moving hundreds of miles away from home, away from my family, and away from Sam? Maybe once I get there and he misses me things will work out. I was not only an idiot, but an idiot out of time and with no options. After all, pride and dignity may not keep a woman warm at night, but they did let her look at herself in the mirror.

The move was painful. Sam helps me drive up and get settled. We unload the last of the boxes and return the rental trailer. He needs to get back to work and can't stay on. I was grateful for his help and show of faith by coming with me but dreaded his departure on the train for home.

The last part of our time together was a blur of unpacking as we avoided talking about anything but the most mundane of topics. We sleep on opposite sides of the bed making the night long and cold. By the time I took him to the train station, I think we were both grateful he had to leave.

The station is nearly deserted when we arrive. Small gray ceramic tiles cover the floor; the grime of a thousand travelers trampled into the crevices. I tried to think of anything but his leaving. We hold hands in the waiting room but don't talk much. We both know this is the end, that our love will never recover. The distance his betrayal had left was almost as large as the distance the miles between us now brought.

The waiting room slowly fills up, the noise echoes off the tile walls while the winter cold seeps in with each entering passenger. We huddle closer putting both hands into one another's, a desperate move of lovers parting. Inevitably the loudspeaker announces his train south. A swarm of passengers head towards the door like birds changing flight direction in mid-wing-flap.

We rise silently. He puts his arm tightly around my shoulder as we make our way to the platform. Once outside he kisses me deeply, I feel my knees get weak as the familiar passion flares under his caress. He looks at me wordlessly, one last time. In his eyes I could see the silent but desperate wish to go back; to have our life returned. I touch the side of his face with my gloved hand and start to tell him how much I love him. He shakes his head and gently places his fingertips on my lips to silence me. He knows my heart is breaking, he knows he is responsible and there are no words to take us back. He turns abruptly and gets on the train. I follow his progress to the back of the car where he takes a seat and lowers the window. I stand on tiptoe to reach his outstretched hands. My breath came in white clouds.

The train whistles and it lurches forward. Sam's hands are wrenched out of mine as the train begins to lumber, smoothing as it picks up speed. He looks at me, but the distance begins to consume the details of his face.

"Don't go!" I shout. But my words were snatched by the Chicago winds and carried away. I thought I saw him mouth the words, 'I Love You' but I couldn't be sure. My breath caught in my throat. The last car passes me. The train swiftly gains speed, moves around the bend, and slips out of sight.

"Are you all right Ma'am?" A kind porter asks. I turn with tears running down my cheeks. He nods in quiet understanding and wordlessly leaves me alone. I stand outside in the cold for nearly an hour, simply wishing the train to return. My feet and hands grow numb. I feel nothing. Finally, I head back to my car and a new life I hoped would help ease the pain.

Eventually, I found a new boyfriend and tried to get on with my life. I thought the distraction of a new lover would help me forget Sam. I was excruciatingly wrong. I wait for Sam to make the first move. He never does.

CHAPTER SIX (1994)

Back at Mom's house, I face the unpleasant task of sorting through the remnants of her life. I drink my second cup of coffee out on the porch as I postpone the inevitable. I hear a car drive up, it's my younger sister Maddie and my younger brother Kyle. As they round the corner of the house, anyone could tell their brother and sister. The distinctive gait to their walk and certain familial hand gestures when talking give their relationship away. As fashion statements, however, they shop on different floors at Filene's. Maddie has her freshly pressed blouse tucked neatly into her creased khaki shorts. Kyle has on a mangled T-shirt with missing sleeves, blue jeans with a large hole ripped in one knee, and a pair of black lace-up Army boots that look uncomfortably hot. The whole ensemble gives him a stray-dog-by-the-side-of-the-road allure. One does not want to stop to pick him up but worries the next car might run him over. I ask them if they want coffee.

Maddie looks uneasy. "Let's just get started. We have a lot to do, and I don't relish having to go through Mom's old things. It feels creepy." She shoves her hands into her pockets. Her hair hangs loosely about her shoulders as she leans against the porch railing. With the sun at her back, she reminds me of the teenager who used to borrow my clothes and filch my jewelry. Some of the awkwardness of youth still lurks behind the professional woman who now stands before me.

As children, Maddie and I had competed for Mom's attention. Mom loved Maddie more, and, as any sister can imagine, it was never more obvious to anyone than me. As an adult, I finally got up the nerve to broach the subject with Mom. I was driving her to the grocery store, and I asked her. I hated myself at that moment. There I was, nearly twenty-one and still I begged the question.

"Maddie was easier to love, sweeter, and more soft-spoken," Mom said, "she was more lovable."

You wouldn't think a grown woman could have her heart crushed so easily. I suppose I thought that if she pretended, I could live with the certainty the first to know, but last to believe. Of course, when she told me, I said nothing. I nodded my head like a spring-headed, plastic dog in the back window of a moving car, but inside I screamed, 'How could you?' The conflict between my grownup rational side and the young girl that still prowled the confines of my heart nearly tore me apart. I was left with unresolved anger I tried hard not to direct towards Maddie.

Kyle draws me back to the present. "Where's Wilkes?"

"He's still sleeping. He came in late last night and I didn't have the heart to wake him."

"What would we say to him anyway?" Maddie asks. "'Hi, Wilkes, don't mind us as we divvy up Mom's stuff.'"

I squirm at the mental picture.

Maddie sounds upset already. "Let's get to it, OK?"

This is going to be a long day.

I lead the way inside. "Where do you want to start?"

"Let's do the attic first while it's still cool and then move our way down as the day heats up," Kyle suggests sensibly.

In the hallway, Kyle reaches up and pulls the rope that dangles overhead, and the stairs magically unfold; the mouth of the attic gapes open dark and beseeching. Maddie and I look at each other, then as if on cue look at Kyle and say: "After you."

He bows dramatically, an impish grin on his face. "Why dear sisters, I'm honored." He grabs the wood handrails and with no fear climbs the stairs. Maddie looks at me and I at her. I raise an eyebrow, issuing a silent sisterly challenge. She winks at me and goes up the stairs while I bring up the rear.

Once I reach the top of the stairs, Maddie nervously grabs hold of my upper arm. "Hey, I thought there was a light up here somewhere."

"There is, hold on a minute," Kyle says. I can see his outline, the sunlight filtering through the eaves highlighting the dust that hangs in the air. His hand swipes the open space above him as he feels for the light cord. "Dang it!" He shouts as his fingertips painfully slap the rafter beam above his head.

Maddie's fingers start to dig into my flesh. I pry them off and hold her hand until Kyle locates the light cord; she has always been afraid of the dark. Kyle finds the cord and turns on the light with a yank. The dangling light bulb swings back and forth, shadows sliding on and off our faces. Strewn around the attic are boxes closed with brown strapping tape, racks of clothes covered in plastic, dusty filing cabinets, and old furniture. Near the top of the stairs and to the left is an old small hard-covered suitcase encircled with woven variegated stripes, the brass latches pitted with rust. A broken leather handle hangs on the front.

I used this suitcase when I tried to run away from home.

* * *

I was nine years old and hadn't gotten my way - a tragic event. "I'll show them! They'll be sorry when they find me gone," I said as I pulled that suitcase out from under my bed. I throw in some clothes, essential dolls and their paraphernalia, and my faithful stuffed brown bear. To make sure that Mom and Dad would hear my impending departure, I drag the loaded suitcase noisily down the hall. Mom comes around the corner as I make my way through the dining room.

Her hands were calmly clasped before her. "Where are you going?"

"I'm leaving home," I say as I wait for her to fall to her knees and beg me to stay. She says nothing for a moment.

"Do you have any money?"

I was immediately indignant. "No, but I can get a job."

"Do you have anything to eat?"

"I'm not hungry."

"Well, Hannah it seems you've thought of everything." She turns and holds the door open for me.

I grab the broken suitcase handle and drag the case forward.

"Don't be draggin' that case across my good parquet floor young lady," she admonishes. She didn't look upset about my leaving. My plan was sprouting a few unforeseen flaws. I bend down, pick the case up in my arms, head through the kitchen, and out the side door into the garage. The garage is dark. Mom shut the side door behind me but didn't lock it. I knew I had her at my mercy.

I decided to sleep in the back seat of the car and get an early start. I retrieved my bear from my suitcase, so he wouldn't be scared, and I waited. Any minute they will realize I was serious about this and run after me with apologies in tow. Two hours later, when all my resolve has dissipated and my hopes of attempted reconciliation dashed, I hear the side door open. Dad comes out and scoops me off the car seat as I keep my eyes squeezed shut in feigned sleep. Even when he accidentally dings my head on the door frame carrying me into the house, I keep my eyes closed tight. By the next morning, my suitcase had mysteriously reappeared in my room. I wordlessly unpack and shove it back under my bed. I guess I had shown them.

* * *

Maddie's shaking my arm: "Where were you?"

"Just being nostalgic," I tell her as we admire the vast collection of stuff Mom has accumulated over the years. Besides antiquated luggage, there are piles of empty boxes for Christmas and birthday shipments. In the middle of the floor sits a large plastic container full of wrapping paper, bows, and ribbons covered with an old sheet to keep the dust off. She has stacked boxes nearly halfway to the rafters. There are boxes with the names of each child on them. Kyle finds a box with his name on it and carefully pulls it out of the pile and sets it on the floor. Inside are meticulously folded piles of his old clothes.

"Wow, look at this. I haven't seen this shirt since junior high school." He rummages a little further and finds an old belt, a raincoat, some worn slacks, and other nondescript items.

"Why'd she keep this junk?" he wonders aloud. "Why didn't she throw this stuff out or give it away?"

I move to Kyle's side and peer into the box for myself. "You know Mom, the original pack rat."

"But some of these clothes aren't even wearable," Kyle holds up a pair of navy-blue slacks with a large rip in the seat. "What do you think she was saving this for?"

I can't resist. I tug on the torn hole in his jeans. "Because she knew it would eventually come back into style, so she saved it for you."

Kyle swats my hand away. "Everyone's a critic."

Maddie goes on the defensive. The voice of the protective older sister, "Hannah!"

"What, Maddie? I was only teasing him."

"Maybe not everyone finds your teasing amusing."

I had the feeling we weren't talking about Kyle anymore.

"Is that right?" I'm full of snappy comebacks.

Maddie grabs the opening "Yeah, maybe Kyle's sensitive about his clothes."

I turn to Kyle before she can stop me. "Is that right, Kyle? Are you sensitive about your clothing?"

"Don't drag me into this, I'm an innocent bystander."

I smile at his wisdom. "You're just a coward, you mean."

He smiles back, "Whatever."

Maddie stomps her foot. "Would you two knock it off?"

I can't tell if she's angry or not, but before I can find out she changes the subject.

"There's one with your name on it, Hannah," as Maddie points at a box to my right. We open it up. Inside are more old clothes, most I recall, some I don't. I find a white cotton dress festooned with rose-colored flowers I wore on my first day of high school.

What could be more horrifying than entering high school? First-day terrors in full swing, desperate to fit in yet destined to live on the fringe of friendships; girls only give me their time when other friends are too busy.

Lunch period presented the greatest challenge: "Is this seat taken?" I dared to ask a classmate. "I'm saving it for someone," she would allege. I struggled through those awkward seconds of rejection as I held my plastic tray with its plopped goodies and acted as though I didn't care about the pettiness of teenage girls who couldn't stand to sit next to me for even half an hour. I sat alone, scarfed down my food, and felt as conspicuous as a zit on a beauty queen. I watched that saved seat out of the corner of my eye. Nobody ever came to claim it and my humiliation drifted dangerously close to rage.

Maddie taps me on the shoulder and ends my reminiscing. "Where do you keep going?" She takes the dress out of my hands and holds it up to the light. "Can't say I'd have saved this one," she says as she clumsily refolds it and tosses it back in the box. "I guess I should be glad I didn't get stuck with that as a hand-me-down."

The stark light in the attic makes her features look drawn and older. It's the first time I have stopped to consider that Maddie is no longer a kid but a grown woman in her mid-thirties. She still looks young, but the first signs of age are sniffing along the edges of her youth. Maddie never married. I wonder if she's sorry now or if she hears her biological clock's tick-tock echo in her ears. Maddie was so thrilled when I had Carly. She played the part of the doting aunt to perfection. She flew up and spent two weeks - almost all her vacation time - helping me after Carly was born. She never failed to send Carly birthday and Christmas presents - always something extravagant. Carly, of course, thought her Aunt Maddie walked on water. I had found a renewed love for Maddie in her love for my daughter. Maddie catches me staring at her. She smiles and winks at me.

I smile back, close the box, and try to stick the tape back on. "I suppose we should open each of these and what we don't want, repack, and take downstairs for delivery to Goodwill."

Kyle generously volunteers to carry the boxes down after Maddie and I go through them one by one. Most are easy to sort through, just old clothes, although occasionally there's a scrap of paper or a photograph that's interesting.

In one box I discover some old newspaper clippings and old letters. I find a letter addressed to me; the envelope is still intact. I slowly pick it up and examine the front and back; there is no return address the postmark's stamped June 30, 1979.

Maddie looks over my shoulder at the envelope in my hand. "What'd you find?"

"I'm not sure?"

"Who's it from?"

I turn the envelope over again in my hand. "Why would Mom have an unopened letter addressed to me?"

"I don't know," Maddie whispers. "Go on, open it."

I hand the letter to Maddie. "Here, you open it."

She sits on the floor next to me, carefully loosens the flap of the envelope, and withdraws a single sheet of paper, the contents handwritten. I recognize Sam's handwriting. I nod to Maddie for her to read it out loud. She unfolds the letter and begins to read.

Dear Hannah:

Your Mom won't give me your new phone number, but I thought she would deliver this letter if she didn't know it was from me. I miss you so terribly and know what a mistake I made in letting you go. I still love you.

I'm not very good at putting my feelings on paper, but I would love the chance to talk with you. Please call me; if you don't call, I'll understand that you want to get on with your life and I won't bother you again.

All My Love, Sam

For a few moments, we are both quiet. Neither of us knows what to say.

"You mean you never got this?" Maddie asks in disbelief.

I shake my head in silence. Sam had sent this letter six months after I'd moved to Chicago.

My post-Sam boyfriend in Chicago didn't take it too well when I dumped him. He began to follow me. At first, I thought it was harmless, but then he started to track me while I was on dates, phoning me in the middle of the night to make sure I was alone. Once I caught him watching me from across a half-deserted restaurant as I ate dinner with a new security analyst from work. It was hard to turn on the charm and captivate my new love interest while a lunatic stared at me. His phone calls became threatening. The police said they couldn't do anything unless he tried to hurt me. I decided not to fulfill their requirement. I moved and got an unlisted phone number. Then I worried he would follow me from work and find my new address, so I transferred to the office downtown. Of course, it was no small accident that the downtown office was also where the new security analyst worked.

And now here I sit in the dust of my mother's attic holding in my hands the road not taken. I have a hard time deciding whether I'm more upset by my mother's duplicity or by the lost opportunity to be with Sam.

"It's awfully quiet up there," Wilkes shouts from the bottom of the stairs.

I look at Maddie. "Please, don't tell anyone about this," I say as I take the letter from her hands, replace it in the envelope, and stuff it in the pocket of my jeans.

"Well, good morning." I sound calm and collected even to me. "Did you have a good time last night with your friends?"

Maddie watches me with a puzzled look on her face.

"Hey, Wilkes how ya doin' man?" Kyle calls out as he comes back into the house for another load.

"Hey Bro' how's it going for you?"

"Not too bad, but it's starting to get awful dang hot in that attic. I think Mom did you a favor."

I hold my breath. I can't believe Kyle would even mention 'the will incident' to Wilkes. But, then again, that was just like Kyle, very straightforward, no secrets. Kyle's an enigma, he couldn't possibly be from the same gene pool; he's too normal.

Wilkes puts his arm around Kyle and steers him towards the kitchen. "Well, let's get a brew and cool off. You've been working too hard."

"Hey," Maddie shouts, "who is going to carry all these boxes down?"

"I will return Sir Kyle in a few moments ladies, so don't get your knickers in a bind, OK?"

"Knickers my ass," I say to Maddie under my breath.

She laughs, then whispers, "Why didn't you want them to know about the letter?"

I try to think of a response. I don't have one. "Let's see what's in those boxes over there." I move off hoping she won't pursue the letter business.

Maddie was never stupid or insensitive, she dropped the subject and helped me sort through at least a dozen more boxes before Kyle showed up again. The attic starts to get unbearably hot; we'll have to move downstairs soon.

"I'm back," Kyle announces, a stupid grin plastered on his face. Something tells me they had more than just one brew and it's only ten o'clock. "What do you need me to do, Fair Damsels?" We both look up, dust in our hair, dirt on our faces as sweat trickles down in all sorts of uncomfortable places.

He looks at both of us, and the smile on his face disappears with comic slowness. "Ouch!" he says, "If looks could kill."

I get up and open the metal file cabinet. It's stuffed with papers. "Kyle why don't you take a few of these drawers downstairs and put them on the kitchen table so we can sort through them where it's not so hot."

I hear the phone ring in the distance. I look up expectantly and Kyle says, "Wilkes's still down there, he'll get it."

"Hannah, it's for you," Wilkes calls up the stairs. "I think it's Jack." I come down the stairs using the tail of my shirt to mop the dirt and sweat off my face. "How could you marry such a dweeb?" He asks.

I look at Wilkes annoyed "I'm not married to him anymore. I hope you didn't say anything to make him angry."

He smiles as I go to the phone in Mom's room and shut the door.

"Hello," I call into the receiver.

"Hannah, is that you?"

It's not Jack.

"Yes," I answer, the hair on the back of my neck begins to prickle. "Who's this?" I already know the answer.

"It's Sam, Sam Lancaster."

His voice sounded exactly as I remembered. The years apart swoosh closed at lightning speed. Involuntarily I say: "Oh my God."

"Did you get the flowers I sent?"

I can't respond because my brain whirls so fast that I don't have any cells left to make my mouth work. I sit on the edge of the bed before my knees give out and I find my butt on the floor.

"Yes," I sound like a bad imitation of Breathless Mahoney.

"Hannah, are you all right?" There is genuine concern in his voice.

"Yes, I'm fine." I clear my throat and regain a modicum of composure. "How are you, Sam?" I stall for time.

He doesn't want to waste any. "I'd like to get together with you to catch up. Can you have a late lunch with me this afternoon? I know it's short notice and all, but it would be lovely to see you."

I fall over my tongue. I can't say no, I never could say no. I chide myself, 'Oh come on, you haven't seen this guy in more than ten years. You're both grownups now. It'll be two old friends getting together for lunch, that's all, nothing more.' I convinced myself. With that argument won, I turned my attention back to Sam.

"That'd be real nice Sam, I'd enjoy seeing you too." I try to sound polite yet casual.

"Look, I know you must be busy so why don't I bring lunch out to you, and we can visit on the beach? I won't stay too long because I have to get back to work. That sound good to you?"

I assure him it does, and we agree on the time and place. We aren't going to meet until two o'clock, so I have a few hours left before I need to start getting ready.

When I come out of Mom's room Kyle has set two metal filing cabinet drawers on the kitchen table. Maddie is already thumbing through some of the papers as Kyle and Wilkes look on being their usual helpful selves.

"What's in those?" I ask.

Before Maddie can answer me, Wilkes interrupts. "Listen you two don't need Kyle to help with that, why he'd only be in the way don't you think?"

I look at him suspiciously. I think I know where this is leading. "Get to your point, Wilkes."

"Well, I thought that Kyle and I could take a walk on the beach and get caught up, you know engage in some male bonding." Wilkes puts his arm clumsily around Kyle's shoulders. Kyle inspects the pattern on the kitchen linoleum.

Maddie laughs at them both. "You mean cruise for babes, don't you?"

Neither answer. I look from one to the other. "True?"

"Well, there may be women there and they may want to get to know us better. Who are we to deprive them of the famous Wheeler charm?" Wilkes says enjoying himself. He knows he's already won the battle, now he's just having fun with the prisoners.

I look from one to the other and say, "All right, get lost."

Maddie chimes in with a smile on her face, "Yeah, beat it you two."

They turn towards the door without a moment's hesitation. Wilkes tries to get Kyle in a headlock to administer one of his famous noogies. Kyle squirms mightily, finally breaks loose, and runs ahead of Wilkes who follows in hot pursuit.

"Was that Jack on the phone?" Maddie asks when they've gone.

"No," I answer evasively.

Her innocence is exasperating, "Who was it?"

"It was Sam, all right?"

"Really? And you weren't going to tell me? What kind of sister keeps that sort of vital information to herself?"

I busy myself with papers.

"Well, don't keep me in suspense. What'd he say?"

"He wants to have lunch with me." I made another show of sorting through the first file folder.

"Well, are you going to have lunch with him or not?"

"Yes," I nearly shout. "I'm meeting him at the beach this afternoon for a picnic lunch."

"Oooh, a picnic lunch, how romantic," she teases.

"Now stop that. We are just two old friends getting together to catch up, that's all." I tell her sternly, as I lift out a stack of files and place them on the table in front of me.

"Yeah, Elizabeth Taylor and Richard Burton were good buddies. Come on, Hannah, this guy was the love of your life, and you haven't seen him in nearly fifteen years. I can't believe you're being so casual about all this." She takes the next armload of files from me and puts them on the table. "Shouldn't you be getting ready? You don't want to go looking like that."

"Gee, you think?" My sarcasm is lost on her. "We're not meeting until two o'clock, so I have a little time yet before I have to start scraping the dirt off me."

"What are you going to wear?"

"Well, I hadn't given it much thought. I suppose clothes would be in order." I kid her knowing she's probably chock-full of ideas.

"Hey, remember the best revenge is looking great so he knows what he missed out on," Maddie says. Her face turns serious. "Why do you think Mom kept Sam's letter from you Hannah?"

"I don't know. She never really liked or approved of Sam."

Maddie marvels at my composure "Aren't you even a little angry that she would do such a thing?"

"More sad than mad. Now I will have to spend a lot of time wondering what if. You know what I mean?"

"You mean, what if you'd married Sam?"

"Yeah, but more than that. All this time I thought it was out of my hands, that Sam had decided he didn't want me and there was nothing I could do to change his mind. Now I find it was fate, be thee named mother, that intervened."

"I'm sorry, Hannah, I know that must hurt." She rubs my back lightly with the palm of her hand to try and make me feel better. Her love and concern make my eyes burn with tears. I try to wave her off, but she stoops down and awkwardly hugs me. My tears roll down my cheeks and land on her shoulder. She holds me tighter.

I let a sob escape. "You know that Mom always loved you the most don't you?"

She lets go of me and sits in the chair next to mine. She doesn't say a word. I feel silly and embarrassed that I said anything. I try to lighten the mood. "Why all of a sudden do I feel like a Smother's brother?" I smile at her through my tears.

Maddie drops her gaze to her lap where her hands busily smooth the crease in her shorts. "I know Mom acted like she loved me more."

"You knew?"

"Yes, I knew. But I bet you didn't know what a burden it was."

"A burden!" I blurt out in disbelief.

Maddie holds up her hands to silence me. "Yes, a burden. To feel your pain when Mom made a display of loving me more."

"You mean you knew what she was doing?"

"Anyone with eyes knew what she was doing. That was her favorite punishment. You screwed up and she'd make me cookies. You sassed her, I got a new nightgown."

"But why?" I ask. The child-like sincerity in my voice slaps her in the face.

"Because it worked," Maddie whispered.

"I don't get it. What do you mean it worked?"

"Every time she did it, your pain was written all over your crestfallen face. She had her weapon and she used it unmercifully."

I could hardly absorb what Maddie was telling me. I couldn't seem to jam it into place.

"You see," Maddie continues, "it wasn't that she loved me more, but she used me to hurt you."

I can only stare at her.

"As a kid, I did think she loved me more, and sometimes when she hurt you, I was glad." Maddie softly strokes my hair. "I'm not very proud of that. But mostly she hurt me as much as you. I never enjoyed what I got at your expense, I always felt sort of dirty and guilty."

I take Maddie's hand in mine. "It wasn't your fault."

"I know, but the pain she caused affected both our lives. She should never have used me that way and she never should have hurt you the way she did. It was just plain mean."

I nod and go in search of a tissue. I found a box by the sink.

"But then," Maddie continues, "when I thought I couldn't take another minute, she'd be at my bedside taking care of me when I had the flu or loaning me money to buy my first house."

I splash water on my face and grab a fresh dish towel from next to the sink. "Do you miss her?"

"Sure, I do," Maddie explains, "I miss telling her about a new lamp I bought or getting her opinion on the new curtains I'm thinking about putting in the living room, things like that. While I didn't relish all her advice, it was a part of my life."

"I know what you mean." I sit back down. "Nothing was ever black and white with Mom. She could be so exasperating to the point of hatred and then she'd help babysit Carly when Jack and I wanted to go on a cruise and our sitter canceled a week before we were to leave."

Maddie slips her shoes off and curls her legs up under her. "I'm sorry Mom hurt you. I'm sorry I hurt you."

"You didn't have anything to do with it. Mom wouldn't let us be normal sisters. In a way, we should thank her because, in the end, it brought us closer together."

"It was a hell of a price to pay."

"Amen!"

A silence settles between us.

"Look, let's not talk about this anymore, OK?" I leaf through the documents in front of me. "What do you think all these papers are?"

"Looks like a bunch of bank statements. I think every bank statement she ever got is here. My God, this woman never threw anything out."

I flip through pages of statements dating back nearly thirty years. "At least she didn't save all the canceled checks."

Maddie laughs. "Hey, don't be so sure. There are six more file drawers up there waiting for us."

I think about all those file cabinet drawers upstairs. "God, I hope you didn't just jinx us, my dear."

"To change the subject abruptly, I have to ask you, did you ever see Sam again, I mean after you moved to Chicago?" Maddie asks tentatively, curious. "If you don't want to talk about it, I'll understand. You can tell me to buzz off."

"No, I don't mind," I say as I set the papers in my hands on the tabletop. "I did see him two more times after that," I tell her. "The first time was more than a year after I moved to Chicago. I broke up with the security analyst at work and unfortunately, because he was also my boss, I lost my job. I moved back home to regroup." Maddie nods for me to continue. "I'd saved enough money to enroll in graduate school. I wanted to become a college professor. Sam must have heard I was back. I hadn't been in town more than 48 hours before he showed up on Mom's doorstep asking for me."

* * *

He was a sight for sore eyes standing there on Mom's porch. My heart began to beat faster the moment I saw his face. We talked and within a week the romance was back on. I fell in love with him all over again. I had forgotten how all-consuming he could be.

He was different, quieter. There was a sadness I couldn't quite put my finger on. He finally told me he'd taken a job in Mississippi and was to leave in two weeks. He asked me to marry him and come along. We got a marriage license and even picked out wedding bands. The thrill of realizing my biggest dream was marred by nagging doubts. I wanted to go to school and become a professor. The irony of finally knowing what I wanted to do with my life and yet I knew if I married Sam, I would never get there. I was torn between my old desires and my new dreams. I knew if I went through with the marriage, I wouldn't go back to school. He would absorb my time and I would live the rest of my life with regrets.

He saw the choice in my eyes, his sadness and resignation almost made me change my mind. I honestly thought we'd get another chance at a different time to be together when things were right for us both. He gave me his love and blessing and even kept me company in the evenings while I filled out applications for graduate school. Soon he had to leave, and our time together came to an end. Once again, I found myself telling Sam goodbye.

* * *

"Did he ever mention the letter?" Maddie asks.

"He never mentioned the letter and he never asked me why I hadn't responded. Seven months later I ran into one of the members of the old band who told me Sam had gotten married."

"No!" Maddie sounds remorseful. "What did you do?"

"Nothing. There was nothing I could do. I guess he couldn't wait any longer."

Maddie tries to lessen the blow. "He wanted to marry you Hannah, but it wasn't right for you at the time."

"He should have married me," I whisper, "I knew he still loved me, but our timing was always off." I'm surprised these old feelings pop to the surface so easily and with such zeal.

I go back to sorting; the paper pile grows larger by the minute as I toss more bank records and other scraps. I find the hospital bills from Mom's having each of us kids.

Maddie prompts me to continue. "I thought you said you saw him twice after Chicago."

"I did. Before I married Jack, I tracked Sam down. I knew I was still carrying a torch, but I hadn't seen Sam in almost four years. Not since he'd moved away to Mississippi and gotten married."

Maddie gets a cardboard box for recycling from the garage and starts to fill it with the papers we have let drop on the floor beneath us. "How'd you find him?"

"I hired a detective."

"A detective, you're kidding?"

"No, I picked one out of the Yellow Pages and told him I was looking for an old boyfriend."

Maddie's curiosity grows. "How did he find him?"

"I still had the marriage license with his birth date and social security number. The detective used that information to find him. He found him in Charleston and got an address and phone number."

"Did Jack know what you were doing?"

"Do I look stupid? Of course not. But I had to know if it was over with Sam before I married Jack."

Maddie has stopped picking up papers and stands still before me. "Was he still married?"

"Yes, he was still married, but he wanted to see me."

Maddie sets the recycle box aside and sits down facing me. "Did you tell him you were getting married?"

"No, not over the phone. I went to see him in Charleston."

* * *

We meet at a restaurant off the interstate. He is waiting for me at a booth when I come in. He stands and gives me a hug and a kiss on the cheek.

"You look wonderful Hannah; life must be treating you well," he says as he takes his seat on the other side of the booth from me.

"You haven't changed at all," I assure him but notice his eyes are bloodshot and his hands shake as he picks up his water glass.

"I'm so glad you called; I've been thinking about you." He reaches across the table and takes my hand. "I'm so glad you found me."

"I'm getting married Sam," I blurt out as I take my hand back.

"No!"

The waitress comes to take our order. When she leaves, he looks at me. I could see he'd aged in the past few years; his face is a sort of a pasty white. He looked beaten down and unhappy.

"Why'd you come to see me, Hannah, if you're getting married?"

I try to lighten things up. "I guess I had to see you one last time before I did the dirty deed."

"Do you love him?"

I go on the defensive, "What kind of question is that?"

"Well, it just seems to me that if you loved this guy, you wouldn't have come down here to see how you felt about an old boyfriend." He aims his arrow carefully and hits his mark.

"Jack is wonderful," I assure him, sorry I came. "He's finishing med school and is going into residency next year." I hit Sam's education button. From the wounded look on his face I can see my aim is also true.

His voice softens. "Look, I'm sorry Hannah. I didn't mean to make you angry. I guess I got a little jealous, is all."

"I'm the one who should be jealous. You were hardly out of my sight before you up and married someone else." Tears come unexpectedly.

"I know." Sadness settles over him. "I shouldn't have married her."

I finally got to ask the long-unspoken question. "Why did you?"

"I couldn't face living alone. It's as simple as that," he says as his eyes plead for understanding.

Sam never could stand to be alone; he isn't the singles kind of guy. I do understand, but that doesn't lessen the hurt I feel.

"I wish I'd married you," He looks at me with those intense green eyes. "I wish you hadn't turned me away." Reminding me it was I who decided to leave.

"I suppose it's too late for regrets."

The waitress brings our food, and we spend the next few minutes in silence as we eat.

"When are you getting married, Hannah?"

"In a couple of weeks."

We finish our lunch, and he wants to take me for a drive. He takes me down past my alma mater, the College of Charleston. I am surprised how little it has changed over the last few years, but I did notice some refurbished walkways and a new dormitory. He then drives down to the Battery in the old part of Charleston where the ocean beats relentlessly against the man-made concrete edifice and the beginnings of the Civil War are but a boat ride away at Fort Sumter. We park on the road at Battery Park. Battery Park is surrounded by old antebellum homes. Well-kept mansions from another era still stand firm and as imposing as ever against both time and Mother Nature. The park was nearly empty, the afternoon picnickers had already packed up and gone. Sam and I walk to the gazebo in the middle of the park where he takes me in his arms and before I can make even a token protest, he kisses me deeply as his arms pull my body tightly against his. My knees go weak, and I hate myself for being such a feeble ninny. When Sam loosens his grip, I pull away flustered and unsure what to do or say.

"Sam, I can't go through this again." I nearly beg for his understanding. "I've got a good life now. You're married and I'm getting married. I can't throw all that away for a few stolen moments with you."

"I'm not asking for anything past today, Hannah. Just let me love you today." The passion in his eyes is fierce, I weaken under its intensity.

"No, you don't understand. It's not only being unfaithful to your wife or Jack but also digging up all those emotions; all the love I have carried around for you over the years inside my heart. If I let those feelings out, I will have to suffer the agony of losing you all over again. I don't think I can live through that again."

He studies my face for a long time. My breath comes in small, ragged gasps, tears roll down my cheeks.

"I'm sorry, Hannah." He takes me in his arms again. "I wasn't thinking. You're right; it would hurt both of us to bring up such deep feelings. But I am glad to know you still love me." He brushes the hair back from my face, such a familiar gesture. "I hope you have a good life, Hannah. I hope Jack makes you happy. I will miss you and love you all the days of my life." He takes my face in his hands and kisses me ever so softly on the lips. Then we silently went back to the restaurant, and I drove to the airport.

* * *

"What incredible love. What incredibly bad timing." Maddie stoops to put more papers in the recycle box. "Do you think it's a good idea to see him even now? Aren't you afraid of stirring up old feelings?"

"It's been sixteen years since we first met. Certainly, after all this time we can enjoy each other's company without it resulting in some heart-wrenching affair." I leaf through the various medical records on the table before me.

"What does he look like now?" I ask Maddie. I was thinking of my extra ten extra pounds and the many laugh lines that have taken up housekeeping on my face.

"He still has his beard, but his hair is graying, and he's put on a little weight. From what I remember though, he looks the same." She glances at me, a worried look on her face. "Just be careful Hannah, you're recently divorced and that makes you vulnerable."

"Don't worry Maddie. After Jack, who is, a self-centered egomaniac and narcissist, I'm not looking for a new love interest."

"And let's not forget cheating scum bag," she adds. "You know I've always wondered why you married Jack?"

"I don't know really. He was so nice to me in the beginning. When he asked me to marry him, I was almost thirty. Mom approved because he was a doctor and that was a big factor. I thought by marrying a professional he would understand my career and not be threatened by my successes." It all sounds like excuses instead of reasons.

At first, Jack was wonderful. Solicitous and understanding of my schoolwork as I finished my doctorate, and he worked as an intern. Carly was born in his last year of residency at the University of Wisconsin, and I started my first-year teaching at the University's business school. The push and pull of trying to balance our careers and parenthood devastated whatever goodwill there was between us. The disintegration was slow, almost undetectable. I didn't leave until he acquired another significant other by the name of Tiffany.

"Jack tries to be a good father. No matter how big of an ass he may be, I know he loves Carly."

"How is Carly taking all this?"

"After the divorce, it was hard for her at first, but eventually she got used to the routine of our living apart. Jack is good about making time for her even though his schedule is incredibly busy. She took Mom's death hard. I remember the cascade of tears and the difficulty in explaining to her about death while simultaneously alleviating her fears that no one else would likely die soon. This was the first time in her life that someone she knew passed away. While they didn't see a lot of each other, Mom did come to visit at least twice a year and Carly looked forward to her arrival for weeks beforehand." I almost envied Carly's sorrow because I felt numb when I heard the news about Mom's death. "I think having the divorce and Mom's death so close together has made her moody and introspective."

Maddie picks up the last of the papers and drops them in the box. "I miss Carly. Maybe she could come to spend some time with her aunt this summer."

"She'd love it. I know she misses Aunt Maddie. She doesn't seem to be having much fun this summer despite my best efforts at trying to entertain her. She wanted to come down here with me, but I thought it would be too morbid. I also thought it would be good for her and her dad to spend a little quality time together and for me to get away for a couple of weeks."

Maddie isn't listening. She's staring at a hospital bill she's retrieved from the pile on the table.

"What's that?" I look over her arm at the document she's so intent upon.

"I don't know. It's an emergency room bill for Mom."

"She got hurt?"

"I don't know. There are charges for a pelvic exam, a suture kit, a set of X-rays, and some miscellaneous charges for bandages and medicine. Looks like they ran some lab tests, but I don't know what any of this medical mumbo jumbo means." Her voice drops to a conspiratorial whisper. "What do you think happened?"

"What's the date on the bill?"

"1964. Do you think Mom was in an accident?" She hands me the papers.

"Gosh, I think I'd remember that. I don't recall her being in any sort of serious accident." I try remembering through the eyes of a eight-year-old. "What about you, Maddie?" I can tell she's doing her best to check her memory.

"I was only six. I don't remember anything unusual." She watches my face for something to click into place. Nothing does. "Maybe she had complications with her pregnancy with Kyle."

"Probably not because Kyle wasn't even born until September, and she would have been a month maybe two months pregnant."

"Well, it must have been pretty serious, this bill is for more than $1,000, and that was nearly thirty years ago." She takes the bill from my hand and reexamines it. "Jack would know the meaning of these medical terms; can we ask him?" Her voice is full of worry and curiosity. "I suppose it doesn't matter now, with her gone, but I wonder if she was seriously hurt. I wonder if this would help explain some things." Her voice trails off.

"I do remember Mom being really sick for a while, but I can't recall what was wrong with her. I just remember tiptoeing around the house for a few weeks trying to be extra quiet so she could rest." I head for the wall phone by the stove. "I'll call Jack and see if he can decipher this for us."

I get Jack's answering service. A half-hour later he returns my call. He sounds peeved and out of breath.

"What is it, Hannah?" Jack's put out with me before I begin.

"Sorry to bother you, but I need your medical expertise,"

"Is somebody hurt?"

"No, but I found this emergency room bill for my mother from 1964. I was wondering if you could tell me what she had done or what might have happened?"

"Why do you want to know? Hannah, I'm sorry about your mom, I always liked her, but who cares what happened to her nearly thirty years ago?"

"Look, Jack, would you just listen? Then you can tell me what I want to know and then you can go on your merry way, all right?" I started to get annoyed with both of us. Me for being stupid enough to ask him for a simple favor and him for being . . . him.

He pulls out a familiar piece from his arsenal. "You haven't even asked how Carly is."

"How is she?" I try to keep my tone even and not rise to the bait.

"She's fine, but it wouldn't hurt you to ask."

"I only left a couple of days ago. Besides I talked with her yesterday AND I told her I'd call tomorrow evening." The annoyance I feel starts to creep into my voice. "Can we please get back to this hospital bill thing?" I told him about the pelvic exam, the sutures, and the X-rays. I also mentioned there are some lab tests whose names I can't pronounce.

"Hannah, from what you're telling me it sounds like your mother miscarried."

"What do you mean sounds like?"

"Jeez Hannah, you just don't quit, do you? All right, fax me the bill and I'll look at it when I get a chance. That's the best I can do. Take it or leave it."

"I'll take what I can get. Sorry, I bothered you." I sound sarcastic even to me. He hangs up without saying goodbye.

"Twit," I say as I replace the receiver with a bang.

"Trouble in paradise?" Maddie laughs at me.

"You bet sister."

"What he'd say?"

"He thinks she may have miscarried, but he said he'd look at the paperwork. I'm supposed to send him the information. When I go out to meet Sam this afternoon, I'll stop by a copy shop and fax this to him." I take the documents from her outstretched hand and go off to find my purse.

When I sit back down at the table Maddie says, "Don't you think you ought to be getting ready for Sam?"

She worries two hours isn't going to be enough time to whip me into shape. "You still haven't decided what you're going to wear." She points out the obvious flaw in my plan to wait until the last minute and hope for the best. "Listen, if you don't mind, I'll look through what you brought and help you pick out something." She tries to be diplomatic, but I can see she doesn't think I'm capable of finding a suitable outfit for such an auspicious meeting.

I tell her to go ahead. For the next hour, as I sit on my bed and sort through some more papers, Maddie regales me with the possible clothing choices I might consider. She finally settles on something as my headache, which took hold when I called Jack, ratchets up a notch from listening to Maddie prattle on about how I should do this or that to various parts of my anatomy to make myself "more attractive" now that I'm single again.

I indeed have a married woman's body and, woefully, a married woman's wardrobe to go with it. I finally get cleaned up and dressed to Maddie's satisfaction. She says I pass muster only when I threaten her with bodily harm if she rearranges one more hair on my now-throbbing head.

The fresh air feels good after being cooped up all morning in the attic. I fax the information to Jack and am on my way to meet Sam for our picnic. We agreed to meet by the pier and then walk to the public picnic grounds. I arrive a few minutes early. My heart begins to race. I can't believe I feel a bit giddy about seeing him. 'Come on Hannah, you're closing in on forty, get a grip. You're too old for this kind of stuff anymore.' Then I check my makeup in the visor mirror for the umpteenth time. 'Forty, schmorty. You're also not dead.' I say to my reflection. 'Stop talking to yourself, it's annoying.'

There is a tap on the passenger window. My compact and lipstick go comically flying. I know it's Sam, but I can't look him in the eye, I'm so embarrassed he caught me primping. He taps again on the glass and then says, "You going to sit there and talk to yourself all day?"

I try to gather what's left of my composure (it doesn't take long). I put my purse under my arm, open the car door, step out, and look across the roof of the car at Sam. He smiles at me. I detect a note of amusement in his still greener-than-green eyes.

"Stop it, Sam." My cheeks start to flame. His smile spreads with my growing embarrassment. "I'm not kidding, I'll get back in my car and go home." I threaten idly.

"In that case, I succumb to the lady's wishes."

"That's more like it!" I straighten, grateful to recover a little of my dignity.

He does look older; his reddish blonde hair I remember so well is rife with gray. He has put on some weight; middle age spread happens to great lovers and charmers too, I see. I remind myself he's now nearly forty-five years old.

He comes around the car, takes my hand, and brings it to his lips. "Hello, Hannah." He kisses my hand and caresses it gently with his own before letting go. Even this little touch is enough to send my heart racing again. "Time has been very good to you; you look just the same," he says, with no mockery or amusement in his voice.

I love every lying syllable that falls from his lips. "Flatterer."

He tries to sound offended. "You know me better than that."

"You forget who you're talking to," I remind him, "I probably know you better than anyone and I stand by my statement. Flatterer."

"How could I forget." He smiles at me, and his eyes sparkle. "But you do look lovely." We stand and stare at each other, and an awkward silence ensues.

"I understand you have a daughter. Do you have any pictures?"

He doesn't have to ask me twice. I pull out my pictures of Carly. One was a family portrait taken two years earlier.

"She's beautiful, Hannah." He admires her pictures. "She looks like you. Is this Jack?" He points at the family photo. I nod. "He doesn't look good enough for you. I'd say I was sorry to hear about your divorce, but we both know I'd be lying," he says as he hands me back the pictures.

I ignore this last statement. "How's your son, Cal? Gosh, he must be seventeen or eighteen years old by now," I wonder where all the years went.

"He's nineteen. I haven't spent much time with him over the years and haven't seen him at all the last five years." A shadow moves over his features, a sadness I hadn't noticed before.

"Why?"

"Remember his mother remarried and I had trouble making child support payments when I lost my job. She wanted her new husband to adopt Cal and threatened to have me arrested for non-payment of child support if I didn't agree. At the time I convinced myself it would be best for him; a stable home life, someone to be there every night. God knows when we were married, I was on the road all the time with the band. I hardly spent any time with him even when I had the chance."

This was a new side to Sam, a contemplative side. I had never seen him wrestle out loud with his contributions to his divorce. I know from experience how difficult it is to concede your own mistakes in a failed marriage. No matter what one might think it always takes two to screw up a marriage.

"God, I miss him." He says simply. "Maybe it's just as well. After you and I split up, I spent a lot of years drinking heavily. When you came to see me in Charleston I was near the bottom of the pit and your visit sent me over the edge. Not anything you did," he reassures me when he sees the concern on my face. "But knowing what I had let slip through my fingers, I couldn't live with the finality, the sadness of losing you for good."

"And now?"

"My liver took a beating, and the doctor convinced me to take it easy. The pain of losing you eventually dulled as the years went by."

"What about your wife, Jamie?"

"She's been good to me. We live separate lives, but she's stayed with me when I'm sure a lot of others wouldn't have. We've been together a long time now, stuck in our marital dance."

"What do you mean?"

"Jamie doesn't work. She stays at home with too much time on her hands."

"What does she do all day?"

"She drinks mostly. Sometimes with friends, but mostly alone."

"Why don't you get her some help?"

"I tried, but she blames me for ruining her life. In all honesty, I do feel responsible for her drinking, and for her being so unhappy. She knows I don't love her, that I stay out of duty, out of habit. I'm not trying to make excuses, Hannah, Jamie, and I both have plenty of fingers to point."

We walk towards the pier and down to the public picnic area by the beach. Sam brought deli sandwiches with potato chips and chocolate cookies for dessert. I don't know quite how to tell him I'm now a vegetarian.

We continue to catch up over lunch. He trades my roast beef sandwich for his chips, nonplused that my eating hierarchy has changed. I'm grateful he doesn't grill me about why I became a vegetarian, there are only so many times you can answer that question.

Sam seems sad and lost, run down by life.

We sit in silence for a while as we watch some kids play catch happily and noisily on the north side of the park. "Sam, what's wrong? I can tell something with you isn't right."

"What do you see?" He asks in all seriousness.

I hesitate. "The truth?"

"Yes, I expect nothing less from you, Hannah."

I look at him for a long time before I answer: "You look unhappy. No, let me rephrase that. You look dead inside, Sam. I don't mean to be brutal, but I don't know how else to describe it." I can tell I've hit a nerve. He looks down at his hands and says nothing. I wait knowing he will come around soon enough. 'Just be patient,' I tell myself; my natural urge to fill in the silence can be overwhelming.

A few minutes silently pass. When Sam looks at me again, I see tears in his eyes; one rolls unfettered down his cheek. He takes a deep breath. When he has himself in control, he says, "Hannah, you always knew me so well. It's scary that you can still see through me so clearly. I do feel dead inside. I'm trapped in a loveless marriage I don't know how to escape. I have a dead-end job and my health is slipping out from under me. I know I don't have much time left and I never got to do or be what I wanted."

"What was that, Sam?" My heart reaches out to him, his sadness almost too much for me to bear.

"To have you, Hannah. To be happy. That's what I have wanted since we first met, but I always screwed it up. I was never good with timing even if my heart was in the right place."

I am truly speechless. My heart skips a beat. I am surprised that blood can course through my body so fast at my age; I feel light-headed. My ego soars above the clouds unchecked. I guess I never really believed that Sam loved me as much as I loved him.

Sam's gaze is unfocused looking out over the ocean; the medley of blue hues and the glimmering sun reflecting off the waves are mesmerizing. I get up and kneel in front of Sam taking his hands in mine.

"Sam, we're grownups now with responsibilities and duties to others."

He looks at me and my heart rips at the look of resignation in his eyes. "You're right Hannah, I'm sorry I laid all this on you." He straightens as he removes his glasses and wipes his face with his handkerchief. We both stand as a frolicking Rottweiler runs circles around us in the grass and then runs off to his master.

I move in closer and put my arms around his waist, place my head on his chest, and hold him tight. His arms slowly encompass me, and he lays his head gently on top of mine. A sigh of contentment escapes him as he moves his hand up and down my back in a soft caress. As I let go and start to move away, Sam takes my face in his hands. I wonder how many times over the years he has done so but find the thrill of his gaze and the delight of his touch no different now than I did in the very beginning.

"Hannah, you are still so beautiful," he whispers. He kisses me languidly. I feel my pulse quicken. I'm pleasantly surprised to feel that old familiar burning sensation racing down my spine. He pulls me closer. His kisses become urgent; our desire surpasses the confines of acceptable behavior at a family park. He finally lets me go, his breath coming in shallow gasps flattering my feminine ego. I still have the same effect on him that he has on me.

"I know you have to go," he says as he distances himself from me. We both know this is dangerous.

We get back to the cars, the afternoon sun has left the interiors scorching.

"Can I see you tomorrow?"

"I don't know Sam," I say as I hesitate, unsure of what to do.

"Please, Hannah, it would mean a lot to me. There are a few things I need to talk with you about. Things that I need your advice on." He's so sincere I can't say no. "Listen, I don't want to pressure you. You think about it, and I'll call you later, all right?"

I agree and he escorts me to my car door and sees me off.

On my way back my mind reels. "My God, what have you gone and done girl?" I say to myself.

When I get back to Mom's house Maddie has put on an apron and is still sorting through file cabinet drawers. Kyle and Wilkes aren't back yet.

"Well, how'd it go?" she says eager for an itemized account of my afternoon with Sam.

"It went OK." I feel awkward and don't want to share.

"OK? That's all you're going to say is, OK?" she asks unbelieving. "No, No, dear sister. You must give me more than that. I want details!" she demands. She smooths her hair back and mops some of the sweat off her brow with the front of her apron.

I notice pots on the stove simmering. "Is Bird here?"

"Yes, she's here. Now give, Hannah, I'm about to bust a gasket."

Bird comes into the kitchen. When she sees my face says: "Oh my Lord, not again."

Maddie looks at Bird then at me and then back to Bird. "What do you mean Bird 'Oh no, not again?'"

Bird eyes me. "I'd say based on the look on your sister's face, she's in a heap of trouble."

"Oh Bird, I don't know what you're talking about," I try to dismiss her and end this uncomfortable conversation.

Maddie catches on to the drift of Bird's unspoken accusation. "You're still in love with him, aren't you?"

The phone rings. At first, I'm grateful to be 'saved by the bell,' then I worry it might be Sam. Bird answers the phone, a truce of silence momentarily in place.

"Just a moment," Bird nods to me. I take the phone.

"Hello." I hold my breath.

"Hannah?" It's only Jack.

"Where have you been? Didn't Maddie tell you I called?"

I look over at Maddie. She shrugs her shoulders sheepishly and mouths silently 'I forgot.' I roll my eyes to the ceiling annoyed at her forgetfulness.

"I just got in."

"How are you?" He catches me by surprise with his solicitous attitude.

"I'm fine. Thank you for asking," I look at Bird and Maddie and shrug my shoulders in disbelief. "Did you get my fax?"

"Yes, I did," he pauses.

"Well?"

"Hannah, I don't know exactly how to tell you this," he begins.

I recognize his tone. This is the tone of bad news; of things we don't want to hear. I can feel life slip out of my voice. "Tell me what?" I whisper.

He hesitates. My temper suddenly flares. "Just tell me." I can't even speculate on what he might have to say as my mind works a hundred miles an hour and comes up blank.

"Well, from what you sent me, there is only one conclusion."

"Please get to the point before I scream."

"Hannah, your mother was raped."

CHAPTER SEVEN

A re you still there, Hannah?" Jack asks, concern evident in his voice. "Yes, I'm still here." My stomach churns, the kitchen becomes stiflingly hot and my headache resurfaces and does a nasty backstroke around my head. Jack sounds far away as the room lurches. My hands and feet feel prickly. Jack's voice becomes more agitated, but I can't make out the words.

After a few moments, the kitchen tilts back into place and the air becomes less suffocating and easier to breathe. I can hear Jack now repeatedly calling my name, a note of urgency in his voice. "Are you sure?" I finally whisper to the phone.

"Are you all right?" He doesn't answer my question.

"Yes, I'm fine, you took me by surprise, that's all." I take another deep breath and let the air out slowly. "Are you sure about this?"

"I'm sorry, Hannah, but from the hospital bill you sent me it's very clear your mother was admitted to the emergency room as a rape victim." He explains his voice is soft and understanding Jack always had a good bedside manner.

"There's no doubt?"

"None," Jack says gently. "I take it you didn't know?"

I slump into the kitchen chair. "No. She never said a word."

"Well, it's probably not something she would have wanted to discuss."

"Yeah, I know, but she never said anything about it later either."

Maddie interrupts, her voice low, but urgent, "What did he say about the hospital bill?"

I put my finger to my lips to shush her so I could hear Jack. She falls silent but I can see the frustration on her face. Bird hasn't heard anything. She hums quietly by the kitchen counter kneading bread for supper.

"Hannah, there's something else." Jack hesitates.

"There's more?" I lean back in the chair and close my eyes. "Go ahead, you might as well tell me everything," I say, resigned.

"She must have been beaten up pretty badly during the attack. There are charges for gauze bandages, sutures, Betadine, and that kind of thing. But it looks like she went home, that she didn't stay overnight which was a surprise."

"Why does that surprise you?"

"If she'd been a patient of mine, I'd have kept her at least one night for observation, you know to make sure she didn't have a concussion or internal bleeding that might not show up right away." I hear him whisper instructions to a nurse before going on. "I bet if I saw her medical chart, it would show she discharged herself, probably against medical advice."

I feel embarrassed to ask, but I have to know. "How do you know she was. . . you know?"

"There was some lab work ordered. Tests to check for sexually transmitted diseases." He says in a crisp professional tone.

I don't want to hear anymore, my stomach is tied in a knot, my head throbs, and my palms are sweaty. I wipe my hands one at a time on the front of my jeans. I look over at Maddie. Her face is pale, but she meets my gaze unwavering waiting.

Jack continues. "Do you remember anything about this time that would tell you whether your mother pressed charges? Do you remember any lawyers, talk of court or that kind of thing?"

I can't think without a pen in my hand. I pinch the phone between my ear and shoulder and search the tabletop for something to write with. "No, nothing. Why do you ask?"

"If she pressed charges and they tried the guy, there would be a paper trail if you wanted the details of what happened. But it sounds like nothing ever came of it. Maybe she didn't see who did it or maybe they never caught the guy."

I stop holding up my end of the conversation and doodle on the back of an old bank statement.

"Hannah, are you there?"

"Yeah," I say distractedly into the phone, "I'm still here."

"Anyway," he continues, "it was a long time ago so please don't let this upset you too much, all right?"

I find his advice irksome. "Sure Jack, I'll try and be cool."

"Hey, I'm only saying, there's no use in getting upset over something that happened so long ago, especially when there's nothing you can do about it now."

My annoyance peaks. "I heard you."

He sounds distracted. No doubt a passel of nurses swooping in and out of his office. He has amazing powers of concentration. "Listen, you asked me to look at this stuff so don't kill the messenger, OK?"

"Sorry, guess I was taking this out on you."

He seems reluctant to hang up. "Do any of the others know?"

I stand and pace the floor as if that will hurry him off. "No, I don't think so."

"Are you going to tell them?"

My annoyance rings crystal clear. "I don't know."

He ignores the warning sign. "That doesn't mean they want or should know if you catch my meaning."

"I can't make that decision for them." I already dread having to face Maddie when I get off the phone.

He's suddenly dismissive "Suit yourself, they're your family." He changes the subject, "When are you coming back?"

"I'm not sure," I try to loosen the phone cord that's twisted up tight around my wrist. "But I'll let you know, all right?"

"Sure, and again Hannah, I'm sorry about your mom," he says.

My anger instantly deflates. "Thanks, Jack."

I gently replace the receiver in its cradle, take a deep breath, and sit down across from Maddie. I wonder how much she's put together on her own.

She reaches across the table and pats my hand. "What is it, Hannah? You look like you've seen a ghost."

Bird is still busy with supper preparations. I feel like Paul Tibbets the pilot of the Enola Gay. I can think of no way to soften the blow. There is nothing to do, but simply blurt out the truth. "Maddie," I take her hand in both of mine, "Jack said the hospital bill indicated that Mom had been raped."

"NO!" Maddie gasps. She lets go of my hand and stands up. Her chair catches on the edge of the linoleum seam and tips over. She stands frozen for a moment staring at me, her mouth open in surprise. I hold my breath as I watch her and wait. Suddenly she clamps her jaw shut with an audible click, turns, and heads down the hall into the guest bedroom. She softly closes the door behind her and turns the lock.

Bird comes over to the table and rights Maddie's overturned chair. "What was that all about? What did you say to that girl?"

Before I could answer, Wilkes and Kyle burst through the screen door. Both of their faces are Barbie-pink from too much sun. Their shorts are still damp from swimming and their shirts are missing altogether. I wince when I see their exposed shoulders already a deep hue of red.

"Hey, Bird!" Wilkes calls expansively. A few more beers have found their way home. Kyle grins stupidly and lists a little to the left.

"Hey yourself, Master Wheeler."

"You're not going to start that Master stuff again are ya, Bird?" He pleads.

Bird smiles and gently pushes his windblown hair off his forehead. "Not today, Hon."

"Did we interrupt something?" Wilkes asks Bird.

Bird goes back to her bread. "I don't know, you'd have to ask your sister."

He turns to me as Kyle successfully navigates the kitchen floor and lands on the nearest chair. "Well?"

I'm not sure what to do or say. The information seems too raw to pass around the room. Kyle saves me when he accidentally knocks a stack of papers onto the floor.

"Jesus! Kyle, watch what you're doing!" I say as I stoop to pick up the mess.

"Sorry, Sis." His voice has the sincerity of a befuddled partygoer.

"For goodness' sake, Wilkes, did you have to pollute your little brother too?" My motherly tone of voice surprises me.

"Hey, he's a grownup. I didn't force him to drink a whole six-pack of beer." Wilkes grins foolishly. They look from one to the other and then burst out laughing. Though Bird's back is to us, I see her shoulders hitching up and down. I even find myself amused for a moment despite everything. Wilkes asks where Maddie has gone.

"She's in the guest room taking a nap," I lie and then wonder why I don't tell them the truth. The weight of the news has started to tackle me again, my fear of having to tell almost more torturous than the culpability of keeping the secret. Bird looks at me with both eyebrows raised in a question mark, but she keeps her silence.

"I'll go check on her." I knock lightly on the guest room door and softly call out Maddie's name. She doesn't answer. For some reason, I feel it's important to talk with Maddie before I break the news to anyone else.

Maddie finally emerges at supper time. Her makeup is in place, but her eyes are puffy and red. Kyle has moved the file cabinet drawers off the table and food is brimming from the serving dishes; steam rises from the plate full of corn on the cob, and mashed potatoes are piled high with a large serving spoon stuffed in the side waiting for a taker. There are mountains of field peas, and a platter of fried chicken stacked up precariously high. The fruit salad has farm-fresh peaches, homegrown watermelon, red grapes, and big chunks of honeydew melon. There is a large plate full of sliced Vidalia onions and thick slices of red-ripe, vine-grown tomatoes. There's a linen-covered basket full of homemade biscuits and cornbread.

"My goodness, Bird," I admire the spread, "you outdid yourself."

Bird grins. "I sure miss cooking for a big family. I haven't had the pleasure in a long time."

I can tell by the glow on her face she means what she says. Bird always did like doing for others. Wilkes and Kyle voice their appreciation and thankfulness for the food and we all sit down and hold hands around the table while Wilkes says the grace like old times.

All through supper Maddie avoids eye contact. Afterward, she tries to elude me, but I follow her outside to her car. "Maddie, what's going on with you? Why did you run off like that?" I ask her.

She fumbles in her purse for her car keys. "I really don't want to talk about this right now."

I can't force her. Although I do briefly consider holding a gun to her head to make her talk. I hate secrets! But in the end, I discard the idea as impractical - no gun.

Bird and I cleaned up after supper with only small talk passing between us. She's too experienced with sibling complexities to badger me with questions. I debate about confronting Bird to see what she remembers. She must know something. I can't form the words to ask: 'Bird you know my mom was raped, don't you?' or perhaps, 'Bird, my mom was raped, what do you know about it?' It sounds too much like an accusation. We finish the dishes and Bird hugs me before she heads home.

"You know I'm always here for you, Sweetie," she whispers in my ear, her arms holding me close.

I nod and squeeze her tight.

I spent the evening going through the file drawers I had the guys fetch down from the attic before they slouched outside to the porch for more beer and conversation. Frankly, I'm surprised they're so close. Wilkes is a successful legal shark while Kyle is a laid-back musician. Where Wilkes is typically fastidious about this appearance, Kyle always has that haphazard look of one who is woefully unaware of the fashion police. Yet, since the brothers' arrival here, they have formed a very tight bond.

When the phone rings, I know it must be Sam. I run into Mom's room to ensure I have some privacy.

"Hannah, I'm sorry I didn't call earlier, but I had trouble getting to a phone before this," Sam explains when I answer.

I realize the implications; he had to steal away from his wife. I can tell from the background noise that he's on a pay phone.

"Sam, I'm not comfortable with this. This feels too much like sneaking around, again, and frankly, I'm too old for that."

He tries to placate me. "We're not doing anything wrong Hannah, but I know Jamie wouldn't be thrilled about us seeing each other. She wouldn't understand we're just old friends catching up."

"Sam, this afternoon was anything but two old friends catching up, it was two lovers coming together." I'm surprised I said the words aloud.

He gets defensive. "I didn't know I was forcing myself on you, Hannah."

"I didn't mean it that way, Sam." I could kick myself for always saying the wrong thing. "I've had an awful afternoon. Look, something's happened. I can't go into it, but I'm afraid I wouldn't be very good company."

He's immediately solicitous. "What's wrong?"

"I can't talk about it, Sam," I say when what I really want is to be in his arms and tell him everything. What a luxury it would be if for a little while I could be vulnerable and put all this at his feet and have him somehow make it all go away.

The hurt in his voice echoes through the phone line. "All right, I'll abide by your wishes, but can I call you tomorrow?" He asks.

I hesitate, torn between what I should do and what I want to do.

"Jamie is going to visit her sister tomorrow and she'll be gone for the whole weekend. Can't you find some time in there for us to talk for a while? I promise, just talk. I'll even bring lunch again, but this time I'll include plenty of vegetables and fruit, OK?" His voice now sounds so hopeful.

I cave in, the words of acquiescence leave my lips before my brain has had a chance to sort through the rights and wrongs. "Call me from work tomorrow morning and we'll work something out." I hang up the phone and sit on Mom's bed for a long time thinking hard about what I'm getting myself into with Sam. I know that to stop things now would require a miracle, only I can't decide whether to ask for one.

The next morning, Wilkes and Kyle sleep late. Maddie arrives, gets a cup of coffee, and then joins me on the porch to watch the tide come in. An unusual morning breeze makes the air perfect for coffee sipping. I give her room for silence, keeping my coffee cup clutched and my mouth shut. She has on an outfit like yesterday's, every item clean and pressed. Today she has on makeup, but she can't hide the haggard look on her face.

She doesn't look at me but gazes out at the swaying marsh grass. "I'm sorry about yesterday, running off like I did."

I'm eager to accept excuses. "You don't have to explain."

"No, I want to. I remember when all this happened."

I turn to face her. "You do?"

"Let me finish," she says impatiently. She lowers her voice to a conspiratorial whisper and continues. "Don't you remember when Dad brought Mom home that night?"

I confess I can remember only vague details.

"There was a bad storm and you and I were snuggled together in your bed."

I think back. "I do remember the storm."

Maddie sets her coffee cup down and tucks her feet under her. "When Mom and Dad came home it was late and Wilkes told us to stay put and pretend we were asleep so we wouldn't get in trouble. We could hear Wilkes and Dad in the kitchen."

"But we couldn't hear what they were saying," I add, the details becoming clearer. That night emerges in my memory like the answer in a child's Magic 8 Ball arising out of the murky ink slow to come to focus but demanding my attention. "I also remember Dad shouting and when Wilkes came back, he looked shaken up but said everything was OK."

Maddie leans forward in her chair, "You do remember."

"Yes," my heart slows, "now I do."

Dad got a call shortly before supper and left without saying a word to anyone except Bird. Bird stayed through supper and helped us clean up. She was upset and distracted. Something was wrong. The evening grew late and finally, Bird left Wilkes in charge so she could get home to her babies before the storm got worse.

I begin to pace the porch as details fall into place. I pick up the story where Maddie left off. "Do you remember Dad telling us Mom was sick? He wouldn't let us in to see her for weeks. Said she was contagious and if we got too close, we'd get infected."

Maddie rolls her eyes, "Dad was always so melodramatic."

I stop and stand in front of her. "I don't think it was melodrama, Maddie. I think . . ."

Maddie interrupts. "That he took care of her at home and hid it from us."

The interlocking puzzle pieces click together with a sickening snap. "That's exactly what I think." I begin to pace across the porch floor.

"Do you think Bird knew what happened?" The idea only now occurs to Maddie.

I shrug my shoulders. "How could she not know?"

"Should we tell Wilkes and Kyle?"

I look at Maddie. "I wrestled with that question most of last night. On one hand, they have the right to know I suppose, but on the other hand . . ."

"Why upset them about something that happened before Kyle was even born." She follows my progress back and forth. "I don't think we should tell them."

I sit down in the rocker next to her. "Did it occur to you that Wilkes probably already knows?" I can see from the look on her face it hadn't "Remember he was nearly thirteen when this happened, he might know more than we do."

"I don't think I want to know anymore," she whispers.

For a while, we both sit in silence and watch a shrimp boat head out to the open seas with its nets tied neatly out of the water. The boat chugs slowly through the waterway, its crew lolls along the boat railings. The sun starts to scorch the morning air and will no doubt be unbearable by this afternoon.

Abruptly Maddie says: "Let's go finish the attic before it gets too damn hot." She purposefully heads through the screen door, plops her empty coffee cup on the kitchen counter, and disappears down the hallway. I follow her. It takes both of us to pull the stairs down. I take a flashlight with me so we can find the light cord without breaking a finger swiping for it in the dark.

The morning's work goes quickly. Neither Maddie nor I say much as we rip open boxes and rummage through their contents. Wilkes and Kyle make unhelpful noises from below shortly before lunch. In their defense, they do carry the rest of the boxes downstairs and out to the potting shed. Gratefully, Maddie and I will soon be done with the attic.

The afternoon sun is relentless. Bird left sandwiches and salads for our lunch. When Maddie and I go downstairs, we find Wilkes and Kyle have already dug in, it's hard not to be annoyed. I must have looked as irritated as I felt because without me speaking a word Wilkes gets on the defensive.

"Don't give me that look, Hannah. We carried down a truckload of boxes this morning."

"Sure, after Maddie and I had already gone through each box in that sweltering attic, then you two waltz in and make like the grand knights of the friggin' round table and offer to carry them off for us." My voice gets louder, my anger starts to match my temperature.

"That's not fair," Kyle jumps in, "we didn't start as early as you two zealots, but we pitched in pretty good. Besides, I don't see why Wilkes should have to help at all."

Maddie wades in with both feet: "He's still getting a fourth of the money from Mom's estate. It's not like he's really missing out on anything. We haven't exactly been bowled over with treasures during all this cleaning so don't talk to me about fair. It seems to me like he's used his poor abused feelings to his advantage long enough."

"Wait!" I shout above the din. "This isn't getting us anywhere."

Wilkes goes to the refrigerator gets out a cold beer for everyone and hands the first one to Maddie as a peace offering. She's reluctant at first, but then grabs it out of his hand and murmurs a thank you.

She tries to twist off the top. Wilkes stands and watches her. She starts to grunt, unwilling to ask for help. He holds up the bottle opener. She keeps struggling and doesn't see the opener in Wilkes's hand. With a loud grunt, she finally gives up and then sees the opener before her nose. Kyle and I stand ready to run for cover. Maddie has the good grace to laugh while Wilkes takes the tops off our beer bottles.

"To us," Maddie holds up her now topless beer bottle in a mock salute.

"The survivors," Wilkes shoves his bottle towards the center of the group.

"To dysfunctionalism!" shouts Kyle, clinking his bottle with ours.

All eyes turn to me. "I can't top that," I laugh and send my bottle in for a good clang with the others.

We settled around the kitchen table to eat lunch. Maddie looks at me and gives a small nod.

"Go ahead," I whisper across the table. Both Kyle and Wilkes look up.

Maddie begins. "Not to spoil the good mood, but there's something Hannah and I want to talk with you two about." She hesitates. The table gets quiet, beer bottles slowly gravitate to the tabletop and stay parked as each listener detects the note of seriousness in Maddie's voice. She looks to me to continue, but I nod my head and tell her to go on. She plunges ahead. "Hannah and I found a hospital bill among the papers in the file cabinet in the attic." All eyes are on Maddie.

I wait for her to drop the bomb. I look at the faces of my brothers and how in repose they do look more alike than I'd realized. The same nose, the same eyes, my sneaking suspicions that maybe Kyle is my half-brother begin to subside. The family resemblance is too strong for Kyle not to be a full-blooded Wheeler.

"Hannah faxed the bill to Jack to have him decipher it." Maddie looks at me, panic on her face.

"Go on," I whisper.

"What did Jack say?" Wilkes asks in a low voice as though he hadn't wanted to ask the question.

"He said that Mom. . ." she hesitates, takes a deep breath, and goes on. "He said that Mom had been raped." Maddie stares at the table and pushes her now empty bottle in repeated circles with her fingers.

"What?" Kyle asks in disbelief.

Maddie doesn't answer. Wilkes says nothing. His face is pale. He takes a long draw, finishes his beer, wipes his mouth with the back of his hand then goes to the 'fridge and retrieves another. I watch him. I find his silence ominous for some reason. Kyle is still in shock. Maddie has stopped twirling her beer bottle on the table and now meticulously peels off the label and makes a small, shredded pile in front of her.

Kyle finally comes around: "What happened?" he asks me.

"We don't know for sure. We only know that in 1964, Mom was treated as a rape victim at the hospital." I get the bill from my purse and hand it to Kyle as proof. He stares at it for a few minutes, but I can tell he's not focusing.

Maddie sneaks a glance at all of us while she scrapes off the last remnants of her bottle label with her thumbnail. "You're not saying much, Wilkes."

"What's there to say? It's not like I can change what happened. And as shocking as the news is, it did happen more than thirty years ago." He takes a long swig from his beer.

His tone grates on my nerves. "I'm surprised you feel that way."

He loudly slams his beer bottle down on the table. Beer leaps out of the bottle and foams on the table and his forearm. "How in the hell am I supposed to feel?"

We are all speechless, awed by his sudden furry.

"For God's sake, the woman's dead, they're both dead, do we have to dredge up all this stuff now? Can't we just leave it alone?" He looks at each of us in turn a silent challenge in his eyes.

Wilkes gets out of his chair and in a few impassioned strides crosses the kitchen, goes out onto the porch and the kitchen screen door slams shut behind him. We can see him pace out there on the porch, his heels digging into the pine boards as he works on his goose-stepping skills. He stops abruptly, the silence more menacing than the pound of his heels. Suddenly he bangs down the porch steps. We hear his car door slam shut, the engine springs to life, and his motor revs loudly as he peels out of the driveway.

The rest of us sit silently at the table and pick at the last of our lunches, lost in our thoughts.

"Kyle, are you all right?" I ask concerned at his reticence.

"Yeah, I'll be OK." He's not too convincing. "Did Jack say anything else?"

Maddie and I look at each other as if to confirm whether we should tell him about the beating Mom went through.

"Tell me," He insists when our silence is evidence there's more.

"From the hospital bill, it seems Mom was pretty banged up in the incident," I tell him.

Kyle looks directly at me as if to dare me to deny it. "You mean this guy beat her up."

"That's what Jack surmised."

"God," Kyle says, his hands holding either side of his head as if to cover his ears to stop the words from coming inside. Neither Maddie nor I know what to say. After a few minutes, Kyle looks up, hands on the table, and his face is grim. He looks first at me then Maddie and then back at me. His face starts to turn from pain to panic.

"What is it, Kyle?" I ask, almost afraid of what he's going to say.

"This rapist could be my father," Kyle says the horror of his words startle. "Think about it," he insists waving the bill at us. "This happened in February. I was born in July."

None of us can completely deny the mathematics of his logic. "But Kyle, she would have had to have you two months early and you weren't born two months early."

"How do you know?" he asks a condemned man reaching for straws.

"Because I checked your birth certificate, you weighed more than nine pounds. That doesn't sound like the weight of a premature baby to me. Mom must have already been pregnant with you when she was . . . attacked." The word leaves a bad taste in my mouth.

Kyle looks amazed, "you've already thought about this?"

"Why didn't you say anything to me?" Maddie asks astonished that I never said a word about my suspicions.

"What did you want me to say?" I feel guilty. "Besides I wanted to be sure."

Maddie gets up to put her empty bottle in the recycle bin. "Maybe we should get back to work."

I worry about leaving Kyle alone, but Maddie frantically waves for me to come along. Reluctantly I follow her to the back of the house. "What's the big idea?" I ask when she has me sequestered in the back bathroom and the door closed behind us.

"I thought Kyle needed a few minutes alone. He looked like he was going to cry, and I don't think he wants his two big sisters to be around for that."

I'm not so sure I agree. Kyle has always been very sensitive; I don't think leaving him alone is a good idea.

When Kyle was an infant and I held him in my arms, he would place his soft, baby-smelling head on my shoulder while he sucked his thumb in utter contentment. In a house where attention was a four-letter word, the lavishness of his behavior was a gift. Later when he was a young boy, he would crawl into my lap with a book and beg me to read to him. While I read, he would absently stroke my hair, a soothing motion that seemed to help him drift off to sleep. While his demand for love was always something to fulfill, I don't think I ever realized how important this physical contact, this unconditional love, was to me.

Kyle's teenage years were especially hard. His vulnerability attracted bullies like flies to a carcass. To complicate matters, after Dad's death, Kyle was the only one living at home and Mom used him to keep from being lonely. She acted helpless or got sick any time he tried to loosen her grip. When he wanted to go away to college ("In California for God's sake!" I could still hear Mom yelling.) Mom claimed she was dying even though her doctor didn't agree. It took all three of us to finally pry Kyle lose from her grasp, a move she deeply resented, and never forgave. Even though she died of old age in her sleep, I knew Kyle still felt responsible as if he alone could have prevented the snatching of her life. Her guilt strings were cast iron.

Maddie sits on the edge of the tub. "Anyway, we do have to finish cleaning out this house preferably in my lifetime. Why don't we do this bathroom while we're here and then move to the den?"

I agree and we spend the next hour folding up linens and throwing away various medicine bottles, toothpaste tubes, and the like and boxing up the salvageable items. We pass the time silently as we sort and stuff. After a while, Kyle sticks his head in and asks if we need any help. He looks exhausted and his eyes are bloodshot. I wonder about the wisdom of telling him the truth.

"Could you take this stuff out to the trash and those boxes in the hallway go on the Goodwill pile." Maddie directs Kyle who seems eager to be doing something.

We finish up the bathroom and move to the den. We spend the rest of the afternoon boxing up books and wrapping knickknacks in newspaper. We reminisce over some of the items but keep nothing. None of us seem nostalgic for family memories and mementos.

"Have you spoken with Sam?" Maddie asks as she packs up a shelf full of paperbacks.

"I talked with him last night and this morning."

She tries to sound casual. "Are you going to see him again?"

I'm diabolically coy, "maybe."

She stops packing and turns to face me. Her face is streaked with dust, her hair tucked under a red bandanna tied around her head. She smiles at me, "You're exasperating."

I toss a paperback book at her, "I know."

She ducks and it lands harmlessly at her feet. She grabs a dust rag and heaves it at me catching me on the shoulder. "Oh, it's gonna be that way is it." I smile and throw the roll of trash bags at her. They bounce off the shelf above her head and unroll across the floor.

"Oh, that was great," she says in mock exasperation and then picks the hard-cover dictionary off the shelf.

"No!" I shout and duck behind the sofa.

She laughs and sets the book back on the shelf. "Just kidding."

The back door opens, and we hear Bird arrive to get supper started. We both go out into the kitchen just as Kyle returns from delivering another box to the potting shed. I casually tell Bird that Sam will join us for dinner. This piece of news brings silence from all.

I think about dropping a pin but feel the humor would be lost. "Oh, come on," I insist with exaggerated exasperation.

"But he's married." Maddie blurts out as though this were a terminal disease - she may be right.

"I didn't ask him over to have sex, only to have supper." They all gawk at me. I begin to feel like an alien life form. "Look, he and I go way back. We have a history together, you know, a common past that makes us friends despite our ups and downs or current marital status." I emphasize. "I want to spend some time with one of my oldest and dearest friends *and* my family, is that so horrible?" They continue to stare at me, and it makes me move from being on the defensive to being plain angry. "If this is a problem for any of you, let me know and Sam and I will go somewhere else to have supper." I issue the ultimate family challenge. There are murmurs of agreement as Maddie and Kyle inspect their shoes and Bird picks imaginary lint off her sleeve. I laugh. "You people drive me nuts." I love each of them, if not for their outright support, at least for loving me enough to let this slide.

Bird gets a clean apron from the drawer and ties it expertly around her waist. She smiles at me - a conspirator. She winks as if to say, 'You can fool everyone else, you can even fool yourself, but you will never fool me.' I find her knowing smile both pleasant and a bit scary.

Wilkes comes home as I'm about to take a shower to get ready for Sam. He looks better, the drive has smoothed some of the tension from his face. He seems glad to see us. Maddie can hardly wait to tell him the gossip.

"Guess who's coming to dinner, Wilkes?" She nearly prances in anticipation of telling him the news.

"Sidney Poitier?" He answers with a deadpan expression.

"Wrong, smart aleck." She swats him playfully on the arm. "Sam Lancaster, Hannah's old flame. Or perhaps I should say Hannah's old married flame." She looks to see if I'll rise to the bait.

I show amazing restraint.

"Sam's coming here?" Wilkes asks.

"Maybe you should try telling him in Spanish," I say to Maddie.

"You're kidding," Wilkes says as if what Maddie said finally sank in. "I haven't seen him in what, fifteen years? Let's see, how old would that make you, Hannah?" He starts to count on his fingers.

"Keep it up, wise guy," I turn and head for the shower before they can heap any more abuse on me.

Sam arrives with an armload of Tiger Lilies. It's the perfect icebreaker. He charms Bird within five minutes and has the rest of the family onto friendly territory by the end of supper. Sam and I go out on the porch with some iced tea and sit on the glider watching the sunset. Everyone else conspicuously disappears.

Sam softly caresses my hand. "You seem distracted, Hannah."

A pleasant shiver runs up my arm. My body can be such a traitor, plotting against me when I least expect it.

"You said you'd had some awful news this afternoon. I hope it wasn't about Carly." His concern is genuine.

"No, Carly's fine. Thanks for asking, Sam."

"Can you tell me what it is?"

"It's about my mother." I look at him. "We found some old records while we were cleaning out the attic." I falter.

"You don't have to tell me, Hannah, if it's going to upset you." Sam puts his arm around my shoulder.

"No, telling you might help get it off my chest." I take a deep breath. "In her records we found copies of an old hospital bill from 1964. It seems my mother was treated in the emergency room as a rape victim."

He squeezes my hand tightly. "Oh, Hannah. I'm so sorry."

"She never said a word to me, Sam. How could she keep such a thing from me?"

"Hannah, you were what, only what eight or nine years old? That's not the kind of thing you discuss with a kid."

"I know." Rationale collides with frustration. "But later, why didn't she tell me later?"

Sam puts his hand under my chin and turns my face to look at him. His eyes are so green in the waning daylight. He strokes my cheek. "You were her daughter, Hannah." He nearly whispers. "That's not exactly the sort of confidence a mother and daughter share. Would you confide about something like this if it were Carly?"

I shake my head. A tear comes loose and drifts down my face.

"There's something else, isn't there?" He brushes the tear away with the touch of his hand.

"Yes." I close my eyes and push back in the glider. The gentle movement soothes me as my body finds a rhythm to keep the glider in motion. "It seems that this all occurred around the time Mom got pregnant with Kyle."

Sam slips off his shoes and pushes against the floor with his toes. The sound of the glider with its soft squeaks reminds me of long summers with afternoon cookouts and evening swims on the beach.

"You think Kyle is the product of your mom's ordeal?" He asks delicately.

"I don't know. I checked a copy of Kyle's birth certificate. He was born five months later, but weighed more than nine pounds, not the weight of a preemie."

"What does Kyle think, or doesn't he know."

"He knows, Maddie and I told him." I curl my legs up under me and the glider slows to a stop. "I think he sees the logic of my argument, but now there's a question about his heritage that he can't ignore."

"What about a DNA test? That would answer the question once and for all wouldn't it?" Sam suggests.

"That's a good idea, but I don't want him to think his parentage makes any difference to me. He might take my suggestion as a sign that I'm suspicious about his pedigree. He's my brother no matter what, no matter who the father might be. Hell, Sam, you know I had no love for the father we did have."

He gently runs the back of his hand down my right cheek. "Hannah, you don't have to convince me."

I realize I've run off at the mouth and dumped all my problems on Sam. I know he'd never complain, but I feel guilty all the same.

"Uh oh, I know that look." He stands, gently pulls me up, puts both his hands on my shoulders, and looks me in the eye, his face only inches from mine. "You are not boring me. You are not dumping on me. I like being here for you, it makes me feel good." He kisses the end of my nose "Being here for you makes me feel important and useful. I love you, Hannah, that has never changed. Remember what I told you long ago? My sanity may waver, but my love for you never will. That's still true, even now."

I'm afraid of his love for me. I'm even more terrified of my love for him. And then for a moment, an overwhelming sadness for all the years we were not together washes over me.

He reads my mind. "Yes, we wasted a lot of years," he whispers.

Suddenly, I don't trust myself to be alone with Sam. I slip from his grasp and go to the edge of the porch with my back to him. I place my hands on the railing and breathe in the salty sea air. I watch the sky as the stars begin to illuminate and let themselves be known. Sam comes up behind me and puts his hands on my shoulders but makes no move to turn me around. He talks softly in my ear as he absently caresses my shoulders. "I apologize, Hannah. You didn't need to hear all that from me this evening. You have so much on your mind with your mother and Kyle."

"Sam. . . ."

He wraps his arms around me and holds me tight. My tears start slowly at first as the stress of the day takes its toll. One falls on the hand that Sam has wrapped around my waist. He turns me around I offer no resistance. He cups my face in his hands and kisses a tear off my cheek. This only serves to make me cry harder. "Don't be nice to me." I insist halfheartedly. "You know how I hate that."

"Go ahead, Hannah, and let it out. I'm right here." He gathers me closer in his arms.

When my tears have worn out and the evening wind has dried my face, Sam moves me to the glider. I sit in his lap with his arms enfolded around me and my head on his shoulder. Simply his being here, holding me close, helps make all the other things seem less important, and easier to deal with. We sit in silence; the house inside has quieted down. Maddie and Bird must have gone out the front door so as not to disturb us. After a while, when sleep seems to rob me of breath, making the yawns more frequent, Sam kisses me and says goodnight. I go inside and barely make it out of my clothes and into a light tee shirt and boxers before I hit the soft feather pillows and slip into a deep and dreamless sleep.

In the morning the heat has let up and a summer breeze wafts through my bedroom window. Wilkes shakes me awake. At least he has a cup of coffee for me. I sit up in bed and gratefully take the steaming mug from his hand - no questions asked. I take the coffee into the bathroom with me and when I emerge, teeth are brushed, bathroom duties performed, and more than half the coffee is already rousing my tired veins. I fluff up a few pillows, push them against the headboard, lean back in relative bliss, and look at Wilkes. He looks worried dang! I hate that first thing in the morning.

"You're up awfully early," I say. I take another sip of coffee and wait for him to tell me what he wants. He sits on the edge of the green overstuffed chair by the window, taking advantage of the breeze. He has his eyes closed nursing his coffee. I notice his face isn't as pink this morning, but I bet his shoulders are aflame. He remains silent and I wonder if he heard me.

"Wilkes, what's wrong? You wouldn't wake me up this early unless you either had a death wish or something important to talk to me about. I'm going to assume the latter because I am not in the mood to kill you right now."

Wilkes looks out the window, no smart aleck retort hurdled my way, now I know something's wrong.

"I wanted to talk to you about Mom," he says so quietly that I can barely hear him.

"About her being attacked?"

He looks at me for the first time. "Yes."

His tortured eyes break my heart and scare me more than I care to admit. "What do you remember?" I forget about my coffee and watch his face. When he says nothing, I prompt again. "You would have been thirteen when this happened. You must remember something." Wilkes turns his face away, but I see his torment. I get off the bed and go sit on the footstool in front of his chair and put my hands on his knees. "What is it? What do you remember?"

"It was my fault." He blurts out, still averting his face from me.

"How could it be your fault?"

"Mom asked me to go with her to the store that day, but I didn't want to go. I wanted to hang out with my friends." His words come in a torrent of confession.

"I still don't get it Wilkes; how can you think this was your fault?"

"I should have been with her!" He nearly shouts and then drops his head into his hand. "I should have been there. I . . . just should have been there." His voice trails off as he roughly wipes a tear off his face.

"Did you know what had happened at the time?" I try to put the pieces together.

Wilkes sits up and takes a deep breath. "I suspected, but I never put any of it into words not even in my mind. I remember when Dad got the news. He complained about Mom being late. She'd gone to the store to pick up a few things. Remember we lived in town then and she usually walked to the store or sent one of us kids. She'd asked me to go, but I was too busy." He parodies himself, his voice full of self-hatred. He catches his breath. "Then she asked me if I'd mind going with her. I didn't want the other guys to see me with my mom, so I told her my best friend, Ronnie Hill, was expecting me at his house. That was a lie. I didn't have to be anywhere. I just didn't want to go." Wilkes looks at me, the anguish of his boyhood guilt visible on his face.

"You don't have to tell me all this if you don't want to." My words don't match my longing to know the truth.

"No, I want to tell you. I'll never forget that night. The phone rang. Dad's face lost all its color as the person on the other end must have told him the news. God, how do you tell someone their wife's been raped?" Wilkes gazes out the window.

"I don't know," I whisper.

"Dad held the receiver so tight his knuckles were white. Then he hung up the phone so calmly almost in slow motion. I wanted to ask him what was wrong, but he looked strange. I was scared. I knew something awful had happened. Truth is, I didn't want to know, I wanted Dad to take care of it, to make it all go away."

"Then what did he do?" I prod.

"He went over and talked with Bird for a minute and then left the house. Bird left a while after supper the weather service had been predicting a bad storm, a possible hurricane. She'd followed its progress on the radio in the kitchen all afternoon. She left me in charge of you girls. Remember?" He looks at me.

I nod.

He continues, "I read Black Beauty to you." He stops, "why do I remember that?"

I smile and shrug my shoulders.

"Anyway, Maddie pleaded to sleep in your room, and you said OK. I think you were grateful not to be alone with a storm coming. We could already hear the thunder in the distance. You two wouldn't settle down and I threatened to tell Mom when she came home. I think we were all scared not knowing what was going on."

I took his now empty coffee mug out of his hands and set it on the table next to the chair.

"Usually when they left me in charge they'd leave meticulous instructions, telling where they would be and how I could reach them. But that night, I didn't know where they were or when they were coming back. Bird didn't know either. She said she'd like to stay with us, but she was already worried about her own brood waiting at home for her."

"I remember the storm," I cut in, "Maddie and I shivering under the covers with a flashlight."

The lightning put on a grand display as it streaked down from the sky like the aberrant harpoons of Zeus. The wind whipped and pushed the treetops. The thunder rolled end over end in a near-deafening sequence. Then the rain began. Scattered fat droplets pummel the roof, then a fierce downpour that drowned out the thunder. We all sat on the bed as we listened and waited. Then we heard the back door slam open.

Wilkes continues with his story. "The kitchen was dark, and Dad had a large brownish-gray poncho slung over Mom. I only knew it was her because I saw the bandages on her arms and face from the hospital. Dad hurried through the kitchen towards the back of the house. He didn't stop to turn on the light and didn't notice I was standing there."

"What'd you say?"

"I didn't say anything. I pushed myself up against the wall and watched them go by. Then they were around the corner, and I heard the door to their bedroom slam shut."

"Then what'd you do?"

He leans back in the stuffed chair and looks at the ceiling. "I didn't know what to do."

He looks at me and I can feel his fear.

"I stood there frozen against the kitchen wall. Before I could move, Dad came back. He turned on the light over the sink. He put water on the stove to boil. Then he went to the 'fridge and got some ice cubes and began to crush them on the countertop with a wooden mallet." Wilkes stops.

"Go on, what happened?"

"He wouldn't stop, he kept pounding those ice cubes, pulverizing them. The whole counter was shaking. I called to him, but he didn't hear me so finally I shouted at him. He turned around holding that dang mallet in his hand and came towards me."

"Jesus, did he hit you with it?"

Wilkes smiles weakly at me. "I thought he was going to. I was so scared, I thought I was gonna pee in my pants. He didn't seem to know who I was. His face was twisted in rage. I put my hands up in front of my face like this and shouted, 'It's me, Dad, it's me!'." His hands dropped to their sides. "You know maybe he couldn't see me because his body was blocking the light. I don't know. Finally, he seemed to hear me, his shoulders slumped and he looked defeated."

"Why didn't you run, for Christ's sake?"

He leans forward and looks out the window. "I don't know, it all happened so fast." He looks at me, but I can tell he's back in that kitchen thirty years ago. "First, he tossed the mallet on the kitchen table and then he grabbed me by the shoulders and rammed me backward into the wall. He knocked the breath right out of me. He wanted to know what I was doing there. I could hardly breathe, and I was so scared I couldn't make any words come out. I don't know if he'd have heard me over the storm anyway." Wilkes laughs, a kind of snort as though he finds something in this vaguely amusing. "You know, here I was worried he was gonna pound me to death when in all likelihood we were all going to get blown away by the storm."

My impatience builds, "did he say anything about Mom?"

"No. He shouted at me again and when I didn't say anything he yanked me forward and shoved me against the wall again even harder this time. My head knocked back and hit the wall."

"You're lucky he didn't kill you."

"I did almost pass out, but he shook me to bring me around. By this time, my fear overrode any inclination I may have had to faint. A bolt of lightning struck close to the house and lit up the kitchen. Dad finally got a good look at me. He let me go and turned back to the sink without a word."

"We're you, OK?"

"I was afraid to move at first. My head and back were throbbing, and my shoulders ached. Finally, the tea kettle squealed, and he took his water and ice cubes and left the kitchen without even looking at me."

I feel an inner chill. I wrap my robe tighter around my shoulders. "Did you see Mom after that?"

"No. A few hours later, the storm petered out as it moved inland, and we all fell asleep." He fingers the empty coffee mug. "The next morning Dad was sullen and distracted. He didn't say anything about our encounter the night before. Only that mom had the flu, and we weren't to bother her."

"I remember that part." I concur.

Wilkes gets up out of the chair and steps over my knees, pulls the curtains aside, and looks outside. "He said if we went into her room if we even knocked on the door, he'd give us a beating we'd never forget." He turns and looks at me. "I believed him."

"We did too."

After the night of the storm, Bird started to come every weekday. Dad worked longer hours at his lumber yard and rarely came home before we were in bed and left before we were up. Bird inherited a lot more of the parental duties with the three of us. Bird wouldn't tell us much and we finally quit asking. She kept saying we needed to be quiet and let time do its work and heal Mom. I never knew what she meant until now. I didn't know she'd been raped, but I also knew she didn't have the flu. I thought maybe someone had died. I was too scared to ask. Eventually things not so much went back to normal as became normal.

Mom finally came out of her room. She was quiet and withdrawn, her skin pale and waxy. Bird walked on eggshells around her, so we did too. Dad's temper got the best of him more often. He'd frequently fly off the handle over seemingly unimportant things. He handed out beatings for the least of infractions, the beatings soon took on an abusive edge.

Dad finally told us Mom was expecting a new baby. He might as well have said he'd dropped a kidney stone. Dad had taken to sleeping on the couch in Mom's sewing room, which in time turned into his permanent bed without anyone saying a word.

Mom came out of her shell as her pregnancy progressed, but she was prone to severe mood swings, sometimes bursting into tears for no reason or locking herself in her room for the whole afternoon. We never questioned any of it. That's not true really. I did ask Dad about it once. He told me to 'mind my own damn business.'

Wilkes looks at me "I wish now I had done more to help. Maybe if I'd paid more attention or if I'd gone with Mom that day it would have made a difference." His voice drops off.

"There was nothing you could have done. This was not your fault and certainly not your responsibility. Even if you had gone with Mom, that's no guarantee things would have turned out differently. You were just a boy."

"I was a teenager!"

"That's right you were a teenager, still a youngster, not an adult. Wilkes, listen to me." I stand up next to him and turn him to face me and look me in the eye. "There was nothing you could have done," I repeat. He looks at me, the pain in his eyes is hard to bear. "Do you hear me?" I ask. He nods his head. "Do you believe me?" I demand an answer.

"Yes," he barely whispers. The morning breeze makes the sheer curtains billow, and a hint of a storm drifts through the screen. He takes his handkerchief out of his pocket and blows his nose, the brusque features of a grown-up Wilkes replaces the tormented child who was before me a moment ago.

"I'm sorry I told you all that, Hannah. I guess I had to finally get it off my chest."

"I'm glad you told me; the truth is never a mistake," I tell him sincerely.

He stares at the floor, then squares his shoulders, stuffs his handkerchief back into his pocket, and turns towards the door. "I'll let you get dressed. I'm heading into town to pick up my plane tickets."

"When do you have to leave?" I feel uneasy about his departure, there is too much still left unsaid.

"Not for a few days yet." He leaves my room and closes the door tightly behind him.

I retrieve my now cold coffee and curl up in the chair that Wilkes has vacated by the window and enjoy the breeze before I have to close the window for the coming storm.

Poor Mom, how I wish I had known. How I wish I could have helped her back then. I also started to grasp the importance of the timing of events. Because it wasn't but about a year later, shortly after Kyle was born, Dad first came to my bedroom in the middle of the night.

CHAPTER EIGHT

The morning sun slowly patrols the earth and scorches everything in sight. The night's rain doesn't cool things off but only makes the day intolerably muggy. Before I get in my second cup of coffee, I hear a car pull up. It must be Maddie. I go inside and fix her a cup of coffee, sugar, no cream. I come back outside and bump the screen door open with my hip as I hold a steaming mug in each hand. When I turn there's Sam. He stands at the top of the porch stairs with a dash of mischief in his green eyes. I haven't even gotten dressed, my robe hangs loose and reveals my skimpy boxer shorts and tee shirt, and my cheeks redden.

He leans lazily on the porch railing and admires my predicament with obvious relish. "I love to see a grown woman blush," he says.

"Damn it, Sam, do you have to sneak up on me like that?" I sound more exasperated than I feel, and he knows it. I'm flattered he thinks I'm still worth admiring, I don't hurry to retie my robe. "Admit it, Sam, your ego enjoys making a woman flustered."

"You drive a hard bargain, Hannah, but all right, I admit it," he says. "Is one of those for me?" He points at the coffee mugs I've set down on the wobbly side table next to the rockers.

"Only if you like sugar and no cream."

"I can live with that. After all, beggars can't be choosy." He blows on his coffee as he sits in the rocking chair next to mine. "Where is everyone?"

"They'll all be clamoring around soon enough. Let's enjoy the peace and quiet while we can."

"You are a beautiful woman, Hannah Wheeler. I can't believe Jack let you get away."

I see the wings of lust flutter across Sam's face. I pull my robe tighter around my shoulders in false modesty, then admonish him for his poor eyesight and for teasing an old woman. I ponder telling him about Jack's cheating heart and that it was Jack who threw me away, but instead say "What brings you by on this fine scalding morning, Mr. Lancaster?"

He softly strokes my arm and then takes my hand. "I have come to whisk you away my dear. For the rest of the day, you're all mine."

"Oh, Sam, I couldn't. There's too much to do here. Maddie only has a few more days off from work to help me and Wilkes has to get back to his firm in a day or two. And Kyle, well, I don't know about him, but he can't stay here forever." I hear myself babble. I do dread today, more stuff to pack and pitch until my head aches. The sound of rustling trash bags and strapping tape being stretched over the top of cardboard boxes dogs me in my sleep. The idea of running off with Sam for the day is appealing and, as usual, impractical.

Sam sets down his coffee. "I knew you were going to give me a hard time, so I have come prepared." Sam crosses his arms and gets that stubborn look on his face. "I'm not taking no for an answer, Hannah."

"Oh no, I know that look, Sam. Please don't do this to me. I really do have to finish . . ."

Wilkes interrupts: "Don't be a stick in the mud, Hannah." He stands just inside the kitchen screen door with a cup of coffee in his hand. The screening distorts his features, but his hair stands on end from sleep. "If the man won't take no for an answer, I don't see what choice you have."

"Where did you come from?" I notice Sam's smile, the smirk of a man who sees victory around the corner.

Sam's grin broadens. "Who cares where he came from? You should listen to the wise words of your older brother."

Wilkes steps out onto the porch. He and Sam shake hands. I wonder if they planned this ahead of time but discarded the idea as too diabolical and complicated for either of them. They start to discuss sports and I become instantly invisible. I go inside and get dressed and when I come back and look out on the porch from the kitchen window they haven't moved.

Maddie calls from behind me. "Hello?"

I spin around, startled. "Hello, yourself." She's at the kitchen table making notes on one of Wilkes's yellow legal pads. "You know, it's been nearly an hour and they're still standing in the same spot." I take the chair across from her. "What are you doing?"

Maddie sets her pen aside and gives me her full attention. "I hear you and Sam are going off to play hooky."

"News travels fast around here."

She smiles. "Gossip loves a well-greased track."

"Well, that's all it is, gossip. He asked me, but I told him I had way too much to do here."

"Are you nuts? You have the chance to go have some fun and you turned it down? What's wrong with you?"

"Nothing's wrong with me, we have so much to do," I repeat stupidly.

Maddie waves her hand at me; "Excuses, Hannah, just excuses. We can take care of things here. We aren't all incompetent you know," she waves off my protests. "Listen, Wilkes and I thought we could hire an auction house to come in and sell Mom's stuff. We'll still have to go through closets and drawers, but we wouldn't have to pack up everything." She pauses, "well, what do you think?" she asks impatiently.

"I don't know." But the idea of finding a way to be with Sam today triggers my imagination. "I like it."

Her voice is full of sisterly affection, "Why don't you go grab your things? Sam's waiting for you."

How can I refuse her? I go around the table and give her a quick hug before going to my room to change my clothes into something that will get and keep Sam's attention. I grab a swimsuit, a towel, a short clingy dress, and heels in case we go out. My cheeks start to hurt from grinning so hard. I put everything into a bag then toss in some makeup, a hairbrush, and a few other items and go back to the kitchen. Wilkes is now sitting at the table with Maddie. Kyle must still be asleep.

"Where's Sam?" The disappointment in my voice is obvious. Wilkes smiles at me, his hair still at attention: "He's out on the porch, Sweetie, waiting patiently for you." Wilkes and Maddie hold up their coffee mugs in a silent salute. I can still feel the grin on my face as I head out the door.

Sam and I drive up to Myrtle Beach. The sun glares down and the temperature is road-buckling hot - a perfect beach day. Sam has the air conditioning on high. I throw caution to the wind and take off my seat belt so I can sit next to him. I put my head on his shoulder and feel like a teenager flush with thoughts of immortality. The radio plays golden oldies. The DJ calls out the dates of each hit single it starts to depress me. How could Mick Jagger possibly be over 50? How could Paul McCartney's face, upon which I had once sworn my undying love, now resemble the jowls of a basset hound? I turn the radio off.

For most of the drive, Sam and I don't talk much. I think we're afraid to break the spell. We stopped to get something cool to drink. I notice with a sinking heart that Sam looks closely at the faces of the people around us to see if he recognizes anyone. I have forgotten the implications for him if we were to run into someone he knows. He sees my crestfallen face - the spell broken. Reality stabs through our lover's haze with the accuracy of Norman Bates. After a few miles, when the trailer parks and convenience stores give way to beach marts and bars, Sam looks at me.

I sit on my side of the car and stare silently at the road.

"You don't understand, Hannah."

I look up at him. "I don't?"

He squeezes my hand and says, "Yes, it's true I don't want anyone to see us. But not for the reasons you think. I want a divorce, but I don't want Jamie to find out this way. I don't want her to hear about us on the grapevine. I should be the one to tell her. I owe her that."

He sounds very magnanimous about dumping his wife of fifteen years. I can't help but wonder if that's what Jack told his girlfriend before he dumped me.

"Hannah, I love you, I always have. I don't want to hurt Jamie, but there is no other way for us to be together."

"I thought we were just old friends catching up," I say caustically as the memories of my divorce come painfully to the surface. Sam doesn't say anymore. He puts both hands on the wheel and concentrates on the road ahead.

I feel rattled, sorry I resorted to sarcasm, but too confused to delve into the possibility of our being together, of his leaving his wife for me - again. I tell myself this sort of thing happens every day; men and women abandon their mates for someone else.

After all, Jack left me for another woman. A year later I find it hard to stay bitter. Of course, when Jack's girlfriend dumped him for someone else that did speed up the healing process. Jack still hadn't recovered from being on the receiving end. I was dying to say, 'I told you so.' The truth is, he was in such a daze and so pitiful afterward I wasn't able to fully enjoy his misery. After Jack was dumped, he was solicitous of Carly and me and even hinted about us getting back together. The hints soon disappeared when he met someone new. This time, I felt only relief. I didn't want to continue with the indecision about what I wanted versus what was good for Carly.

Sam's voice is full of regret, "Can we just forget all this and have a good time today? I really want us to have fun, OK?"

I'm grateful to put our awkwardness aside. "Sure, Sam." I scoot back over to his side of the car. There is one thing my divorce taught me maintaining your pride doesn't keep you warm at night.

Our first stop is the crowded beachfront. Lounging tourists of all shapes and sizes cover the sand. Children are everywhere with plastic buckets and shovels in hand. They diligently move precious mounds of beach-front property from one square foot to another as they erect sandcastles dangerously close to the incoming tide.

Sam and I head into the pavilion to change into our swimsuits. The sand blisters our feet and forces us to perform the burning-sand hoochie-coochie down the strand as we look for an empty spot. Sam carries a cooler, and a tote bag with our street clothes, and has given me the beach towels and umbrella. We sandwich ourselves in between two blobs of people.

On one side is a young family with two little girls, one of which is maybe three years old and the other is closer to five or six. They walk down to the water. The two girls run ahead while Mom and Dad follow closely behind. On the other side is a deeply tanned couple in their early twenties. A tan woman lays face down on an aluminum lounge chair with her black bikini top unhooked. She looks asleep with her eyes closed, head resting on her hands, while her skinny elbows poke off either side of the lounge. The guy is on a beach towel lying next to her on his back. He wears mirror sunglasses and a Speedo swimsuit that leaves practically nothing to the imagination. Neither of them moves when we start to set up camp. I feel like a beached albino whale next to them and give Sam a glare for his choice of spots.

"What did I do?" he asks. Sam shrugs his shoulders and shoves the beach umbrella into the ground. When he opens it, he blocks part of the sun on "Tan Woman's" feet. She instantly comes out of her catatonic state. She holds her bikini top in place, squints into the sun, and holds her hand over her brow in search of the culprit. My eyes fixate on her breast that has popped out the side as she looks up at Sam. I notice she has no bikini line; her breast is as tan as the rest of her.

She squints into the sun. "Hey, what's the big idea?"

Sam looks down at her, her breasts a sort of beacon, and begins to apologize profusely as he quickly readjusts the umbrella. She lays back down, her breast tucks itself back underneath her. Sam stands with the umbrella in his hand and his mouth slightly agape. We both stare at this form that has now returned to its former slug-like self.

Eventually, Sam finishes wrestling the umbrella securely into the ground and we spread out our beach towels. The sun is relentless, and the suntan lotion feels like cooking oil on my skin. Sam's watching Tan Woman no doubt hoping for another glimpse of her tanned breast. I give him a swat on the arm and shout, "You're it!" I make for the water, careful to weave in and out of the tourist piles.

"The last one in is a rotten egg," I call out. He chases me and I squeal with child-like delight as I hit the water at full speed. He catches hold of my ankle and I do a belly flop into the surf. I sputter salt water as I get up. Sam laughs it up; a dangerous move for a man who only has his feet wet. He realizes too late he's going to get wet and tries to turn back for shore. I grab his wrists gently, but firmly and begin to pull him deeper into the water. He begs for mercy as only an out-of-shape middle-aged man can I dutifully point this out to him. In a move to save face and not prolong his agony, he gives up and dives into an oncoming wave.

We swim for a while then stand in chest-deep surf that is conveniently away from the crowds. He puts both arms around my waist and pulls me close. His kiss becomes more demanding as he holds me tighter, and my arms reach out to encircle him. When he loosens his grip, I am breathless. "Sam," I whisper in his ear as he hugs me gently. "Please don't do this. You know I have no willpower when it comes to you."

He kisses me again. My hesitation begins to melt. Suddenly he lets go. I lose my footing and take in a mouth full of sea. Sam laughs as he helps me up. He confuses me with so little effort. Then I remembered he was as ensnared with our kiss as I was, and I smiled at him with this knowledge.

He is taken up short. "Well, well, Hannah Wheeler, we are sure of ourselves, aren't we?" he comments playfully. "I think that's the thing that's changed the most about you over the last fifteen years; you have much more confidence now than you did as a young woman."

"Are you calling me old?" I ask as I chase him towards the shore.

We rest under the umbrella and lay next to each other on our beach towels. Sam hands me a romance novel and says: "I remember when we were living together, how you used to love these."

The man and woman on the cover are in the forest locked in an embrace. His shirt is off detailing his rippled muscles. Her nearly undone bodice reveals a plump bosom that threatens to escape its confines. Her long auburn hair flows loose in the wind. His hands encircle her impossibly thin waistline. Her gypsy-like dress is hiked up and reveals slender thighs, perfectly tapered calves, and delicate bare feet. Her palms are against his bare chest. His lust is evident in his sculptured features; she has a look of wanting with a dollop of fear.

I look up at Sam, "Wow, where did you get this?"

"In the gift shop at the pavilion while you changed your clothes."

I don't tell him I haven't read a romance novel in more than a decade. Who knows, a trashy novel might do me some good. I open the cover and dive in. A few minutes later I'm caught up in the story as I root for the heroine, hate the dastardly bad boy, and cheer my chiseled-chin hero towards the predictable finale.

Sam dozes while I read. The wind blows off the sea and keeps our bodies cool. Later, Sam gets us lunch from a boardwalk vendor. There is enough sand in our food to remind us that we're at the beach; the occasional crunch jars the teeth. The day passes quickly. I finish my book. Sam smiles at my tears when the two lovers get together at the end and then he calls me a hopeless romantic.

Sam has reserved a room at the Holiday Inn for us to freshen up and change our clothes. He already has reservations for dinner. I put on my clingy dress and get the hoped-for looks of appreciation. Sam looks so handsome and desirable in his starched white shirt and black slacks. I'm glad we're running late for our reservations and must hurry; no time to linger over the possibilities the hotel bed presents.

The dinner is exquisite with a delectable vegetable dish that Sam also orders for himself; I'm touched by his gesture of solidarity. The wine is marvelous, the ambiance intoxicating. Our table is by the window and gives an unobstructed view of the darkening shoreline. Outside we can see there are still a few stragglers on the beach; couples holding hands, young families searching for seashells. The restaurant is dark and cool. A small brass

Victorian lamp with a delicate, pink-fringed shade sits in the center of the linen cloth-covered table. Fresh gardenias float in a shallow dish of water. A seasoned piano player softly caresses the keys of a baby grand piano. A gentle blues tune emanates from her expert fingertips. I'm entranced; this is the mood to fall in love by and I'm not disappointed.

After dinner, Sam and I go for a stroll on the boardwalk and admire the wares of the small shops stuffed with custom-painted T-shirts, hand-woven baskets, and other beach paraphernalia. We enter an arcade and although overdressed we engage in fierce competition over pinball. I surrender when my thumbs and fingers hurt from pushing the flippers. Sam makes me say out loud that he's the all-time champion. I do but I keep my fingers crossed behind my back.

Around ten o'clock Sam walks us to a nightclub called The Blue Note Jazz Club. We can feel the pulse of the music from inside. "You game?" There is a hint of mischief in his eyes. "Or are you too old?" He asks a direct challenge.

"I'm never too old," I assure him.

The club is dark and the band's going on a break. The jukebox blasts a country tune I don't recognize. A couple vacates a table near the bandstand, and we slip into the empty chairs. A waitress appears and takes our drink orders. It's too loud to talk over the music so we hold hands, sip our drinks, and take in the surroundings. The club is a local establishment free from the clamor of tourists. Most of the people are in their mid-thirties. The band is a native blues band and, according to the club's poster board PR, is on the cusp of discovery by a national label. I wonder if Sam misses singing with a band. He said he'd given it up more than five years ago when he got too old to hit the high notes and the pressures of work made it impossible to get away for rehearsals and weekend gigs.

Before long the band returns and begins to play. They're very good; the members have worked together awhile as their banter and across-the-stage gestures attest. The singer is especially gifted. She conjures up low lazy notes and makes the high notes dress up formally before they leave the stage. Sam and I both admire her ability to work with an audience.

Couples crowd the dance floor; some practiced and others, with too much to drink, simply hold one another up. Other couples merely push up against each other as they steal a private moment amid a dozen bodies. I hesitate at Sam's invitation. Before I can get out a breath of protest, he has me on the dance floor with his right arm around my waist, holding me close. He tells me to relax. I follow orders and give in to the rhythmic sway of the beat and Sam's body. He holds me tighter, whispers his love for me, and kisses me lightly on the ear. A delicious chill runs up my spine. I give myself away when I let my body sag for an instant with the delight of his touch. He kisses me on the lips, softly at first. As my caution starts to pack up and head towards the door, he kisses me deeper and holds me closer still, without ever losing time with the music. He lets me go momentarily when the song ends, and we both clap our appreciation. The bass player looks at me and executes a small bow. I blush at the attention.

Sam pulls me close for the next song and whispers in my ear: "Looks like I'm not the only one who thinks you're irresistible tonight." He then looks me in the eye and says: "But don't forget, I'm the one who takes you home tonight." Before I can answer, he kisses me on the lips.

I feel my knees get weaker as I break away and playfully say, "Sam, not here."

He smiles down at me. His hands caress my back as we finish the dance.

When the band takes another break Sam looks at me and asks: "Are you ready to go?" There is so much unspoken in his words and his eyes that I simply nod, and we head out into the night. The ocean breeze is cool against my skin as we make our way back to the hotel.

When the door to our room closes shut, I quietly but firmly push Sam back against the wall. I touch his cheeks softly as I look at him, I'm sure the lust in my eyes is unmistakable. Without taking his eyes off mine, he lifts me in his arms and sets me on the bed. I begin to panic. What if he's disappointed? What if I'm disappointed? I needn't have worried. All these years have not diminished our mutual lust for each other. He murmurs soft verbal caresses nearly as silky as his touch. I look at his face and see the love he feels for me as clearly as it was fifteen years ago. I know in my heart I will love only this man for the rest of my life. The prospect both elates and terrifies me. I wonder how I ever let him get away. I vow never to let him go again.

Reality begs us to come back; we resist the call, but eventually, as good slaves to a master, we heed the summons, get dressed, and head home. As we leave, I have the uneasy feeling that my life will never be the same.

The next morning the packing resumes. Maddie has to be at work and leaves me to pack boxes while Wilkes and Kyle talk with auctioneers. Once the auctioneers leave, Kyle and I do most of the packing while Wilkes acts as a consultant about the disposition of various articles Kyle and I pull from the closet and drawers.

Kyle takes a break and joins Wilkes on the sofa. "You know, I hardly remember Dad. I was so young when he died. What was he like?"

Wilkes fidgets with the paperweight on the end table." I don't know, sort of large and loud I guess is how I'd describe him."

"You never want to talk about him," Kyle notes. "Why is that?"

"What do you want to know?"

"Nothing specific. I guess I want to know more about what the family was like before I came along. I want to know more about Mom and Dad and what happened after the attack."

I watch Wilkes's face. He says nothing for a moment, but then he looks at Kyle and says, "She was different afterward." He sets a paperweight back on the table. "But she doted on you. Gave you all her energy and attention."

"Did that bother you?" Kyle asks.

"Bother me? Heavens no! I was almost thirteen when you were born." Wilkes crosses his legs. "Besides it made me feel good to see Mom happy and she only seemed happy when she was taking care of you."

Kyle turns to me as I sit on the floor cross-legged and wrap a collection of porcelain figurines I want to keep. "Were either of you girls jealous?"

I think long and hard before I answer. "I think at first Maddie may not have appreciated all the attention you received. But you must remember that we were all older than you. It's tough to be jealous when we all loved you and helped take care of you."

Kyle sits silently for a few moments. I notice how fidgety Wilkes is as the foot on his crossed leg wiggles back and forth like a windup toy with the key turned too tightly.

Kyle absently fingers his earrings. "What about Dad?"

"What do you mean?" I ask.

Wilkes interrupts. "Dad got more violent afterward."

"Did he ever hit Mom?"

"Oh, no!" Wilkes says emphatically, "he'd never hit Mom. Just us kids mostly."

"Mostly you, you mean," Kyle observes.

"Yeah, mostly me I guess." Wilkes sloughs it off.

They seem to have forgotten I'm even here.

Kyle continues to ask questions. "Did Mom do anything to stop it?"

Wilkes lets out a deep sigh. "Dad was the disciplinarian and whatever he said was law. That went for Mom as well. So, to answer your question; no, she never did anything to stop him. In her defense though, I don't think she knew how tough he was on all of us."

Kyle nods and traces his finger along the flower pattern on the arm of the couch. "How did Dad die?"

Wilkes gets off the sofa. "You know how Dad died, Kyle."

"Mom said he died in a car accident, but over the years everyone's been vague about exactly what happened. I just wondered why, that's all."

I stand up and try to enter the conversation.

Wilkes ignores me. "What's there to know? He was in his car, it skidded off the road, went over a cliff, hit a tree, burst into flames and the man died. What is so tough about believing that?"

"I didn't say I didn't believe it. I just don't know exactly what happened. Like I didn't know the truck burned." Kyle grasps for details. "How long did it take you to find him?"

"I didn't find him." Wilkes declares loudly. "I wasn't even near the place when they found him. I was at school."

I interject. "Kyle, the police found Dad."

Kyle doesn't seem to hear me. "I didn't mean anything by that, Wilkes. I was only wondering how long Dad had been missing before someone found him?"

Wilkes paces the porch like a caged animal. I wonder what has him so upset.

Wilkes stops pacing and turns to Kyle. "Why do you want to know all this stuff? Why would it make a difference to you if Dad was human toast for Christ's sake?" Wilkes stands in front of Kyle with his feet spread apart and his hands on his hips. He looks like a drill sergeant as he dresses down a lowly private and the memory of my father painfully resurfaces. Lord how we tend to turn into our parents despite our best efforts to stop the metamorphosis.

Wilkes is silenced when he sees Kyle close to tears and immediately begins to apologize. "I'm sorry, Kyle. I don't like these questions. It brings up the whole ugly mess all over again. I was the one who had to identify Dad's body; if it hadn't been for the silver ring on his right hand, I probably couldn't have been sure it was him." Wilkes shudders at the memory.

Kyle looks stymied. All he probably wanted to know was how the fabric of this family was put together, to catch a glimpse of what life was like before he arrived so late on the scene. All he must see is estrangement and resentment among the family members towards Dad. Even my memories of Dad are filtered through cheesecloth. I only remember him as hulking and loud our lives punctuated by his flaring temper.

I knew Wilkes had told Kyle about the night Mom was attacked. I guess he felt that there was still so much he didn't know. He must feel disconnected and ungrounded as he looks for some pieces of the puzzle to help him understand the workings of this family - his family.

The key was that fateful night. How it changed us all remains a mystery one I hope to unravel before I go home and pick up the thread of my life again. Wilkes's anger bothers me. I can't help but feel that he's hiding something, but what and why?

The next morning I'm the late riser. When I do wake up, I stay in bed and languish on the memories of my day at the beach with Sam and especially of our night together. I smile at the ceiling and think how wonderful life is and how lucky I am to get a second chance. There was a gentle knock at my bedroom door right when I was reliving the really good part. "Yes?" I call out irritated with the interruption. Maddie asks if she can talk to me and reluctantly, I give in. She didn't bring coffee with her, but I decided to forgive the indiscretion since this is one of the most perfect mornings I've had in recent memory.

"Are you going to get that lazy butt out of bed or what?" she asks as she pulls back my covers.

"Or what!" I snatch them back.

"Well, you must have had a good time," she says a bit smugly.

"It was all right," I concede.

She plops down on the end of my bed. "From the glow on your face, I would say it was better than all right. So, give dear sister. I want details and I'm not moving until you produce."

"I haven't even had coffee yet," I complain.

"OK, I'll get you some coffee, but then you have to spill your guts."

She leaves the room and I get out of bed and get myself together. I'm sitting up in bed when she returns with a steaming mug in hand.

"Well?" She says as she expectantly resumes her place at the end of the mattress.

"I know it sounds like a cliché, but it was the most wonderful day of my whole life. I had more fun than I've had in the last ten years put together. We went swimming, we had a romantic dinner and then we went dancing." I say dreamily as I recall the details.

"And...?" she insists.

"There is only so much that sisterly duty can force me to confess."

"No holding back, Hannah, or I'll tell Sam you had a tummy tuck."

"You wouldn't!"

"Don't try me."

"You are such a heartless woman Maddie. All right the sex was great and there was plenty of it. There, are you satisfied?" I ask as I sip my coffee.

"I'm not the one looking satisfied this morning." She says as she raises one well-plucked eyebrow.

I throw a pillow at her.

She catches it, throws it back, and nearly spills my coffee.

"Look out!" I shout as I grab the pillow and roughly stuff it back behind me. "I'm not telling you another thing. I don't want my love life to become a spectator sport."

"Spoilsport. Now what room are we going to tackle today? Wilkes has meetings planned with two auctioneers. One is supposed to arrive sometime this afternoon and the other is to come on Monday morning I think."

I hear the phone ring in the distance. A moment later, Kyle sticks his head in my door and tells me that the phone is for me.

"He can't live a minute without you I see," teases Maddie, as I climb out of bed and head into Mom's room to get the phone.

"Good morning," Sam says brightly when I pick up the receiver. "I hope you slept well. I miss you already."

"It's good to hear your voice. I miss you too." I tell him sincerely.

"Can you have lunch with me today?" He asks and then hesitates before continuing: "It's the last time I'll be able to see you for a while."

I don't ask any questions; after all, ignorance is bliss. I eagerly agreed to meet him for lunch.

When I get back to my room Maddie is still perched on my bed and leafing idly through a magazine. She doesn't ask about the phone call. We decided to do Mom's bedroom today; the one room we've silently avoided all week. I get dressed, have some breakfast with Kyle, and then join Maddie in Mom's room. She already has a collection of empty boxes stacked in the corner and a fresh roll of trash bags at the ready. Kyle is going to clean out the garage and help us carry out boxes and bags. Wilkes has disappeared. Kyle said he was gone when he got up this morning.

The day is hot and humid and soon Maddie and I are drenched with sweat and getting irritable. Maddie finds Dad's sword scabbard lying in the back on the top shelf of Mom's clothes closet. "I found it at last. I thought maybe Mom had thrown it out. Now it's mine." She declares carefully as she sets it aside, her prize claimed.

"Don't forget that Wilkes wanted that too." I remind her, annoyed with her proprietary tone.

She lays the scabbard on the bed. "I found it!" She points out contentiously.

"Big deal. That doesn't make it yours."

She puts her hands on her hips. "Mom said he couldn't have anything."

I pull big-sister seniority. "Well, then maybe I want it, did you ever think of that?"

"You never said anything about wanting it before," she says, immediately suspicious.

"I don't want it silly, but I have the right to want it," I tell her. "Just because you found it doesn't make it automatically yours."

"Why not?!" She demands petulantly.

"Just because! Christ Maddie, how about some gratitude?"

"Gratitude!?" Maddie shouts suddenly outraged. "What have you done for me!?"

"What have I done for you?" I ask, surprised.

"You want me to be grateful?"

Her intonation tells me that somehow, we're not talking about the same thing anymore. She seems way past the discussion of the money I sent to her every week to help cover incidentals while she was a college student.

"How long do I have to be obliged, dear sister?"

Her voice has a dangerous quality to it that I've never heard before; she starts to scare me.

"What, no answer? That's not like you at all big sister," she says between gritted teeth. "You always have an answer. So, tell me how long I have to go through life giving you my dang gratitude?"

"What are you talking about, Maddie?"

"We both know what I'm talking about, Hannah. Don't play stupid with me. Don't you dare play stupid," she threatens menacingly. She throws down the roll of strapping tape she had clutched in her hand. It bounces harmlessly off the arm of the wing chair and rolls under the bed. "Answer the dang question, Hannah. How long do I have to go on being grateful? Or better yet, tell me what I can do to even the score, so I don't owe you anymore. I'm sick of owing you, sick of you holding it over me, and just plain sick of you, Hannah."

I feel like I've walked into the middle of someone else's fight. "Owe me for what, Maddie? I don't understand." I plead innocently.

I honestly don't know where this is coming from. This is more than sibling rivalry; this is deep-seated anger that's been festering. I've never seen Maddie get so angry so fast. I have no idea what she's talking about. I'm afraid to ask; afraid of what is about to land in my lap.

"OK, I'll explain it to you." She calms down a little in the face of my obvious total ignorance.

"I wish you would."

She takes a deep breath. "I'm grateful that you protected me from Dad. Grateful you kept him away from me." She says in a near whisper, as her body physically melts into the chair next to the phone all her anger gone as quickly as it came.

I'm speechless. I had no idea she ever knew anything about any of this. She never said a word until now. I cautiously ask her to tell me more, trying to find out how much she knows.

"I saw Daddy going into your room one night after everyone was in bed. It seemed odd, he looked, I don't know, like he was up to something; like he was being sneaky. Then a few weeks later I saw him go into your room again." She gets up grabs the box of tissues off the bureau and continues. "As I was watching him shave in the big bathroom one day, I asked him 'Daddy, why do you go into Hannah's room in the middle of the night?' You know what he told me?"

I shake my head.

"Nothing. He just picked me up off the floor and spanked the hell out of me. I couldn't sit for a week afterward. I never asked him again; I can tell you that." She blows her nose and sits back down with the box of tissues clasped in her lap. "Sometimes, late in the night, I could hear you cry. I couldn't bring myself to come see what was going on. I knew somehow that what Daddy was doing was wrong, but I was scared, too scared to do anything about it." She stops as the tears get hold of her.

I sit on the floor next to her and pat her knee. "Maddie, there was nothing you could've done," I assure her. "I'm sorry you even know the truth." Tears come unbidden to my eyes tears of anger that the ugly demons have dared show their faces in the daylight.

Maddie reaches her hand out to me and continues. "I remember one night when I was about ten years old, and you must have been twelve; Dad came into my room." Her grip on my hand tightens. "I remember how my heart froze in my mouth when he opened the door. I was too terrified to scream or do anything but pretend to be asleep. I knew a bad thing was going to happen to me, but I didn't know what and I was terrified. But then, when I thought I was going to scream, when I thought, I was going to die, you called out to him. He backed out of my room and closed the door. He never came back." Maddie stops and looks up at me her cheeks are streaked; the dust washed partially off her face by her tears. Her eyes are the pleading eyes of a ten-year-old. "You saved me, Hannah. You deliberately kept Dad away from me. We never talked about it, but I've always felt grateful and exceedingly guilty."

I gently reach up and smooth her hair back from her face. "What do you mean you felt guilty? For what?"

She looks at me for a moment and says nothing. Then she says, "I was just so glad he left me alone. She stops and takes a deep breath, "but I did nothing to stop him from hurting you."

I wrap my arms around Maddie and in the emptiness of our mother's bedroom, while the family skeletons loudly rattle all around us, we hold each other close.

With her head on my shoulder, Maddie whispers. "I was so glad when he died and then, if you can believe it, I felt guilty about that too."

I never dreamed she knew - that anyone knew. Years later I confronted Mom. I thought she could help me understand what had happened and why. She denied the whole thing. Slapped my face when I insisted it was true. She refused to talk to me. I left the next day and we never spoke of it again. I eventually saw a therapist who said I couldn't do anything about my mother's denial, but I could get better, and I did. Now I realize that my dad only terrorizes me in my sleep.

I tell Maddie all this and suggest she talk with someone about it. There is certainly no reason to feel guilty. I had also celebrated when Dad died and refused to feel any remorse.

Maddie gets up to go wash her face. When she stands in the doorway I tell her, "Somehow I feel I've come full circle, so let's consider the debt, however big or small, paid in full."

If only I had known then that Maddie and I were not the only ones who knew about Daddy's secret.

CHAPTER NINE

Maddie and I finally get Bird alone. We're both eager to hear what she remembers. We hope she knows substantially more than we do and will tell us. Bird confirms she knew what happened, but Dad had warned her not to utter a word. I can tell she's sad we've discovered the truth but has resigned herself to answering our questions.

The house is unusually cool this afternoon as the three of us sit around the kitchen table. The cool front that's tried to wedge itself in all week has, for the moment, gained the advantage.

Bird fidgets as she talks. She reminds me of a reluctant witness for the prosecution. Her hesitation to lay the ugly truth before us is tempered with her relief to abandon the secrets she's guarded all these years.

After Bird has told us what she remembers Maddie asks, "Bird did they ever catch the guy who raped Mom?"

"No Honey. Nobody even looked for 'em. Your mother say she didn't see who attacked her other than to say he was a white man. Besides, your daddy wasn't exactly rushin' her to pursue it, I guess 'cause he couldn't face the humiliation."

My temper immediately flares, "What do you mean his humiliation?"

"Don't go gettin' all huffy on me girl, I'm just tellin' you what I know. Remember this was in the seventies and things was different back then. I think your daddy was afraid of losin' business if what happened to your momma got out," Bird explains.

Maddie holds up her hand to silence me, "I don't understand Bird, how could what happened to Mom hurt Dad's business?"

"Well, your daddy did most of his lumber business with locals. Now these are good ol' boys and they might've hinted that maybe your daddy wasn't takin' care of business at home. You follow what I'm tellin' ya?" Bird hesitates. "Let's just say that a lota folks with whom your daddy did business wouldn'a been gushin' with sympathy."

"Oh my God," Maddie covers her mouth with her hands in disbelief. "Is that why they kept it a secret?"

"One of the reasons, yes," Bird acknowledges. "But your momma was deeply ashamed and didn't want no one to know what happened to 'er."

"It wasn't her fault!" I exclaim.

"No Sweetie, it wasn't. But she felt guilty all the same. Said she felt like she'd brought disgrace down upon the family. Things ain't like they is now, with victim's rights and survivors poppin' up all the time on them talk shows tellin' their stories. This was the kinda of thing a family kept hush-hush."

"Was Kyle. . ." I falter not sure quite how to put this. I pull my chair a bit closer and drop my voice to a whisper "Was Kyle legitimate? Was he Daddy's son?"

"Is that what you thought? Lord child, you sure does have an active imagination. Yes, Kyle is your Daddy's son. Your mother was pregnant with Kyle before that man got ahold of her." Bird affirms.

"How do you know?" Maddie asks. "According to the hospital records and Kyle's birth certificate, she would have been only about two months pregnant. Back then didn't you have to wait at least six to eight weeks and then kill a rabbit or frog or something to tell if you were pregnant?"

Bird smiles at her. "Yes, the white folks always wantin' to know; never willin' to let the Good Lord tell 'em in his own time. But I seen she was expectin' before any tests, I'd already told her she was gonna have another baby."

"How did you know Bird?" Maddie asks intrigued.

"Why I could see it in her face, child. I'd had four babies of my own and I'd been around for the birth of you all so I knew what she look like when she gonna have a baby. I even told her it was gonna be a boy."

"Did she believe you?" I ask.

Bird pats my shoulder as though she feels sorry for me because I refuse to see what's as plain as the nose on my face. "Sure, she did and why not, I ain't never been wrong about a thing like that. The sad thing is that your daddy didn't believe me."

"Why not?" Maddie and I both ask at the same time.

Bird looks down at her lap and absently smooths down the pockets of her apron. "He thought it was just a bunch of colored-folk mumbo jumbo and told me to keep my opinions to myself." She looks at Maddie and me, "Your daddy, God rest his soul, was not a warm man." Bird finishes diplomatically.

"Why was it sad he didn't believe, Bird?" I don't really want to know the answer, but I'm too drawn in not to ask the question. "Did he blame Mom for what happened?"

"Well, once he'd decided Kyle wasn't his, someone had to take the blame."

"Bird, do you think that's why Daddy was so abusive?"

"How do you mean?" she asks. "I don't think he ever hurt your Momma."

"Well, Dad sure took enough swings at us, especially Wilkes. Don't you remember?" I ask her.

Bird's face is frozen, the shock of our words almost too much to absorb. "I never seen your daddy hurt any of you." She whispers, never taking her eyes off my face. She takes a deep breath and swallows her hurt. "But you have to remember, except for night after your momma got hurt, I wasn't at your house but three days durin' the week and then for only part of the day and hardly ever when your daddy was home." Bird pauses as a tear slips down her face. She pulls a hanky out of her apron pocket, blows her nose, and says: "I'd never known anybody who'd hurt their little darlins' on purpose. I jus' never put it together. I remember Wilkes havin' more than his share of bruises, but he always had an excuse when I asked him about it. When you all got moody and sullen, I didn't think nothin' of it. Why it was natural that you'd be withdrawn with your Momma not payin' you hardly any attention, what with her hol' up in her room most the day. After a while I guess, I got used to it." She looks up at both of us, her eyes full of tears. "I'm sorry, so sorry ol' Bird let you down."

"Bird, you didn't let us down. You were the one safe place there was to be." I wrap my arms around her and lay my head on her shoulder as my tears start to slide down my cheeks. I sit up and look at Maddie and Bird.

Maddie wipes a tear off her face with the back of her hand. "There was nothing you could have done even if you'd known Bird," she says taking Bird's hands in hers.

For a few minutes the three of us hold on to each other Bird mourns our lost innocence and Maddie and I hold on to her grateful for all the times she was there for us.

Bird helped me keep my sanity. When things were at their worst, only Bird's love gave me hope and I couldn't have gotten through a single day without hope.

Bird pats me on the back and says, "Would you look at the three of us jus' carryin' on like a bunch of hens whose rooster's flown the coup." Maddie grabs a box of tissues off the kitchen counter and passes it around. We wipe tears and blow our noses, each of us feeling a little self-conscious.

Bird sits down between us again and Maddie takes her hand. "What about the sexual abuse?" she asks before I can stop her. "Bird, did you know anything about that?"

Bird gets visibly upset again. "What are you talkin' about young lady?"

"Maddie!" I try to cut her off.

"You mean you didn't know?" Maddie asks Bird, astonished.

"Know what, child?" She asks. She looks up at us; one on each side of her. She looks back and forth from me to Maddie and waits for one of us to explain. We're both silent as we stare at each other a battle of wills.

"Please, one of you girls tell me what's goin' on?" Bird implores.

"Hannah, you were the one who said we should get all our secrets out in the open."

I'm speechless, caught between my darn pontificating and the horror of exposure.

Maddie doesn't take her eyes off me, "Daddy sexually abused Hannah."

To have it said out loud by someone else in such a matter-of-fact tone of voice is a shock.

Bird takes my hands in hers, leans forward, and whispers: "Is that true, baby?" She asks me, the concern and heartbreak evident in her voice. I can only nod my head. "I had no idea, Sweetie; I swear I didn't or I would have killed him with my bare hands."

From her tone, I believe she would've tried.

"You poor darlin', why didn't you tell ol' Bird?"

Maddie looks at me too as they both wonder why I never told her.

I take a deep choking breath, the knot in my stomach tightens with sickening strength, and the heat on my face rivals fire. "At first, Daddy said that his visits were to be 'our little secret.' Then he convinced me that all girls did these things for their Daddies." Maddie and Bird listen silently. "When I began to ask questions, he simply said that if I told, he'd kill Mom. I believed him."

For a moment I feel twelve years old all over again; humiliated, powerless, and lost.

Maddie raises her hand up and softly strokes my cheek. "I'm sorry, Hannah." She puts her arm around my shoulder as Bird squeezes my hands to console me. "I thought you'd talked this through with a therapist. I thought you were better," Maddie's surprised and confused at the depth of my anguish.

I don't know how to explain to her that you don't get better. The most you can hope for is that it doesn't haunt you day and night, that it doesn't run your life and taint every darn thing you do. Kyle and Wilkes's arrival home saves me from having to make explanations.

Wilkes puts a bag of groceries on the counter. "What do you three have your heads together about?"

Maddie casts a glaring look at them both.

"What's wrong?" Kyle asks concerned.

Maddie tries to lighten things up before they start to ask too many questions. "We were just talking about a bit of family nostalgia."

"I want to know," Kyle states a bit harshly, tired of being left out.

Maddie tries to head him off. "Kyle, I don't think this is the time."

"When is it going to be time?" Kyle asks, annoyed at being put off. "When are you going to stop keeping things from me?"

"Stop it! Just stop it!" I jump to my feet, my tears almost instantly replaced by anger. "How dare you pity me." I look at Maddie and then at Bird. "I'm not some wounded animal who needs to be rescued. I get to decide who I want to tell! I get to decide who should know! Do you all understand!? It's up to me!" I look around the room at each of them. They have all stopped dead at my emotional outburst. Wilkes has stopped unloading groceries into the refrigerator. Maddie and Bird sit with stunned looks on their faces. Kyle is the only one who moves, and he backs up out of my way.

I take a deep breath and as calmly and clearly as I can I say, "We were talking about Dad and how he sexually abused me."

Kyle gasps while Maddie and Bird look at the floor. Wilkes stays perfectly still, with no reaction at all. I fix my gaze on his face the others are forgotten. He knows. I can see it in his eyes, there is no surprise, no perceptible flinch at the suddenness of the news or the crudeness of the mental pictures sure to flash through his mind. I cross the room, place my hand lightly on his arm, and whisper loud enough for him to hear. "You knew, didn't you?"

He takes a long time to answer. "Yes, I knew." He says loud enough so everyone can hear. Wilkes leads me gently back to the kitchen table, gets me seated and squats in front of me holding on to the arms of my chair. I never take my eyes off his face. Everyone silently stares at Wilkes. He doesn't say anything at first, but you can see the inner turmoil on his face as he wrestles with his demons. He looks at me. I try to smile, but I think all I'm able to muster is a half-lip sneer.

Maddie breaks the silence: "Wilkes you don't . . ."

Wilkes holds up a hand to ward off further comment. "No, I think it's time the whole truth came out. I can't keep these secrets anymore." He stands and begins to pace. He stops and looks directly into my soul. "Yes, I knew about the abuse. But I didn't want to face the truth. I suspected but found it easier to keep my head in the sand than to deal with the consequences of facing reality." He turns to me, "I'm sorry, Hannah. I'm sorry I didn't do something sooner. I've always felt awful that I didn't intervene long before I did."

The air in the room suddenly gets thicker. "What do you mean, long before you did?" I ask.

"I think I knew from the beginning, but I didn't confront Dad for almost three years."

"How did you know?" The fire on my face comes back.

"I saw Dad go into your room one night, I heard you crying afterward, it didn't take much to put it all together," Wilkes says dejectedly.

The fire moves from my face to the top of my head. The air in the room is suddenly too thick to breathe. I can't get my breath and my hands start to shake uncontrollably. I have this sick fear that I'm going to suffocate. I stand up as my panic moves to hysteria. My arms start to flail as my frenzy rises. In the corner of my mind, I notice the lights get darker and I think a storm must be moving inland. Everyone stares at me, they get up and move towards me, I wonder why they move so slowly. I feel clammy and dizzy.

Why doesn't anyone help me? Then I feel a calmness come over my body and the lights go out. I don't even feel my body hit the floor.

I hear the rumble of a window unit as it loudly spews cold air. The smell of Freon is unmistakable. The room is too cold. I try to roll over away from the icy air flow and a blast of pain rocks my head and brings me completely awake. I can't see very well because one eye is blocked. Oh my God, I'm blind! I raise my hand to my head and feel my eye. There is a huge gauze bandage and tape over my forehead that covers my left eye. I vaguely remember the scene in the kitchen and wonder where I am.

"Hey, she's awake," I hear someone call. The voice sounds like Kyle. Someone takes my hand. The touch is soft. I try to open my eyes again and see who it is. I'm finally able to focus my good eye and see Maddie swim into focus. Kyle and Wilkes stand behind her.

"Good morning sleepy head," Maddie grins from ear to ear. They all grin.

They look like a bunch of hyenas. "What's so damn funny?" I ask annoyed with all their happiness while I lay here with my head pounding. I lie back on the pillows and wait for the excruciating throb to stop.

"We were worried about you, sweetie," Maddie pats my hand. Kyle and Wilkes nod in agreement like a couple of nitwits.

I feel my bandages again, "What happened?"

"You had a little accident," Maddie says.

"No kidding." Sarcasm drips from every word I speak. "Wilkes, what the hell happened?"

"You fainted and hit your head on the edge of the kitchen table." Wilkes moves around to stand beside me and puts his hand gently on my shoulder.

"Am I blind?" I ask worried.

"No, Sis, you're not blind, but you do have about seven stitches holding the right side of your forehead in place. You really banged yourself, you have a slight concussion, but the doctor said there wouldn't be much of a scar. She also said the stitches are very near your hair line so what scarring there maybe won't show up on your beautiful face." Wilkes assures me.

I look at each of them and see the concern on their faces and their love for me and say: "How come one of you idiots didn't catch me?"

There is complete silence for a minute, then they all burst out laughing, and then all start to talk at once. A nurse pushes her way through the crowded room. She's a large middle-aged woman who looks like she could pick us all up and comfortably throw us over her shoulder. Her reading glasses hang from a silver chain draped around her neck. Her gray-streaked hair is short and curly with a white starched nurse's cap perched securely to the top of her head with a mass of bobby pins.

"This is a hospital," she barks. She glares at each of us as she bustles to the side of my bed and displaces Maddie and Wilkes. She moves to straighten my sheets. She tugs on the sides and neatly stuffs the loose ends under the mattress with military precision. She pulls the top sheet so tight you can see the outline of my body underneath. I'm afraid to breathe as I might inadvertently cause a wrinkle. She seems to loom over me with her silver name bar indicating her name is Martha Cummings. She asks, "How you doin' Hon?" in that mother/nurse/terrorist voice I remember from when Carly was delivered by cesarean.

"My head hurts and I want drugs," I tell her without blinking. That's the only way to deal with these hospital people. Hit them early and hit them hard with requests for pain medication. If you let them see you weaken, if you show any fear, they'll dilly dally until you're a dead woman.

She straightens up and tugs her uniform down tightly over her ample bosom. "You'll have to wait for the doctor." She answers crisply. "Now, all you people are going to have to leave." She tries to shoo everyone out the door.

"Excuse me!" I yell above her shoo noises; my head quickly pays me back for the outburst. "I want these people to stay," I say a bit softer as I hold my head in my hands.

I have offended the nurse. "You're only allowed two visitors at a time," she crosses her arms and stands her ground.

All three volunteer to leave. "I want to talk to Wilkes alone for just a few minutes," I tell them. Then I look again at the nurse who hasn't moved but looks pleased with herself for having won that round. "Could you please get me some pain pills," I ask her again.

"I told you; you'll have to wait for the doctor."

"How long is that going to be?"

"I'm not sure. Dr. Stewart is very busy this morning."

I motion for her to come over to my bed. Kyle and Maddie take the opportunity to leave the room. She comes and stands beside me with her arms unfolded, a bit of concern on her face. I shut my good eye, lie back on the bed, and let out a soft moan so she can appreciate how weak I am. I crook my finger for her to come closer. She leans down. I grab her by the lapels on her nurse's uniform and hiss loudly in her face. "I don't want to wait! I want something now! Do you hear me?"

I let go of her uniform as she backed up abruptly both angry and embarrassed. She knocks the end table with her hip. She turns on her heel and goes to the door. At the door, she turns around and says to Wilkes, "Visiting hours are almost over."

She gives me a parting glare to let me know this is far from over and disappears around the corner as the large wooden door silently closes behind her. When she's gone, I flop back on my pillows worn out from the exchange.

"Why don't I come back later," Wilkes says when he sees my exhaustion and obvious pain.

"No stay," I put my hand on his arm as if I could physically keep him there. I close my eyes to rest for a few minutes. A different nurse enters the room and gives me a shot for the pain. "See, squeaky wheel always works," I smile and whisper to Wilkes as the room starts to get a bit hazy. The last thing I remember is Wilkes kissing me on the cheek and saying he loves me.

The next time I wake up the pounding in my head has lessened. I lie awake for a few minutes before I open my eye. Then I hear the door to my room open and someone comes in. I don't want to deal with that nurse, so I pretend I'm asleep. I can tell though when I hear the footsteps that it's not the nurse. I feel the air particles charge and my heart starts to beat faster making my head achier. I slowly open my left eye and peek out. There's Sam. He stands awkwardly not sure what to do; whether to come or go.

"Hello, handsome," I startle him.

A big smile breaks out on his face. He pulls up a chair and sits beside me. He takes my hand and holds it against his cheek, closes his eyes for a moment, and says: "I'm so glad you're OK. They wouldn't let me in to see you. Are you all right?" he asks, worry written all over his face.

"I'm fine. It'll take more than a lousy kitchen table to break this stubborn noggin open," I say as my head begins to throb in earnest now.

"You're hurting pretty bad, aren't you?" he asks. "Have they given you something for the pain?" He doesn't wait for an answer but stands and heads out the door. I can hear him in the hallway accosting a passing nurse and demanding they do something for me, that they get me some pain medication immediately. I smile to myself, glad to have Sam in charge.

A nurse is in my room in less than five minutes giving me a paper cup with two painkillers inside. Sam gets me a glass of water and I take the pills. He insists I stay quiet until the medicine can start to work.

"I dropped by your mom's house to see you. I know I should've called first, but I thought you might tell me you were busy, and I had to see you. When I got there, Bird was the only one home and she told me what happened." He gently sweeps my hair back from my face. "She said they'd taken you to the hospital. I came right away, but because I wasn't family, they wouldn't let me in to see you. I came back the next day and they still wouldn't let me see you. I've been so frustrated."

"Wait a minute," I start to say, but Sam tries to keep me quiet.

"No, Sam, I need to know. How long have I been here?"

"You've been here three days," he says.

"What?"

"You were out like a light for almost two full days Hannah. We were all worried sick. Maddie, Kyle, and Wilkes took turns staying with you. The doctor said she thought you'd be fine, but also said that the longer you remained unconscious the more likely you were to have some permanent damage. But from the reaming out Wilkes said you gave the nurse yesterday, we're not worried about any permanent damage; you're still your same old ornery self."

I called Carly from the hospital and told her what happened. I assured her I was all right and that I was so sorry I hadn't called her when I'd promised. She sounds worried and I have trouble convincing her I'm fine. Then Jack gets on the phone and wants all the medical details. I tell him what I can but warn him that all this talk about my condition might scare Carly and he lays off. I give him the name of my doctor and tell him to get any gory details he wants from her. Two days later the hospital let me go home.

Maddie has all my belongings moved into Mom's room so I can have the phone by my bed. The auction is planned for the following week except for Mom's bedroom furniture, so I will have a place to sleep. We will give the remaining things to Goodwill once I'm ready to leave.

I take a nap after we get home, but the throbbing continues. I take a few pills Dr. Stewart prescribed and the pain eases off some. I then make my way out to the kitchen so I can be in the center of the comings and goings.

Maddie is at the kitchen table making lists and Wilkes and Kyle are going through the buffet drawers together, the familiar boxes and trash bags nearby.

"Well, look who's up and about," Maddie puts aside her list and comes to help me into a chair. "How about some coffee?" She doesn't wait for an answer but heads towards the stove.

"Are you feeling better?" Wilkes asks.

"Yes, but I want the license number of the truck that ran me over."

"Oh, a smart mouth. We are feeling better, aren't we?"

I stick out my tongue at him.

He gives me a demented grin truly enjoying himself.

"You're deranged Wilkes, do you know that?"

Kyle interrupts. "Sam was here to see you earlier, but he didn't want to disturb you."

I'm sorry I missed him and worry about his taking chances like that to come out here and see me in the middle of the day. "Sam wants you to call him at work when you're up and about. He said he didn't want to call here because he's afraid he'll wake you."

"Thanks, Kyle, I'll call him a little later," I say as I gratefully accept a steaming mug of coffee from Maddie. I take a sip and try not to burn my tongue.

"Damn, that's good!" I say as they all laugh at me. My hair's dirty, a bandage is still plastered to my face, and I don't have on any makeup. "I must look like death warmed over," I say to them.

"Yeah, I've seen you look better," Wilkes teases, "but maybe if we tie a pork chop around your neck the dogs will play with you."

I pick up a placemat and throw it at him. It flutters harmlessly to the floor. "Smart aleck," I mutter going back to my coffee.

I don't want to see Sam again with my bandages still on. I want a chance to at least clean myself up. He says I'm being vain I agree. Two days later the doctor lets me take off the gauze bandages but says the stitches won't come out for another few days. I must keep the area clean and covered to protect it from dirt. She gives me a prescription for more painkillers and sends me home with permission to wash my head. I never appreciated a shower more in my life. The bathtub's all right, but my scalp itches. I wash my hair three times and scrub my face until it's beet red. Only when I run out of hot water do I finally emerge. It feels so good to be clean all over, so good to be alive.

Wilkes says he's going home in another day or two. He stayed on when I got hurt but is eager to get back and take care of business. I know he worries about how the merger's going in his absence. Talking on the phone and sending faxes back and forth isn't the same thing as being there. His partners are shouldering all the work, and he worries that before long resentments will start to build up.

I'm very grateful for his willingness to stay with us while we finished up the last of the details of Mom's life. I also know we all have a very important conversation to finish; the one we started before I cracked my skull open.

Sam comes for lunch at the house the next day. The others suddenly have errands to run and discreetly leave us alone. Sam brings me a vegetarian sub, pastrami on rye for himself, and a big bag of potato chips. I see my cholesterol work is cut out for me but indulge anyway as I stuff chips in like they were going to quit making them. After hospital food, they taste like angel-sent cuisine.

"Whoa, slow down." Sam snatches the chip bag and holds it out of my reach.

"Never snatch away a woman's chips," I try to sound menacing and reach for the bag at the same time.

"I love larger women, but I want to be able to get my arms around you." He rolls the top of the bag and keeps it clearly out of my grasp.

"Mr. Pastrami on Rye tells me the dos and don'ts of nutrition?" I say with all the sarcasm I can muster.

"No, I'm saving you from yourself." He grins much too broadly for my taste.

"You're just lucky I'm too sick to hurt you or you'd be wearing those chips by now," I assure him.

"I hear ya," he says unconcerned.

"I'll get even," I promise.

"I have no doubt," he says as one who speak from experience.

I look deep into his enchanting green eyes. "Sam, what are we going to do about us? I'm going to be leaving soon and to be honest, I don't want to lose you again."

His smile slowly leaves his face, his arm lowers the chip bag to the floor where they are deposited and forgotten. He takes my hand: "I don't want to lose you either. We'll just have to be patient. If Jamie finds out there's another woman, she'll dig in her heels. I've got to get her to ask me for a divorce. She's asked me before, but I've always said no. This time I'll agree."

"Why does she keep asking you for a divorce?"

"She's not happy either, Hannah, but I knew she didn't have anywhere to go so I always said no."

"What's so different this time? Where is she going to go now?"

"Now, I don't care," he says and then softens, "That's not true. I do care, but I don't love her, Hannah. I can't live the rest of my life being miserable so that she has a roof over her head. She could get a job, she's still young and very pretty; she could get married again. I just know I have to be with you."

Neither of us says anything for a while. I nibble on my sandwich.

"I worry how I'll fit into your life, Hannah. How are all your professor friends going take to a country boy like me who has never even been to college?"

I'm silent. I don't know how to respond. His concerns are genuine and don't have an easy answer.

"Well, Hannah how would I fit into your life up there?" he asks, more worried by my silence than anything else.

"Painfully," I answer, and then am immediately sorry when I see the hurt look on his face. How do I tell him that my love for him is all that should matter? Realistically we both know that won't be enough for either of us, but I don't know what to expect. It would be painful at first with his heavy southern accent and non-literary background, but he overestimates the amount of time I spend socializing with my colleagues and how much their opinion matters to me. My real friends would welcome him with open arms glad to see me happy and in love. He could take the heat and so could I, but I wasn't sure he could stand to watch me get harassed on his account. The differences in our backgrounds could be a bone of contention between us, but I believe we could get over that hump in time and achieve a joyous rhythm in our lives.

"Would I embarrass you, Hannah?" he asks, the hurt evident in his voice as he gets on the defensive.

"Of course not! You could never embarrass me. I worry how happy you'll be transplanted in the north with a bunch of boring, and I do mean boring, intellectuals and stuffed shirts like me."

"You are anything but boring my love." He grasps my hands and gently pulls me out of the rocking chair onto my feet. He puts his arms around me and softly kisses my forehead.

"How did you fall and hurt your head anyway? Wilkes was vague on the details of exactly what happened."

"That's a can of worms Sam and I don't really want to get into it right now, OK?" I ask, not wanting to stray from our present conversation and certainly not wanting to get into my family's complications right now.

"OK," he kisses my cheek, "but can you tell me how much longer you'll be able to stay?"

"Probably until the end of next week."

"After you leave, when am I going to see you again?" he asks. "It could be difficult for me to get away. This is the busy time of year for me at work and Jamie's getting suspicious and wants me to account for where I am each moment of the day."

"We'll work something out," I assure him wondering for the first time if I've been naive. Is Sam really in love with me or am I a marital diversion of some sort? He seems to want to be with me but now has excuses and reasons for not pursuing this further. Am I just being paranoid? I'm suddenly scared; a chill runs down my spine causing me to shiver.

"What's that look on your face?" Sam asks, tightening his grip around my body.

"Nothing Sam, I guess someone must have walked over my grave," I say lost in thought. He doesn't pursue it. His lack of pursuit makes me feel as if I've lost him for good. I wrap my arms around him and hold him tight worried it may be the last time I get to have him to myself. I whisper a silent prayer. 'Don't leave me, Sam. Don't waste our second chance.' I hope someone hears me.

CHAPTER TEN

The next morning Kyle, Maddie, and I are sitting at the kitchen table when Wilkes bursts in from outside.

I thought he was still in bed asleep. I take in his happy face. "Where have you been?"

He waves a wad of papers in the air. "I had to go to town to pick up a fax of the merger contract."

"Well," Maddie interjects "Is it going to happen?"

"Yes, Ma'am, and the terms are precisely what we were asking for." He straddles a chair, puts his arms on the back of the chair, and eyes all of us; a big grin plastered on his face. "I think this whole thing is going to turn out all right even without me there to babysit."

"All this happiness is going to make me nauseated," I tease.

"You're just jealous because I'm able not only to consummate my little merger but legalize it as well." He hits the bull's-eye.

"Ouch."

Maddie's disgusted with both of us. "Would you two please knock it off? You're supposed to be injured," she waves a hand at the stitches in my head, "and you're supposed to be a grown-up," she stabs a well-manicured finger at Wilkes.

"Did you hear that?" Wilkes asks me aghast. "She called me a grown-up!" He leaps to his feet and dramatically sweeps his arm about the room. "I have witnesses, this woman called me a grown-up. Clearly, a slanderous remark causing me grievous injury and immeasurable monetary damages."

We all groan and almost on cue tell Wilkes to shut up and sit down.

Maddie and Kyle make lunch from leftovers. When the plates are empty and we're all relaxed, I look at Wilkes.

He lets out a resigned sigh and slowly stands up. "I guess it's time we finish the conversation we started before we were so rudely interrupted. Hannah, do we have your assurance that you won't fling yourself on the floor and bash your head open again?" He tries to lighten the mood.

"Yes, I promise that the next time I throw myself on the mercy of this court I will do so only figuratively."

There is an awkward pause as we all adjust ourselves for whatever is to come; an uncomfortable silence settles over the table as we wait for Wilkes to begin.

"Where was I?" Wilkes wonders aloud, his voice somber.

He looks older all the sudden, more like the professional lawyer preparing his remarks; the transformation is unsettling. I can picture him in a court of law as he ponders his opening statement. The gravity of the moment starts to fill my chest. I take a deep breath to get hold of myself and try not to let my panic overtake me again. Wilkes looks at me anxiously. I am touched by the concern on his face.

He asks me again. "Are you sure you're going to be all right with this, Hannah?"

I take Maddie's outstretched hand. "Yes."

"I knew about the sexual abuse," he begins. "It's also true I ignored it at first; clear denial all the way around. But when I got to college, I realized what I had allowed to go on." He looks at me and I nod for him to continue. "I came home one weekend and saw clearly for the first time Hannah, your sunken cheeks, and the black circles under your eyes. I knew I was as guilty as Dad."

I start to protest but Wilkes holds up his hand for me to stop. I swallow my words and wait in agonized silence.

"It was a Saturday," Wilkes continues, "and everyone had gone to the beach but me and Dad. We were at the old house in town, and he was fixing the roof. I waited until he came down." Wilkes goes to the refrigerator, retrieves a Coke, and pops the top off with the kitchen drawer handle. He takes a big gulp and then holds the cold glass bottle against his forehead.

I can imagine the headache that must be pounding behind his eyes.

He takes another big swig, finishes the soda, sets the bottle on the counter, and continues. "Now that I'd been away for a while, I saw him more clearly. He wasn't the large brute I remembered, but that didn't take away my fear. I couldn't forget the many beatings I took as a kid growing up."

Wilkes sits down with us at the table and Maddie reaches over and pats his arm. "Weren't you scared of him?"

He smiles at her, the sadness in his eyes makes my heart wrench. "When I entered that kitchen, I was scared to death. I knew Dad would go into a rage, but I was determined to protect my little sister, and the consequences be damned."

I can't look at him, my guilt overshadows my reason; I feel responsible, I feel at fault.

"What did you say to him?" Kyle asks.

"My only weapon was to threaten him with exposure."

"Weren't you afraid he'd beat you again?" Maddie asks.

Wilkes laughs a sardonic chortle. "I wasn't worrying whether he was going to beat me, I was worried he would kill me."

I look at Wilkes for the first time since his story began. "What exactly did you say to him?"

"I went up to him in the kitchen and told him there was something important I wanted to talk to him about. He told me he was busy, and it'd have to wait. I told him this couldn't wait."

"Jesus!" Kyle exclaims. "What'd he do?"

"Let me tell you that got his attention and in a bad way. He said, 'Are you talking back to me, boy?' Years of training almost made me say 'no sir' but instead I said, 'I'll talk to you any way I see fit.' I wish you could have seen the look on his face. If he'd beaten the crap out of me right there it would've been worth it to see that expression. That was the first time I'd ever talked back to him. His face got red, and his fists started to clench; all the warning signs that I was in for it."

Maddie interrupts, "Why didn't you run for Christ's sake?"

"Because I noticed something else. For a moment, he looked unsure of himself. I told him I knew about his visits to Hannah's room, and I wasn't going to keep quiet anymore."

My voice sounds like a plead for answers. "What did he say? What the hell was his excuse?"

Wilkes looks at me, "He denied the whole thing, Hannah. He said I didn't know what I was talking about. When that didn't work, he blamed Mom and then you."

I stand up, and the chair from the table noisily scrapes out from underneath me. "My God, you mean he tried to paint himself as the victim?"

Maddie takes hold of my hand and gently pulls me back into my seat. "Hannah, let him finish," she says.

I sit back down and put my head in my hands not wanting to hear anymore.

Wilkes waits in silence and then asks me, "Hannah, do you want me to stop?"

I whisper, "No, go ahead and finish it."

Wilkes sits next to me at the table, clears his throat, and then continues. "I waited. I wanted him to make a move that would let me lay a solid fist on that smirking face. I was champing at the bit. I wanted to make up for all the times he'd left me bruised and battered for all the times he'd hurt you, Hannah." His fists on the table slowly begin to uncurl.

"What happened?" Maddie asks, barely able to contain her curiosity. I understand her feelings. I feel like a traveler craning my neck to see the bloody accident at the side of the road. I'm both repulsed and absorbed at the same time.

Wilkes goes to the refrigerator and gets another Coke. He brings the bottle to the table and sits down again in the chair he vacated. He continues. "Before I could do anything he shoves me hard and knocks me off my feet. I was up again in a second, but he got me scared and then he came after me. I thought I would pee in my pants. But then my anger took over and without even thinking about it I swung my right fist at his jaw with all my might. I heard a snap and wondered if it was his jaw or my knuckles. I never realized how much it hurt to hit someone. I waited for him to get up, I wanted to kill him." Wilkes stops and looks at each of us. "Do you understand what I'm telling you?" Wilkes takes a deep breath with his hands clenched together in a ball; his knuckles white. "I wanted to kill him."

I can see how painful these memories are but know he must go on. He must finish telling the story for his sake as well as ours.

"What'd he do after you hit him?" Kyle asks.

"He didn't get up, he sat on the floor and looked at me rubbing his jaw where I'd punched him. We looked at each other, our eyes locked in some sort of father-son battle of nerves. He finally lowered his gaze, and I knew I'd won."

I raise my head and ask, "What do you mean?"

"I mean, I told him to get out." Wilkes rubs the back of his neck and doesn't look at any of us when he says, "God I was cocky, so sure I was right, so sure I had won."

I feel the hard wood of the chair underneath me. My knees and ankles ache from wrapping my legs too tightly around the chair legs, yet still, the story draws me. "What'd you do after you told Dad to leave?"

"I left the house. It took me more than an hour to get to the beach. I stayed there a while, but then all you kids went to friends' houses for the night and only Mom and I were in the house."

Maddie leans forward and asks, "What'd you tell her?"

"I didn't tell her anything. But when we got home, I knew something was wrong the minute I walked into the house. Dad's pickup was still in the driveway, but it was too quiet. I thought maybe he'd fallen while he was fixing the roof, so I looked out back. While I was in the backyard, I heard Mom scream. I rushed inside and there, in Mom's bedroom, was Dad hanging from a rope."

"Wait a minute," Kyle interrupts, "you mean Dad hung himself?"

"That's right. I found Mom standing in the doorway screaming her head off. I had to put my hand over her mouth to stop her."

Maddie can't seem to accept the finality of his story. "Was he dead?"

Wilkes looks at her disbelieving, "Of course he was dead! I couldn't stop looking at his face. His eyes bulged, his face was blue, it was hideous. Mom kept repeating 'Oh my God, Oh my God.' I took her into the living room and sat her on the sofa. She got quiet after a couple of minutes and then she looked at me the accusation already on her lips."

I interrupt, "What do you mean accusation? You didn't kill him."

"No, but somehow, she knew I was responsible. She asked me and I hesitated. That was my first mistake. I might as well have admitted the whole ugly truth right then and there. She was on me like a June bug demanding answer. I finally broke down and told her the whole story."

Wilkes stops and takes a swig of his Coke. I put my hand on his arm, "What did she say when you told her the truth?"

"She went completely over the edge. Not screaming and hysterical like I expected, but calm and collected. She said I'd killed him with my ugly lies. I was almost glad to accept the blame. I never . . . I just wanted him to leave."

"It wasn't your fault, Wilkes," Maddie says protectively.

Wilkes stares at the table, his shoulders slumped in defeat.

I rub his back with the palm of my hand. "I can't believe you stuck up for me that way," tears fill my eyes, "knowing that someone cared, that someone tried to help me that makes all the difference."

"Wait a minute," Kyle interrupts, "I thought Daddy died in an auto accident. You even told me you identified his burnt body."

Wilkes takes a deep breath and slowly raises his head to look directly at Kyle. "Dad was in an auto accident, he did get burned, and I did identify the body. All of that was true, Kyle," he says his words measured as if the sheer weight of this conversation makes it hard for him to breathe. "What I left out was that dad was already dead when his truck flew into that ravine."

"I don't understand," Kyle says, his voice going up an octave. "You mean you staged his death?"

Wilkes squares his shoulders as though preparing himself for the onslaught. "Yes, that's exactly what I mean. Mom said she wasn't about to explain why her husband had decided to take his own life. Said she wasn't going to live with that kind of stigma." Wilkes explains.

Maddie's voice is full of cynicism; "Let's not forget the double indemnity policy. How convenient for her that Dad died in an accident."

"What does double indemnity mean?" Kyle asks.

"It means, little brother," Maddie says, "that if Dad died in an accident Mom would collect twice the life insurance."

I encourage Wilkes to go on with his story. "What did Mom do?"

"She got hold of herself quickly. One minute she's the grieving widow and the next minute I saw a determination in her I'd never seen before. She told me to cut Dad down. I can't tell you how much I didn't want to go back in that room."

"Why didn't you call the police?" Kyle asks.

Wilkes laughs. "And tell them what? That my dad was a child molester and hung himself because I'd said I'd tell on him?" Wilkes takes a deep breath. "Besides, have you forgotten how Mom can be when she has it in her head, that she wants something done?"

How could we forget?

"I'm sorry, Wilkes," Kyle starts to apologize.

"Forget it little brother, no harm done."

I look at Wilkes and touch him lightly on the arm. "Finish the story. Did you do what she said?"

Wilkes smiles at me and pats the hand I have resting on his arm. "I was a compliant slave. I would have done anything to gain her forgiveness for killing Dad."

"But you didn't kill him," I point out the obvious once again. Wilkes says nothing and he doesn't seem to hear me. Everyone around the table stops moving as we wait for him to go ahead with the telling.

Wilkes pulls his chair closer to the table, rests his arms on the smooth top, and continues. "Somehow, when I opened that bedroom door, I thought he'd be sitting on the mattress putting his shoes on wondering why the hell I hadn't knocked. The room looked the same as before his body slowly twisting. There was an overturned step ladder, and his shoes were on the floor. I wondered why he'd taken his shoes off." He looks at me and shrugs his shoulders. "I know it sounds stupid to wonder about a thing like that, but I must've stood there a whole minute thinking about it. He'd punched a hole in the plaster in the ceiling with a hammer and put the rope around one of the ceiling joists."

"How'd you get him down?" Kyle leans back in his chair, his expression inscrutable.

"It wasn't easy," he continues, "I righted the ladder, stood on the top step, and sawed at the rope with a kitchen knife. It was spooky. I swear I saw his eyes move and then suddenly the last twines of rope snapped under his weight. His shoulder hit the step ladder and knocked me off and he landed on my legs pinning me to the floor."

Maddie says to no one in particular. "Oh my, God?"

"I was frantic." Wilkes looks at each of us around the table. "I tried to pull myself out, but he was too heavy. I finally had to roll him off. Mom wanted to know what was taking so long. She opened the door a crack, threw in an old yellow blanket, and ordered me to hurry and wrap him up. I did as I was told, grateful to be able to cover up his face."

Kyle stops him, "What made you think to put him in the truck?"

"It was Mom's idea to fake the accident. She told me that once it got dark, I was to take the body up to one of the logging roads and make it look like an accident. That was all she said, make it look like an accident."

"How long did you have to wait?" Maddie asks.

"A couple of hours. It started to rain and while we waited for dusk, Mom made me patch the ceiling in her bedroom. I did the best I could, but anyone could see an amateur had made the repair. Finally, she told me to get going. Her last instructions were to make sure that everything burned in the accident. I took Dad's truck up to Dead Man's Hill."

We all look at him in disbelief.

"The irony didn't escape me either," he says. "I parked the truck at the top of the hill. I had a hell of a time getting him from the back of the pickup and into the driver's seat."

I interrupt him. "How did you get the pickup to go over the hill with him sitting in the driver's seat?"

Wilkes explains. "I was going to start the truck, put it into gear, and then leap out. I got in on the passenger side but when I turned the key in the ignition it only sputtered. I thought it wasn't going to start and that I'd just have to let the truck roll down the hill and hope for the best. But the engine finally caught. I reached down to put Dad's foot on the gas pedal. I froze staring at Dad's stocking feet."

Maddie is already ahead of him. "You forgot his shoes."

Wilkes looks at Maddie, "Yes, I forgot to bring his shoes. I imagined being taken away in a police cruiser with Dad's shoes in an evidence bag. But then I realized that nobody would probably notice whether a charred body had shoes on. Dad's foot wouldn't stay on the accelerator, and I needed to be sure the pedal would be all the way down. I found a small log and jammed it into place. I put the truck in to drive, released the emergency brake, and jumped out the open passenger door. The pickup sprung forward. My foot got caught in the door and it dragged me about a hundred feet. Finally, my foot came loose, and I barely missed getting run over by the rear tires."

Kyle interjects. "You're lucky you weren't killed."

"Don't I know it," Wilkes agrees. "The truck wasn't going very fast because of the mud from the rain, but finally it went over the edge I didn't hear anything for a moment and then there was a sickening thud."

"Did it explode?" Kyle asks.

"No. I waited for the explosion, but nothing happened. Then it began to rain again. I got up and tried to walk and then slid down to the edge. There was the truck, at the bottom, nicely smashed into a tree but no flames and so no cover-up. I didn't know what to do so I ran."

Maddie has her chin resting in the palms of her hands, "Where did you go?"

He looks at her and shrugs his shoulders. "Where else, I ran home. By the time I got there, I was soaked through. I found Mom on the side porch sitting in the dark, smoking cigarettes. She took one look at my face and knew something had gone wrong. She grabbed me and I told her what happened. She slapped me across the face and called me an idiot."

"Oh my, God," Maddie repeats under her breath.

Wilkes goes to the refrigerator and opens the door. He changes his mind and lets the door snap shut. "She took me to the garage and gave me a can of gasoline, some matches, and a large camper flashlight. She said to make sure it burned and to remember to bring the flashlight and gas can home when I was done."

I turn in my chair to watch him. "Did you go back?"

He faces me, leans against the counter, and crosses his arm. "Yeah, I went back. I was so scared that Dad wasn't going to be in the truck anymore, you know maybe he hadn't really been dead after all."

Kyle empathizes. "Like those movies where the corpse disappears and comes back to murder everyone."

Wilkes smiles at Kyle. "Yeah. I made my way down that hill with the gas can and flashlight clutched in my hand. I was sure he was going to jump out at me. I turned on the flashlight and pointed it into the cab of the truck. He was still there."

The rest of us let out the breath we've all been holding, and a nervous titter goes around the table.

Wilkes continues. "His head and shoulders had gone through the windshield and there was a lot of blood. I took the top off the gas can and poured gasoline all over dad and the truck. I remember worrying it wouldn't catch fire because of all the rain. I had trouble getting the matches to stay lit. I would get one going and it would go out before I could get it next to the gasoline."

Maddie leans forward in her chair and asks in disbelief. "You mean you went through all this, and you couldn't get the dang matches to burn? What did you do?"

Wilkes looks tired and worn. "I decided I had to light the entire book of matches. When I got them lit, I heaved the whole thing at the truck. The matches bounced off the hood and landed in a puddle. I stood there staring at that wet book of matches. I cursed, jumped up and down, and then sat down in the wet leaves and cried."

Kyle gets up, turns his chair around, straddles it, and rests his arms and chin on the back of the chair. "Did you leave him there?"

Somehow the brutality of our conversation seems removed. It's hard to believe that we're talking about our father. It sounds more like we are discussing the twists and turns of a murder mystery with the oldest sibling acting as the narrator.

Wilkes goes on. "I couldn't face Mom again and I didn't have anywhere else to go. I kept seeing her sitting on that porch silently smoking those cigarettes and then I thought that's it! cigarettes! Every car and truck has a cigarette lighter."

I couldn't contain myself anymore. "Did it work? Did the cigarette lighter work?"

"No, not at first. I had a terrible time getting the wet leaves to burn. I finally got a handful going and put them on the floor next to Dad's feet. I reached behind him to put the lighter back. The leaves landed in a pool of gasoline on the floorboard and exploded sending flames up the driver's seat. As I tried to pry myself loose from behind him, the sleeve of my poncho caught fire. I panicked, jerked myself free, and started shaking my arm trying to put it out. I tried to smother the flames with my hand and caught my other sleeve on fire." Wilkes closes his eyes at the painful memory.

We wait silently for him to go on.

"I finally dropped to the ground and rolled in the wet leaves but not before I got burned pretty badly." He unbuttons his shirt cuffs, pushes up his sleeves, and holds up his arms. You can see the now-faint scar tissue on the bottom of his forearms and imagine his agony.

Now I understand why he prefers long-sleeved shirts.

He slowly lowers his arms and absently buttons his cuffs. "When I finally stopped rolling, I noticed the truck was burning and the flames were getting close to the gas tank. I got up and started to run. I was so busy looking over my shoulder that I ran face-first into a tree." He points to a small white scar on his forehead. "Laying on the ground I watched the truck more whoosh then explode. Then the passenger door blew off and came down a few feet from the car. I decided I better get out of there before someone reported the fire."

"What did Mom say when you got back?" Maddie asks.

He runs both hands through his hair and shakes his head a little as though he's trying to get rid of the memory. "When I got home Mom was still on the porch. I told her I had taken care of it. She took me into the bathroom and took care of my burns and cuts as best she could. She didn't say a word but then I noticed she was crying." He takes a deep breath and stares at the ceiling as he tries to get his emotions under control. "I hadn't expected that you know. I could take her coldness, her hysteria, her anger, but not her tears and when I tried to comfort her, she waved me away." He brusquely pushes a tear off his face as though it was lint he'd accidentally found on his cheek. He takes a deep breath before he continues. "She gave me some of her pain pills and helped me change my clothes. She told me to get the rest of my belongings and head back to school as though nothing had happened."

"Then what?" Kyle asks.

"I did as I was told, I went back to school and acted as though nothing had happened."

"How long before they found Dad?" Maddie whispers.

Wilkes gets a handkerchief out of his pocket and blows his nose. He replaces the hanky in his pocket, then puts the palm of his hands on the counter behind him and pushes himself up on the countertop. His feet swing in the air like a kid and bang against the bottom cabinet doors. "Three days," is all he says.

My back starts to hurt, and I get up out of the hard wooden chair and lean against the table. "Did Mom call you?"

"No. The police came to school to tell me. I thought they'd come to arrest me, so I didn't have to pretend to be upset. They said the body was so burnt they didn't want to put Mom through the ordeal of identifying the remains, so they asked me to come home."

"Why didn't you tell anyone about this before?" Kyle asks.

"Because Mom collected the insurance money on the loss of the truck and Dad's life insurance policy. She thought if they knew it was a suicide they wouldn't pay. Besides, remember Dad had a double indemnity clause in his policy."

"So, she collected twice the benefits," I remind Kyle.

"That's right. How do you think she paid for this water-front house and lived so well for so long?" Wilkes finishes. He looks nearly wrung out.

I stand, walk over the counter, put my arms around Wilkes's waist, and hold him tightly. "I don't know how to thank you. Not just for what you did, but for all you must have gone through. I love you Wilkes and I'll never forget your love for us."

His arms slowly encircle me, and the warmth of his love surrounds me. After I let go, Wilkes slides off the countertop. "Kyle, you're not angry?" Wilkes asks surprised.

"Angry? Angry that you threatened to expose a maniac? Angry because you tried to protect all of us? I don't think so, dear brother. I only wish I had been old enough to help you."

I don't know what Wilkes thought we would say, but it's obvious he didn't expect us to be understanding. His relief is evident.

"Is this why Mom cut you out of the will?" I ask.

The smile on Wilkes's face disappears. "Yes. She said she'd never forgive me for what I'd done. I guess she never did."

"What you'd done? How could she say such a thing?" Maddie asks dumbfounded.

"Look," Wilkes says, "warts and all, he was the only father we ever had. Despite everything, I guess I still loved him in a way. Maybe you don't understand. Maybe because I'm the oldest I remember a time when Dad wasn't obsessive and violent."

We're all quiet as we let everything Wilkes told us sink in. I know I'll never love Dad. In my heart, he died the first night he walked into my bedroom when I was twelve years old. I'm not angry anymore and I don't begrudge Wilkes his love and devotion. All this leaves Kyle with more history about his father than I'm sure he wanted to know. Maddie is left with the horror she hears and the reality of growing up in a house full of dirty secrets. We all try to reconcile what we know against what we can live with knowing.

Maddie leaves the room and a moment later is back with the scabbard we found in Mom's closet. "I wanted to keep this for myself, Wilkes, but now I see it really belongs to you." She hands the engraved scabbard to Wilkes. He looks at her and smiles. He lovingly touches the engraving running his fingers gently over each inscription of every place that

Dad had gone during World War II. I smile at Maddie, so proud of her gesture when I know how much she wanted that memento for herself.

Bird comes in the door and takes one look at us and says: "What are you all up to this afternoon? Ya'll got your heads pressed together like when you was little and plottin' some scheme or another?"

"We aren't up to anything Bird, we're just getting to know each other a little better that's all." I smile at my brothers and sister proud we all came through this; glad to have each of them in my life.

"We love you, Bird," Maddie says. We all nod in agreement.

She gets flustered by the show of emotion. "Shoot, ya'll just a bunch of trouble."

"Bird, what are you going to do when we aren't around anymore?" Wilkes asks.

"Yeah, Bird, what are you going to do when everything here is settled, and we've all gone home?" I ask worried about Bird. "You going to be all right Bird? I mean financially. I don't mean to pry."

"I'll be fine," she interrupts, "don't you be worrin' 'bout me. I'm planning on movin' in with my sister Mimi once I'm through here. Besides the money your mother left me, I did manage to put away a dollar here and there. After your father died, your mother, God rest her soul, set up a retirement fund for me and each Christmas she put in a right hefty sum to 'help me along in my old age' she called it. I sure do miss her though." Bird shakes her head and looks sad.

I get up and hug her close. "Believe it or not, Bird, so do I."

CHAPTER ELEVEN

Wilkes went home two days later. I like to believe he returns to his life with a cleaner slate; guilt no longer gnawing so hungrily on his psyche. Maddie returns to work the day after Wilkes goes home. Kyle decides to stay for the auction. For the first time, I realize I'm the only one among us who ever got married and even that didn't work out. I wonder about the connection between our dysfunctional parents and the lack of ties outside the family.

The auction is morbid and absorbing at the same time. People come out of the woodwork to pick over the bones of my mother's life. The auctioneer warns us not to be present during the auction itself. He says we might find it upsetting to see our mother's belongings being sold and then carried off by strangers. I'm not that attached to any of her possessions and I'm not sure I trust the auctioneer Wilkes has hired. I get angry at him all over again thinking about it. This is just like Wilkes; I sputter to myself; hire some low-life and then leave me holding the bag.

The auctioneer, whose name is Fred, is shifty and too smooth-talking for my tastes. He has black hair that's slicked back and held in place with God knows what, but the end product looks like hardened plastic. He always has a toothpick stuck out of the side of his mouth. I guess that wouldn't bother me so much, but he keeps taking it out and pointing it at me when he wants to emphasize something - a physical punctuation mark. I can't take my eyes off that chewed-wet end as he stabs the disgusting thing at me. Worst of all though is he keeps calling me 'little lady' which makes me nuts. I ask him not to. He apologizes profusely and two minutes later, does it again. I try calling him 'little man' and that only makes him laugh. I hope he gags on that toothpick. Kyle and I think Fred has ulterior motives for wanting us out of the house during the auction. We decide to watch the bidding, so we know exactly what he owes us. Kyle keeps track of the bids while I keep my eye on Fred. Despite all my misgivings, the day goes off without a hitch and nearly everything is sold and carried off. It amazes me what people will buy - one woman's trash is another woman's treasure.

The day after the auction, I take Kyle to the airport, and we have a tearful goodbye. This is the first occasion I have spent time with him as an adult. He's generous and spirited; a person I would want as a friend even if he weren't my brother. After I drop off Kyle, I come back to find myself in the big empty house all alone.

I stayed a few extra days to meet with the realtors about putting the house on the market. I also hope I can see Sam again before I leave. I spend most of my time thinking about him, wanting him - I seem to think of little else. I'm afraid of what may happen. What if he asks me to move here? Would I willingly throw my old life away to be with him? I find his power over me frightening.

I can't forget about my daughter, Carly. A pang of guilt punctures my insanity. I have barely considered her in all this. My quest has been simple; be with Sam. How do I tell her that her mother has fallen in love? What if she doesn't like him? What if he doesn't like her? How can he not love her? As a headache looms on the horizon, I decided to put my worries aside. I feel like Scarlet O'Hare I'll worry about it tomorrow. Besides, I only have a few days left to be with Sam.

My head feels much better. I tell the doctor this news when I see her on Wednesday. She takes out the stitches and says she doesn't think there'll be much of a scar. The following Friday Sam can get away for the day and night and comes to spend both with me. Somehow a sleeping bag is not nearly as romantic as a real bed, but with all the furniture now gone there is nothing else. I am to leave on Tuesday morning.

Sam arrives on Friday at first light with coffee and breakfast rolls. I'm grateful for the delivery service. He even brought my favorite gourmet coffee. There isn't any food or utensils left in the house. I did manage to salvage two of the porch rockers, a couple of coffee mugs, and a spoon, the essential items for a day of relaxing in the South. For the past two days, I've had to dress and drive to a not-so-convenient convenience store for my morning dose of caffeine, so I'm especially thorough about showing my gratitude.

We sip our coffee on the porch and avoid any talk of my leaving or his marital dilemma. I decided not to press. I want to enjoy the day as it unfolds. I have a lot to be thankful for all the people who truly love me and who stuck up for me when it counted most. That seems like a gift enough for now.

The morning glides by as we drink our coffee and catch up on our lives. Sam puts my feet up on his lap and absently caresses my legs and feet while we talk. The day is warm. As I lull peacefully in the shade of the porch with the soft ocean breeze caressing me and Sam's company, I think I may be having the loveliest day of my life. I close my eyes and breathe it all in. When I open my eyes Sam smiles at me.

"I don't think I've ever seen you look so happy, or so contented," he announces.

"I don't think I've ever felt this wonderful."

He sets my coffee mug on the ground next to his and pulls me out of my rocking chair and into his lap. "I love you, Hannah Wheeler." He nuzzles my neck sending tingles of warmth down my spine. He kisses my forehead, my cheeks, and my lips. Each kiss is so exquisitely soft that it feels like an angel passing over my face. He takes my hand and leads me inside. When I try to talk, he puts his fingers to my lips to shush me. He undoes the buttons on my blouse and slides my shorts off my legs. He runs his hands over my naked body the breeze from the open window whispers across my skin. We make love slowly, enjoying the thrill of being with one another; our senses are heightened by the knowledge that we have only a limited time together.

I must have drifted off because when I wake up the sun is high up in the sky and Sam sleeps soundly next to me. I study his face and try to memorize every feature. I take in the soft pout of his lips and the curve of his jaw. He opens his eyes and catches me staring. He smiles, reaches out, and pulls me close. I lay my head on his shoulder as he wraps his arms around me, smoothes my hair, and kisses my forehead.

The morning passes by too quickly as time plots against us. After lulling about all morning, we decided to take one last trip to Myrtle Beach for some tourist shopping and swimming. Rain ruins the afternoon swim, so we play arcade games and eat junk food on the boardwalk. Sam presents me with an exquisite heart-shaped pendant made of garnets hanging from an antique gold chain. I wonder how he's able to afford such an extravagance. But I had always been told not to look a gift horse in the mouth and never ask questions. It's beautiful and his thoughtfulness touches me beyond words.

He stands behind me to hook the necklace on, his fingers brushing the back of my neck giving me goosebumps. From behind me, in a soft voice,

Sam says, "Always remember I love you, Hannah. That I've always loved you and always will, no matter what happens."

His words sound ominous, and I turn to look at his face. He looks sad and far away. "What is it, Sam?" I whisper.

He shakes off his melancholy and smiles at me. "Nothing's the matter." He kisses my cheek then takes the garnet heart in his open palm, his fingers touching my collarbone. "I wish it could be more," he says wistfully, his words full of regret.

"I'll cherish it always," I tell him honestly. I can't forget the look I saw in his eyes. There's something he's not telling me. I don't pursue it. I don't really want to know. Why spoil my perfect day with the painful trivialities of real life? I want my fantasy to stay alive and true; ignorance can be blissful.

Neither of us is hungry anymore so we go to a local tavern, have a few drinks, and soak in the atmosphere. I feel relaxed again as I finger the necklace Sam gave me. Once it gets dark and the evening breeze cools everything off, we go for a stroll on the beach. There's a full moon and the tide is out. When the vendors start to close around midnight we head back to the car.

We are nearly silent on the drive home as I sit next to Sam and put my head against his shoulder. It's enough for us to be together. Instead of heading back to the house Sam drives to a deserted part of the island and we go for another walk. He stops and looks at me, a funny grin on his face. Then he starts to peel his clothes off. He stands before me stark naked. My jaw drops open when he says: "The last one in is a rotten egg." He turns and runs for the water. I watch his white backside shining in the moonlight as his legs carry him to the water's edge. He hesitates for a moment; the prospect of cool ocean water on bare parts gives him pause. Then I can see him make up his mind as he squares his shoulders and runs into the ocean without slowing and finally dives headfirst into a breaking wave. I look around and see no one in sight. I take off my clothes and compulsively fold them into a neat pile next to Sam's which I also fold but hate myself for doing it. Then I head for the water feeling silly, exposed, and happy. I stop at the water's edge.

Sam shouts from beyond the breakers. "It's fine once you get used to it!" Everyone says that to the uninitiated. I let a few waves break over my bare feet. Then I see Sam point frantically at something on the shore.

Convinced someone is about to see my bare buns, I run into the water and leap in to cover myself. When I reach Sam, he's laughing so hard he's holding his sides. I realize he's tricked me, there was no one on the beach, it was just a ploy to get me in the water.

The water feels wonderful against my bare skin. The silkiness of its caress titillates. I swim away from Sam kicking water at him and laughing as he sputters. He catches me and pulls me to him, the water barely above my waist. He kisses me, no more playfulness but a deeper need. His hands and the water soothe my burning skin as the moonlight lays a golden blanket on the dark rolling waters that surround us.

"I can never get enough of you," Sam whispers.

"Nor I you," I confess.

He smiles at me. "When we do finally get together how are we ever going to get anything done?" He pinches me playfully.

I flit away giggling, hoping this night will never come to an end. But soon we're both tired and head back to the beach for our clothes. On the drive home, Sam holds my hand tightly in his as though he never wants to let me go. When we get back, we crawl into our sleeping bag, both of us exhausted, but the feel of his body next to mine flares my passions once again. We make love quickly as though to miss the moment will mean a missed chance to be together. I fall asleep in his arms certain I will never have this kind of love or happiness with anyone else.

In the morning when I wake up, Sam is staring at me.

"What are you doing?" I ask, embarrassed to have him looking at me before I've had a chance to splash on a few fluid ounces of makeup.

"It's only fair. You ogled me while I was sleeping and now it's my turn." He kisses the tip of my nose. "I don't want to forget a single beautiful feature. I want to always be able to recall the exact hue of your blue eyes, the beautiful swell of your breasts, and the gentle curve of your hips," he says, his hand following his voice. I move closer hypnotized by his touch, and we make love one last time.

Later showered and dressed Sam and I stood together on the porch of my mother's home for one final moment. Sam won't be able to get away again before I leave for Wisconsin on Tuesday morning.

He holds both of my hands in his and kisses each tenderly. His voice falters a little when he speaks. "Is there anything you need before you go back?"

"No, I have everything."

He's reluctant to leave. "What are you going to do for the next two days out here all alone?"

"I'm meeting with realtors. I am also having lunch downtown with Maddie on Monday. In the meantime, I have a lot to think about and some goodbyes to make before I leave. Don't worry about me, I'll be fine." I watch his face closely. I didn't tell Sam about Wilkes's revelations; I'm just not ready to share yet, at least not until I've had time to sort it through myself. I also didn't want to spend our last day together discussing my father. I won't let my father ruin one more day of my life; his power over me is gone. I offer to walk Sam to his car.

He shakes his head no. "I want to remember you as you are right now, standing on this porch like I have seen you so many times over the years. You look so Southern standing there with the breeze blowing your white cotton dress, your bare feet on the naked wood floor, with your tanned skin and sun-streaked hair. You look so beautiful this way; this is how I want to carry you around in my heart."

"That sounds so final," I whisper to Sam.

"No darling, I promise you this is far from over," he assures me.

My heart starts pounding at the prospect and I push for dates and details.

"I'll have to work something out," he says vaguely, "I don't want you worrying about it, all right?"

We discussed my departure and arrival times, and he said he'll call me Wednesday morning. We stand there awkwardly for a few moments, neither of us wanting to say goodbye. Then suddenly Sam grabs me, wraps his arms around my body and kisses me hard on the lips. My mind screams for him not to leave, for him to come with me to Wisconsin. He lets me go as abruptly as he grabbed me, turns, and heads down the porch steps without looking back.

"Goodbye my love," I call after him, but my words fall short of their mark. It seems the last year of my life has been filled with farewells; first Jack, then Mom, and now Sam. I'm sick of goodbyes, tired of people leaving empty holes in my life. I listen to Sam's car pull out of the driveway. I stand on the porch for a long time and numbly watch the sun work its way overhead. When my tears on the porch floor have all dried, I turn and go inside.

The rest of that afternoon and most of the next day I spent on a tour of the island. I visit old haunts and relive the more pleasant times of my youth. On Monday I spend the early morning packing my belongings and have an appointment with a realtor. I'm to meet Maddie for a farewell lunch this afternoon. The rest of the morning I go through the empty house to make sure I leave nothing behind. I linger in each room; the house feels almost alive.

We moved to this house after Dad died. Mom wouldn't sleep another night in her room, and now I know why. She bought this house only a week after the funeral. Her friends advised against her buying the place saying she should wait a year before she made any big decisions, but Mom was determined. She sold the lumber business for a handsome profit. Between that money and the cash payoff from Dad's life insurance policy, she was able to live very comfortably. We spent a lot of peaceful, if not confusing, years growing up in this house. I was already fifteen when we moved here with all the scars a father can inflict on his daughter. I suppose Mom did the best she could. I'm tired of being angry for her lack of intervention or her vehement denial that any of it took place. Once we moved out to the island, Mom was more loving and open. While it was all too little too late for me, Kyle thrived under the attention. Even Maddie came out of her shell once the looming threat of our father disappeared from her life.

Later that afternoon I drive into town to go by our old house. Somehow this one final pilgrimage is important. It isn't a path I want to take but one I feel I must travel if I'm going to rid myself of this nightmare. I park my car several blocks away and walk. I remember as a little girl roller skating on these sidewalks. They were new, flat and square. Over the years, tree roots have pushed against the concrete and left the walkway cracked and crooked with grass spilling out of the crevices. The concrete curbs have crumbled and are barely visible from all the layers of asphalt piled on over the years. I hesitate at the corner reluctant to see the old house. Maybe I've made a mistake coming here again, but it seems important as if an inner voice urges me on. Suddenly, there it stands, innocuous. There are no looming dark gargoyles and no inky shadows springing from blackened windows. The house now has white aluminum siding instead of Williamsburg blue slathered on clapboard. The windows have flower boxes that bloom with red gardenias. A little girl rides a tricycle in the driveway. A thigh-high picket fence encircles the yard. On the steps sits a young mother rocking a baby in her arms as she cheers on the older girl. The scene is almost picturesque. I'm glad for them. I'm glad for me. I compliment the young mother on the beauty of her children. She gets up, places the now sleeping baby in the bottom of a playpen, and waves me over. I let myself in the gate. Her name is Anna, and we talk idly for a few minutes. The tricycle rider pedals over full of curiosity. She has shoulder-length, light-brown hair, and saucer-sized brown eyes, and she's full of information and questions. She tells me her name is Sarah and that she's three-and-a-half years old. Anna finally shoos her inquisitive daughter back to her tricycle and we talk a while longer.

I tell her I grew up in this house. She invites me in for a guided tour. Not waiting for an answer, she reaches down and plucks up her sleeping baby, and leads the way inside. We leave Sarah making repeated circles on her tricycle singing a silly tune over and over at full volume. The baby does not wake.

Once we're inside she's eager to show me all the changes she and her husband Gregory have made to the place. I am a reluctant tourist. To exorcise my remaining demons, it seems I must perform this last goodbye ritual. Fortunately, Anna is a talker who requires little feedback other than an occasional nod. She prattles on discussing each change they made, detailing the decorating nuances of every room. We finally entered my parents' old room bedroom. The walls are eggshell white and there are sheer curtains draped loosely at the windows with ruffled valances traversing the top of each curtain rod. The fierce pumping of my own blood drowns out Anna's voice. I feel the heat rise on my cheeks as the darkness of memories begins to threaten. I force myself to look up at the ceiling. They've installed a ceiling fan in the center of the room, but there, just to the right, is a rough spot of plaster evidence of a novice repair job; an amateurish attempt to cover up a grownup's resolute quest for destruction.

I suddenly feel claustrophobic. I hear Anna ask me a question, but I can't make it out because my heart is thumping too loudly. I turn my head towards her. She looks concerned so I try to read her lips but feel the impish fiends inside my head begin to turn out the lights. Then just as suddenly my ears pop, I hear her words and the room gets bright again.

"Are you all right?" she asks, obviously scared. I hear the baby in her arms start to cry. "Please, I have to check on my little girl, will you be OK for just a moment?" She doesn't wait for an answer but turns and leaves me alone in the room. I get a hanky out of my purse and wipe the sweat from my forehead. She's back in a minute with her little girl in tow.

"Are you sure you're all right? Can I get you a glass of water or something?" She asks.

I can see by the worried look on her face that she wonders if she's let a nut into her house. It's time to leave. "No, I'm fine. I guess the heat made me a little dizzy that's all." I hope I sound convincing. "Thank you for letting me see your charming home. I really love what you've done. When we lived here everything was always dark and gloomy." I wind my way down the hall retracing my steps to the front door.

I hear her little girl ask: "Is the nice lady sick, Mommy?" Anna tells her to shush.

I call over my shoulder "Thank you again." I make my way out the door, through the gate, and down the sidewalk. Two blocks later my heart finally stops battering the walls of my chest and my breath isn't coming in gulps anymore.

It's true. It's all true. I never really thought Wilkes had lied, but somehow the realism of that patched hole makes it all so real; too real. Dad really did hurt me and then kill himself rather than face exposure for what he'd done. Was he sorry about what he did? Did he care that he was hurting me? Did he care what he was doing to my life? I already knew the answers were no, all no. Men who hurt little girls do so for their own gratification; no reasons, justifications, or excuses are accepted. I walk the rest of the way to the restaurant where I'm to meet Maddie for lunch. By the time I arrive, I'm feeling better, but the heat and humidity have ruined my makeup and clothes.

"What happened to you?" Maddie asks. She's already staked out a table for us in the small cafe-style restaurant. The tables are wrought iron squares set upon black and white floor tile. The air conditioning is set on stun.

I take my seat and order an iced tea from the perky young waitress who appears the moment I land in my chair. I set my purse on the floor and pat my forehead with a couple of napkins tugged out of the tin dispenser in the middle of the table. "I went by the old house," I tell Maddie as I try to regain my melted composure.

"The one on Dogwood?" she asks, obviously surprised.

I nod and gratefully take a long sip from the iced tea set before me. Maddie and I both order Caesar salads and the waitress disappears again. The thickening crowd makes it difficult to hear one another and we almost virtually must put our heads together.

"Why did you go there?" Maddie asks, still amazed I would voluntarily make such a journey.

"I had to see it one more time. I guess to make Wilkes's story real I had to put it into the context of that house. I hadn't seen it since we moved away. It was smaller than I remembered. The couple that lives there now had redecorated the inside. . ."

"You went inside?" Maddie interrupts.

"Yes, a lovely young woman was sitting outside, and she was nice enough to invite me in to look around once she knew I'd grown up there. They've done a lot with the old place. Wilkes's old room is now an office. The sewing room's a nursery."

"You wanted to see the hole didn't you," Maddie asks horrified at the prospect. "You wanted to see where Dad hung himself."

"Yes."

"Why?" she asks uncomprehendingly.

The waitress brings a breadboard with a fresh loaf of bread and butter and sets it on the table without comment.

I put my napkin in my lap. "I had to see for myself. I had to know if it was really true."

"Did you see it?" Maddie asks, unfolding her napkin and smoothing it meticulously over her skirt.

"Yes, Wilkes's patch job was plainly visible."

"That must have been creepy." Maddie reaches for the bread, cuts off a slice, and then lays it on her bread plate before reaching for the butter.

She slides the breadboard over next to me. "I did start to hyperventilate and practically ran out of that house. That poor woman must have thought she'd let in a lunatic."

"I'm sure it wasn't that bad," Maddie tries to soothe.

"It was Maddie. It was horrible to see that spot. I knew I had to go but I'm not sure it resolved anything or eliminated any doubts I may have had."

"You thought Wilkes made it up?" She asks confused.

I take another sip of tea and welcome the cool feel as it travels down my parched throat. "No, I never thought for a moment that he made it up. I guess I was hoping he'd exaggerated or gotten his facts wrong. To have proof means I can't hide under a bushel basket and deny it happened. That patched hole in the ceiling said it all."

Our salads arrive and we eat in silence for a while.

"What time do you go home tomorrow? I'll be glad to take you to the airport." Maddie offers.

"Bless you darlin' but I need to return the rental car anyway, so you don't need to take off work on my account. My plane doesn't leave until ten o'clock tomorrow morning, so I'll have plenty of time to get ready and get to the airport."

"I'm going to miss you, Hannah," she pauses. "I can't begin to apologize for my outburst the other day about owing you. I do owe you. I owe you a huge debt for keeping Dad away from me. I don't know what I'd have done. I think I would have killed myself." She says and then realizes she's been insensitive. "I'm sorry, Hannah, I didn't mean to imply that you should have

. . . I mean. I don't know what I mean. I only know that I will always be grateful."

I rub her shoulder and smile at her. "I told you Maddie, the debt, if ever there was one, is paid in full. I didn't kill myself and my guess is you wouldn't have either. The fact is, you find a way to survive when there are no other choices. I honestly never thought about killing myself then"

The color drains from Maddie's face. "What do you mean 'then'?"

I take another sip of tea and think about what to tell her, how to explain. "As a young woman in college, I sank into a horrible depression. And then I did seriously consider ending it all. Anything to get rid of the pain and humiliation."

Maddie slips her hand into mine and holds it tightly.

I look at her. "Incredibly, I even blamed myself for what happened. You know, if I'd been a better daughter, that kind of thing. Then I went into therapy and found out the only person who was to blame was Dad."

"What finally decided you to go into therapy?" Maddie asks.

"I had migraines that wouldn't go away. I took pills, I got x-rays, I got tests and shots, but nothing helped. The headaches got worse until I could hardly function. When my doctor first brought up the idea, I was stunned by the notion that my own body had turned against me. The more I thought about it though the more my gut said this was going to be what would save me."

Maddie smoothes the napkin in her lap. "Weren't you scared to talk to someone you didn't know about all this?"

"Terrified would be a better word. But then I thought, what the hell, I'm paying them to listen, and they can't tell anybody; so, I've got nothing to lose." The waitress refills our tea glasses. When she leaves, I continue. "My biggest fear was that I'd be overcome with emotion and not be able to function. But then I realized for all practical purposes I already was a walking veggie. I had to face my fears head-on, and this was the only way. Besides I was sick of pain pills and shots and feeling sorry for myself, anything seemed like an improvement."

"Do you think I should see a therapist?" Maddie asks in a low whisper.

"Yes."

"You do?" She seems flabbergasted by my response.

"Yes, I do. Our family had some serious problems. Do you think that because Dad didn't put his hands on you, you weren't affected by any of this? The guilt you feel about me keeping Dad away from you is a symptom of his impact on your life."

"I'll think about it," she says noncommittally.

I look her in the eye, "Don't just think about it, Maddie, do it."

We finish our salads and fight over the bill Maddie wins. We step outside into the blazing heat. Our lengthy talk over lunch has made her late for work. She hugs me tightly. She smells sweetly of jasmine perfume. "I love you, Maddie."

"I love you too, Hannah," she says close to tears. "Please let's not wait so long to see each other again. Maybe now with mom gone, you can come here to see me occasionally instead of meeting every few years in Chicago.”

“Maybe so,” I concede, entertaining the notion.

“What are you going to do about Sam?” She asks about the weightiness of other things having pushed him to the side.

I answer honestly. “I don’t know.”

“You know, at first I was against you two getting together because of him being married and all, and so much time passing by,” Maddie says, as people walk around us on the sidewalk. “But after everything that’s happened, I don’t know how you could let this second chance pass you by. You may not get another opportunity to be with the man you truly love. I think you should go for it.”

“What about his wife?”

She smiles, “It’s my humble opinion that you had him first.” She says echoing my sentiments exactly and then kisses me one last time before she hurries back to her banker’s office.

I watch her go until I lose sight of her in the crowd. Then I slowly head back to my car. I approach my car from the rear, so I don’t have to go down Dogwood again; one trip down memory lane is quite enough for today. I don’t mind the long walk. I need time to think. Maddie’s right. I am going to go for it; I’m going to be with Sam and let everything and everybody else be damned.

CHAPTER TWELVE

I go for a drive to clear my head and then run some errands. When I arrive back at Mom's house it's late evening. Bird is sitting in a rocking chair on the porch waiting for me.

"Bird, I swear I don't think I've ever seen you sittin' still," I say as I climb the porch steps. I notice what a graceful woman Bird is as she stands and walks towards me. She's been like any parent; as much as you love them, it's hard to think of them in any role other than the one in which they exist for you. She seems pensive and vulnerable. I hug her and ask. "Is something wrong?"

"No, Sweetie, I brought you some supper." She seems flustered. "Thought maybe with an empty kitchen and you bein' so busy gettin' ready for your trip you wouldn't be thinkin' about a proper meal," she says as she turns towards the kitchen.

"Wait Bird, I'm not hungry right now. Why don't you sit and keep me company for a while?" I sit in the rocker next to hers. "Bird, what's bothering you?"

"There's nothin' wrong darlin'," she says. "Just ol' Bird feelin' outta sorts wonderin' what I's gonna do with myself now that your Momma has passed on, God rest her soul, and all of you are grown up and gone. Even my brood has flown the coop." She sits down and picks at the fabric of her dress. The familiar apron is nowhere in sight.

My heart breaks to see Bird so somber. I take her hand hoping for once I can give back some of the love and understanding she has given me over the years. "I'm sure it's difficult to take such a sharp turn in your life, especially now."

"It's not like I ain't lookin' forward to restin' a bit; Lord knows my hands and knees need a bit of a rest, but I been workin' all my life, always done for others. I ain't so sure I'm cut out for a life of leisure." She absently strokes the arms of her rocker running the palm of her hands over the smooth wood. "But it ain't like a gotta choice; who'd hire an ol' wore-out woman likes me."

I gently pat her shoulder and softly say. "You're not old, Bird. The point is that you need to start taking care of yourself now. You've been doing for others all your life and you did a great job. I love you, Bird." The truth of my words is the only gift I have to offer.

She stands, walks to the edge of the porch, and looks out over the waterway. I get up and stand beside her. She looks at me and puts her arms around me. We hold each other gently comforting one another for perhaps the last time. She stands back from me and takes my face in her hands.

"Lord child you still just nothin' but breath and britches," she smiles at me.

"Bird, you always say that," I limply protest.

We stand for a spell on the porch and watch as the moon begins her ascent.

"I better get your supper; I left it on the counter. It's probably already cold but I ain't got no way to heat it up."

"Bird, you stay put. I'll eat it later. Right now, I want you to start thinking about yourself, you hear me?" I wait for an answer.

"Yes Ma'am, Miss Hannah," A smile creeps onto her face.

"Very cute, Bird." I pretend to be annoyed.

Bird changes the subject and asks me: "What you gonna do about Mr. Sam?"

I don't answer her right away. She waits patiently watching my face in the growing brightness of the moonlight. "I don't want to lose him again, Bird," I murmur.

"That boy loves you, Sweetie."

"What about his wife, Bird? I should feel guilty about her, but I don't."

"She done had her chance. You were with him long 'fore she come 'round. Besides he doesn't love her, darlin,' he loves you. Always has loved you, why any fool can see that." She waves away my concerns with a flick of her wrist.

"You really think so, Bird?" I want to hear the words again.

Bird sits, rocks back in her chair, and looks at me. "Don't be silly child, that man has always loved you. I don't know how you let him get away the first time, but you sure ain't plannin' on lettin' him get away again are you?"

"No Bird, I ain't plannin' on lettin' him get away again," I confirm as we smile at each other conspiratorially.

Bird gets up out of her rocker and smoothes the front of her dress. "Well, I better be gettin' on home 'fore they start a worrin' about me. Now don't forget your supper child, I don't want you wastin' away to nothin'." She puts her hands on her hips comfortably resuming her role of provider. "Remember I'm always here for ya. If you need me, Sweetie, you just call on ol' Bird, ya hear?" Her old confidence seems to return.

"I hear you, Bird, thank you. If you need anything you got my card right?" I ask.

She assures me she does and then hugs me tightly. "You look after yourself now and tell that Mr. Sam he better take good care of you, or he'll have to answer to ol' Bird."

I hug her harder, afraid to let go, afraid to go on alone from here. "I will, Bird. I'll tell Sam what you said."

She kisses me one last time and quietly slips down the porch steps. I watch her until she turns the corner around the house and the night settles down around me like a silken glove comforting and suffocating at the same time. I fetch the supper Bird left and take it out on the porch and eat under the full moon. The last vestiges of its light remind me of my midnight swim with Sam. The warmth of his love sifts through my tired veins and makes me want him all over again. I take a cool shower and go to bed early. In the morning I pick up the phone to call Sam, but the phone company has already disconnected the line. I curse Wilkes's efficiency.

The trip home was uneventful. I don't arrive until after 8:00 p.m. Jack and Carly are to pick me up at the airport. I had wanted to take a taxi, but Jack insisted he would pick me up. He said not only did Carly want to be there, but that it would be a waste of money to take a taxi when he could just as easily come and get me. I argued we were divorced and that I could look after myself. He dug in his heels and said I needed to learn to be more careful with money, an old argument. Then I pointed out, to his total incomprehension, that this was one of the many reasons why I divorced him. I could tell from his voice on the phone that this argument went voluntarily through both ears as he repeated the details of my flight schedule in that droning, over-organized voice of his.

I dread facing Jack. I'm afraid he'll see my love for Sam written on my face. I know that somehow, he'll take one look at me and be able to see I've fallen in love with another man. This will be the first time I've been with someone else since our divorce was final only three months ago. Well, he did leave me for another woman, I remind myself! Women worry about their men falling in love with someone else. Men worry about their woman having sex with someone else; love and care about a guy all you want just don't sleep with him.

I have two drinks on the way home to loosen up. Jack seems glad to see me as Carly wraps herself around me and won't let go. Before we even retrieve my luggage, Jack can tell that something is different. He whispers in my ear that he can smell the alcohol on my breath. He doesn't say anymore with Carly there, but I know I'm going to get the third degree later.

Jack drives in silence on the way home while Carly and I catch up. She tells me about her new friends at her day camp, the various field trips they've been on, and her adventures in swimming. I didn't realize just how much I missed her until she was with me again. Jack drops us off at the house, unloads my luggage, and helps carry in Carly's gear.

"Sorry, I didn't get a chance to wash her clothes." He says, handing me a plastic garbage bag full of dirty laundry. Such a joy to face on my first night back.

"Is everything all right with you?" he asks.

"Just fine, Jack. Why don't we have lunch tomorrow and we can catch up and talk about Carly, OK?" I ask too tired to go into anything tonight.

He nods silently, gets into his car, and backs out of the driveway. This is going to be harder than I thought. I wonder how Jack's going to take Sam coming here to visit. I decide not to think about that now and I put my energies into getting Carly bathed and ready for bed.

Sam calls first thing in the morning after I get Carly off to day camp. He asks about my plans for the day and makes me laugh despite myself. My ache for him grows. He makes plans to call me at the end of the day but says nothing about coming to see me. I didn't tell him about my meeting with Jack.

Jack and I meet at The Herring Bone for lunch. I arrive first and take a booth away from the central dining room. The booth fabric and wallpaper are done in tasteful contrasting herring-bone patterns and their specialty, of course, is Pacific herring. Jack arrives five minutes late, a flurry of activity as he accepts his menu from the waitress, takes off his suit jacket, and stuffs his beeper on the waistband of his slacks. He seems flustered and distracted. I notice he's put on a little weight, but being the ever-courteous ex-wife, I say nothing. He hardly looks at me as he finally takes his seat and puts his face in the listing of lunch specials.

"How was your trip?" He inquiries from behind his menu.

"Well, it wasn't exactly meant to be a pleasure cruise." I point out hefting my menu up to my face - two could play this game. The waitress takes our drink order. Jack orders a Coke and I order a glass of wine. After the waitress leaves, Jack rearranges his silverware, still avoiding eye contact.

He asks somewhat accusingly, "Since when do you drink during the day?"

"I didn't know I had to clear it with you." I retort defensively.

"Well, first you're drinking on the plane and now you're drinking during lunch. When did you turn into a lush?" he asks clearly on the offense.

"I hardly think a drink on an airline flight and a glass of wine with lunch puts me in the lush category," I say genuinely annoyed. "Jack, why don't you tell me what's really bothering you?"

He takes a deep breath. "I guess I resented you being gone so long." He confesses. "I missed you and I've been worried about you. Are you all right?" He looks at me for the first time since he sat down.

I smile at him, glad to have all the cards on the table. "I'm OK, Jack, but thanks for asking. It was hard at first, but we all managed to cope and even get a bit closer now that we know why Mom and Dad were so crazy back then."

"I felt bad about being the one to tell you." Jack searches for absolution.

"It wasn't your fault, Jack, and besides I asked you, so you're in the clear," I tell him. He looks relieved.

"How is everyone? I bet they were glad to hear I was out of the picture." Jack pouts, hoping I'll reassure his battered ego. I don't.

"Jack, I think there's something we need to talk about." My stomach starts to gather up the ropes for the first knot.

Jack looks at me, his expression impenetrable. "Go ahead," he says warily noting my tone of voice; the details of ten years of marriage not completely wasted on the man. "I'm listening."

"Do you remember Sam Lancaster?" I feel the first knot tighten. "You know, the guy. . ."

"You mean the red-headed guy, the one you went to see before we got married?" Jack interjects.

"Yes,"

"What about him?" Jack asks, suspicious but still not suspecting the blow to come.

"I saw him again when I was at my mother's."

"Oh?" The first niggling of doubt begins to creep into his voice. "How was it to see him again?" When I don't answer immediately, he asks "Do you still have feelings for him?"

"Yes. I still have feelings for him." I say as the waitress arrives with our drinks.

Without missing a beat Jack orders a Manhattan and stares at me silently, his face frozen. Neither of us speaks until she returns with his drink. Jack downs half of it in the first swallow then loudly places the glass back on the table in front of him leaving his large hand tightly wrapped around the glass like a fire extinguisher at the ready. "Is he divorced?" An iciness has replaced his indifference of a few moments before.

"Yes, two years ago," I say surprised and disappointed at how easily the lie slides off my tongue. I try not to fidget or avoid his gaze, both of which I know will tip my hand.

"Well, how convenient. Now I suppose you two can pick up where you left off. Is that what you have in mind?" Jack tries to appear uninterested but to the practiced ear, he sounds wounded.

"Something like that," I murmur sipping my wine and admiring the wall hangings.

"I see. I guess you were quite the busy girl down there while I was home watching your daughter." He has the nerve to snipe at me.

"Jack, that's not fair. She's our daughter too and where is it written that I must be the only one to care for her, the only one to take responsibility for her? Why do I have to do all the arranging, worrying, and carting her back and forth to friends and events." I say, loading both the anger and guilt barrels and pointing them in Jack's face.

"I didn't know Carly was such a burden," Jack says.

I try to keep a lid on my anger. "She's not a burden and you know it. But sometimes it'd be nice not to have to explain to you where I'm going or what I'm doing every time I ask you to watch her. It's intrusive."

"Are you in love with this Landmaster guy?" he asks, incredulous.

"Yes," I answer quietly. Then I fruitlessly add: "And his name is Lancaster."

"You're in love with him?" Jack repeats, disbelieving. "My God, you were only gone a couple of weeks. I mean I know you two have a history, but it's been what, at least ten years since you've even seen this guy. How can you be so sure you're in love with him? Have you slept with him?" Jack asks, the awful just occurring to him.

I nod, saying nothing.

"How was it?" He asks a testosterone challenge in his tone.

"It was wonderful." I blurt out trying to keep the smile off my face. I don't want to enjoy his pain, but I can't resist reveling for a moment. Jack always said that it was because I was frigid that he had to seek solace with another woman. It feels good to have proof it wasn't true.

"I see." He says his voice is devoid of emotion. "I guess it's pretty serious then."

"Yes," I whisper and refold the napkin in my lap.

"How did this happen? I mean I know you two were serious at one time, but I didn't think you were that serious." Jack searches for answers.

I try to explain the unexplainable. "Sam and I lived together for almost a year. Christ, Jack, I almost married the man."

"You never told me that." Jack accuses.

"Yes, I did."

Jack finishes his drink in another gulp and sets the glass down without taking his hand off it. "You never said you had lived with him. I would remember a detail like that."

"Why would I keep it a secret?" I mistakenly try to argue with logic.

"What else don't I know?" He doesn't seem to hear me anymore. "Were you pining for him all the time we were together? My God! Did you see him while we were still married?"

I look him straight in the eye. "No."

Jack shakes his head in disbelief. "Why didn't you marry him then? You could have saved us both a lot of grief."

"Then I wouldn't have Carly." I point out trying to turn the conversation back to friendlier ground.

His voice gets louder. "Sounds to me like she's in the way of your grand plans."

"Jack, please don't make a scene. I came here to talk about Carly. This is going to affect her too," I point out.

"I don't want that son of a bitch near my daughter!" Jack shouts. He gets out of the booth and throws his napkin on the table.

"Jack, please." I cajole. "Please sit down and let's talk about this." His eyes tell me he already wishes I were dead. Jack stomps out of the restaurant. Our food arrives a few moments later as the rest of the patrons turn back to their dining companions. The waitress is nonplused and simply asks if the gentleman will be returning. I tell her I don't think so and she whisks away Jack's plate of food and leaves me alone with my salad. I feel conspicuous and silly but determined not to leave until I've finished my lunch.

Sam calls that evening and I find myself angry with him for putting me off. I feel I've ruined any goodwill I have worked to build up with Jack and perhaps for nothing if Sam's no longer interested.

"What's wrong, Hannah? I can hear the anger in your voice." Sam says annoyingly bewildered at my attitude.

I hesitate. "I fought with Jack today," I finally tell him.

"Jack's an idiot," Sam declares as a matter of fact.

"What makes you such an expert?" I defend Jack, which is even more unnerving and annoying.

"He let you get away, didn't he?" Sam says, "Any man who'd let you slip through his fingers is an idiot."

"Don't be nice to me Sam, you know how I hate that." My anger melts away.

Sam's voice is smooth and soothing. "All right now, tell me what you and Jack fought about. Did you tell him about me?"

"Yes."

"Well, there you go, you wounded the man's pride," Sam says the whole thing neatly put to rest in his mind.

"It's more complicated than that." I insist.

"Do you still have feelings for Jack?" Sam asks, the hurt evident in his voice.

"No, of course not, but I don't want to hurt him either. It's important for Carly that Jack and I remain on good terms and rubbing you in his face is not the way to accomplish that."

Sam is silent for a moment and then says. "Exactly how are you going to get him used to the idea that we're together now?"

"Are we together?" I ask, a hint of anger resurfacing.

"I'm surprised you need to ask such a thing, Hannah. You've only been gone a day and already you're impatient?"

"Well . . .?" I feel stupid and hurt.

"Is that what's bothering you?" He makes me feel silly and insecure. "Hannah, I was going to surprise you. I didn't want to say anything until I was sure I could get the tickets, but I hope to be there in less than two weeks. How does the weekend after next sound to you?"

"Really?" I say, sounding like a child who has just gotten her way. "I can't wait to see you."

"I miss you too, Hannah, but you've got to be more patient."

"How are you going to get away?" I ask, not wanting to know but the curiosity of a rubberneck makes me inquire.

"I told Jamie I had to go to a trade show in Madison."

My enthusiasm overflows. "I'm so glad you're coming; I can hardly wait to show you around."

"I can hardly wait to get my hands on you and feel your body next to mine." He says the desire in his voice is difficult to ignore.

"Me too, Sam. Me too."

Jack comes to pick up Carly on Saturday. We haven't talked since our fateful lunch on Wednesday. Leaving him alone to cool off was the best tactic. He comes in all smiles. You'd never know we'd fought only a few days ago. I'm immediately suspicious as only an ex-wife can be in such a situation. While Carly goes to fetch her things for a night over at her father's, Jack pulls me aside and says: "So when are you seeing lover boy again?"

"Jack, come on, knock it off. We both knew this would happen sooner or later. I need to get on with my life and if I want Sam to be a part of it then that's my business." I tell him firmly but without rancor.

"So, when are you going to see Mr. Lambaster again?" He ignores my pleas for civility.

"It's Lancaster and he's coming next weekend," I answer.

He looks indignant. "What about Carly?"

"She'll be with you," I point out.

He keeps a straight face and says, "I don't know Hannah, I've got plans for next weekend, didn't I tell you?"

I try to keep my voice low and even. "No, you didn't tell me. As a matter of fact, I was even hoping you'd keep her Friday night."

"That's out of the question," he says as though I've asked him to put me on a space shuttle. "I couldn't possibly do that," he reiterates annoyingly.

"Well, it's your daughter who'll be subjected to having a stranger stay at the house." I point out hoping my guilt trump card will motivate Jack to clear his schedule.

"Why doesn't he stay at a hotel?" Jack asks furiously.

"Because I want him to stay here with me," I say, equally angry.

Carly's arrival with her suitcase in hand and smile on her face forces us to pull apart like boxers hearing the bell at the end of a round. We're instantly all smiles and politeness. She asks what we are talking about, and Jack is quick to think of something believable and boring.

They sail out the door in a flurry of activity as she runs back and forth gathering one more stuffed animal or toy, she insists she can't live without until I instruct her to get her little behind moving, that her dad's waiting for her. At last, blessed silence.

I lay on the couch and tried hard to think of nothing for the next few hours. I'm not successful and finally, give up and go to the movies for distraction. When I return, the flashing light of the answering machine draws me eagerly to its side. I am hoping for a word from Sam but know that on the weekends it's difficult for him to call me. The message is from Jack, his tone angry and menacing.

He says: "Don't push me Hannah, or you'll be sorry!" I am caught between fear and anger not sure what to do and wondering what he means. Later, I mistakenly decided he was merely letting off steam.

CHAPTER THIRTEEN

Jack relents and agrees to take Carly for the weekend. Sam arrives as promised. The few days we have together fly by as though time is in a hurry. On Friday we go to a nightclub and enjoy being together as a couple. On Saturday night Sam cooks dinner. I find his cooking for me to be incredibly sexy. For ten years my dinner table was a utilitarian piece of furniture, now it's a romantic place adorned with burning candles and food cooked for me instead of by me.

After dinner, he takes me in his arms, and we dance slowly and reminisce about the years gone by. The evening does eventually end.

We head upstairs. I feel girlish pleasure not having to say goodnight; to be able to keep him here with me. To sleep in his arms is a luxury I hope never to take for granted.

Sunday comes and already he must leave. There is so much we didn't talk about. I hoarded the weekend not wanting to spend a moment on anything but being with him. But too soon I must take him to the airport. As we wait for the boarding call, I try not to act desperate or dispirited.

Sam takes my hands in his and looks at me. His expression is a mixture of hope and sorrow. "Hannah, I know we've avoided talking about any of this, but I want you to know that I'm going to ask Jamie for a divorce. I want to be with you. That's if you'll still have me."

I throw my arms around his neck and hold him tight. "When?" I whisper impatiently. "When can you come?"

He takes my arms from around his neck and looks at me silently before speaking. "You're going to have to be patient, Hannah. I have a lot of things to settle and take care of before we can be together."

"What do you have to do?" I sound like a pouty tyke.

He brushes my hair back from my face. "I need to sell my house and work some overtime to pay off some of my debts. And I need to take care of Jamie too."

"What do you mean take care of her?" I ask immediately on the offense.

He looks out the window and then turns his green eyes back to me. "Look, Hannah," he says slowly. "I may not love her anymore, but I promised her I'd take care of her for the rest of her life. She has no real skills. She's going to need help starting over."

I try to sound even-tempered and not like a shrew. "What kind of help exactly did you have in mind?"

He let go of my hands. "Come on, Hannah, you know I can't just dump her," he sounds angry.

The hurt on my face must be evident. He takes my hands in his again his voice is softer. "In the long run, you wouldn't think much of me if I did just dump her. I need to give her a hand to get back on her feet. Look, she's still young and pretty, I have no doubt she'll get married again."

"When are you going to ask her for a divorce?"

"When the time is right, Hannah. Please don't get impatient," he pleads to deaf ears.

The ground crew announces Sam's plane. He stands and takes me in his arms one last time and says: "I had a wonderful time, Hannah. This weekend proved to me that we were meant to be together. I have loved you almost all my life and even after all this time, I still love you; now more than ever. Please wait for me. Don't forget that I want to be with you as much as you want to be with me."

"Oh yeah? Well, don't flatter yourself," I tease him.

"Is that right?" He pulls me closer and tightens his arms around my waist as he lowers his lips to mine and kisses me, demanding I respond. My body gives away my true feelings and I'm left breathless by his affections. He smiles at me, his green eyes proud and amused at his effect on me. I don't mind his gloating because I know I have the same effect on him.

"Sam, people are starting to stare," I tell him feeling my cheeks flush.

"Let them." He kisses me again.

The plane begins boarding and Sam must go. Tears fall down my cheeks before I can stop them. Sam wipes them away, kisses each eyelid tenderly, then kisses me softly on the lips and says: "I'm not going to say goodbye, Hannah, only that I'll call you tomorrow morning. Remember, I love you."

"And I, you," I say with all my heart. Then suddenly he's gone. He heads toward the gate. Without turning back, he shows his ticket to the attendant and then walks out onto the tarmac and boards the small commuter plane that will take him on the first leg of his journey home. I watch as the engines roar to life and the plane begins to taxi down the runway. I can tell my feelings are going to get the better of me, so I make a hasty exit. I go for a drive to get hold of myself before I have to go home alone and before Jack brings Carly back.

Jack is polite but barely speaks to me when he arrives with Carly in the late afternoon. He asks me about my weekend and I'm insensitive enough to tell him it was the most wonderful weekend of my entire life. I don't blame Jack for being irritated. I remember how I felt when he was in love with someone else. I was hurt and angry nearly all the time. It wasn't until I fell in love with Sam that I was able to forgive Jack for hurting me so deeply. I'm so in love that I'm feeling magnanimous towards everyone - even Jack.

The next few weeks go by quickly as both Carly and I get ready for school to begin. Carly is starting kindergarten; I can't believe how fast she's growing up, the years slipping past as though time were chasing us. I feel age, silent and aloof, borrowing more of my time, leaving less time ahead and more behind. We shop for school clothes and do other mother-daughter outings as summer draws to a close.

Jack calls and asks me to have lunch with him. He's vague about what he wants but I agree. We meet at a restaurant close to his office. We chat at first about this and that and about Carly starting kindergarten. It surprises me how pleasant he's being. I try not to be suspicious.

After our food arrives Jack gets to the point. "The main reason I wanted to talk with you today is to discuss your mother." He says idly folding his cloth napkin and laying it neatly on the table.

"What do you mean? Is there something you didn't tell me?" I feel panic start to build.

He pats the top of my hand. "No. No. I told you everything. But we never really got a chance to talk about what happened. The news must have been hard on you, and I've been worried. Look, I know that maybe it's not my place to worry about you anymore and I don't want to get in the way of your happiness with Sam, but I still care about you, Hannah."

"Jack, you surprise me. I thought you hated Sam and hated me for loving him. Now here you are all solicitous and I don't know what to make of it." I feel confused and unsure about how much to tell Jack.

"Hannah, I know I can be an ass, but my heart is in the right place. Even though you love Sam maybe you don't feel comfortable yet talking with him about some things. I thought maybe you needed someone to talk to." He takes my hand across the table and gives it a quick gentle squeeze of encouragement.

Tears come to my eyes as my guard falls around my ankles. He's right. I didn't talk with Sam about what Wilkes told us or about Dad. I never even told Jack about my dad because I thought I had put it all behind me before we met. I didn't want the memories of my father sharing our marriage bed.

"What is it, Hannah?" Jack whispers with genuine concern in his voice. He quickly moves to my side of the booth and puts his arm around my shoulder to comfort me. This makes it harder to get my feelings under control.

"I'm OK. Really," I insist, putting up my hand to ward him off. "Would you order me a glass of wine please?" I ask.

Jack calls the waitress and places the order. By the time the wine arrives, I have gotten a grip on myself. I take a swallow to help steady my nerves.

"Come on, Hannah, tell me what's got you so upset."

"Oh, Jack. I feel so sorry for my mother. How awful it must have been for her. My father . . ."

"What about your father?" Jack asks.

"After the rape, he moved into another room," I explain.

"Did he blame your mom?"

"I don't know. I think he just couldn't get over what happened."

"How did they get along afterward?"

"They fought a lot, but Dad took it out mostly on us kids."

"What exactly do you mean took it out? You mean he hurt you?"

I turn my face away from Jack. "Yes."

Jack's voice is nearly a whisper. "You mean he beat you?"

"Yes, he beat us."

Jack's voice is dull, and his words are measured. "What else did he do Hannah?"

Bitterness fills my voice. "He beat all of us, but he had a special kind of hell for me if you get what I'm saying."

Jack keeps his voice low. "Are you telling me that your father molested you?"

I put my hands in my lap and look Jack directly in the eye. "Yes, Jack, that's exactly what I'm telling you."

"Why didn't you tell me before or did you just remember it?"

"No, I never forgot. I didn't tell you because I didn't want you to look at me differently. I thought it was all behind me, but finding out about Mom brought it all back."

Jack is alarmingly solicitous. "I'm so sorry, Hannah. I wish you had told me about this sooner, I would have understood."

"That's not all," I murmur wanting to get it all off my chest, glad to have a sympathetic ear.

"My God, Hannah, what else can there be?" he asks in disbelief.

I plunge ahead. "My Dad didn't die in a car accident."

"What do you mean your dad didn't die in a car accident? How did he die?" Jack asks cautiously.

"He killed himself."

"Oh my God. Why?"

"Wilkes knew Dad was abusing me and confronted him, threatened him with exposure. I guess rather than face public humiliation my dad hung himself; in my parents' bedroom."

"Christ, Hannah . . ."

I hold up my hand to stop him. "Let me finish. Mom insisted that Wilkes make it look like an accident."

"What? Why?"

I swivel in my booth seat, to face Jack. "Dad had a double indemnity clause on his life insurance policy. She had Wilkes make it look like an accident."

Jack's training as a physician climbs into the questioning. "If your dad was already dead how could Wilkes make it look like an accident? It's hard to disguise a hanging."

"Not if the body's burned beyond recognition."

"Jesus!" That is all Jack can manage to say as he absorbs everything that I tell him.

I finish my wine and order another glass.

"That's a hell of a story, Hannah," Jack says. I nod in agreement. "Is there anything else I should know? Anything else you want to tell me about?" he asks nervously.

I smile at the idea. "You up to hearing anymore?"

"No, I don't think I am," he confesses.

"Good because that's it. That's the whole enchilada." I sip my second glass of wine and the welcome buzz relaxes me. "Thank you for listening, Jack. I think it helped to get all that off my chest."

"Sure, Hannah I'm glad I could be here for you," he pauses. "Not to make you angry, but why didn't you talk to Sam about this?"

"I don't know, this isn't the sort of thing I think he would take very well."

Jack is immediately curious. "What do you mean?"

"Well, Sam is old school. You know, Southern gentleman with all the pride and prejudices. While he was great when I told him about what happened to my mother, I don't think he could handle the truth about my dad molesting me. I worry that if he knew he'd split." I say in a rare moment of candor the wine loosening my lips.

"Gee, Hannah, that doesn't sound like he loves you very much," Jack observes.

"He does too," I say, immediately on the defensive. "It's just that . . . . I don't know, it's just the way it is I guess." I finish lamely getting irritated with Jack.

"Whoa," Jack holds up both hands to fend me off. "I didn't mean to upset you, Hannah. I guess I shouldn't have said anything about Mr. Landermaster."

"It's Lancaster damn it!" I shout feeling tired and flustered. "Look, Jack, thanks again for listening, but I need to get back and I know how busy you are these days. I'll see you on Saturday at the usual time, all right?"

"Sure, I'll see you then." He takes care of the check as I make my way out the door and head home emotionally drained.

The days begin to meld together once classes start. Sam calls faithfully every morning and every late afternoon. It has been three weeks since his last visit. While he doesn't seem to be making excuses, he isn't making any progress either. I get more frantic with each week that passes by. Schoolwork fills my schedule and hardly leaves time for anything other than Carly. I don't have as much time for Sam, often missing his calls or having to cut them short because of deadlines or other commitments. I feel him slipping through my fingers and there's nothing I can do.

It's two o'clock in the morning and the phone rings waking me out of sound sleep. I rush to answer it before the noise wakes Carly. It's Sam calling collect. He sounds agitated.

"What's wrong, Sam?" I come instantly wide awake. "Are you all right?" I ask, frantic, for an answer.

"Yes, I'm fine. Jamie found out about us and kicked me out." He sounds exhausted.

"How'd she find out? Did you finally tell her?" I try not to sound thrilled.

"I fell asleep on the couch, and she went through my wallet. She found your name and number."

"Are you OK? Did she hurt you?" I ask suddenly filled with dread.

"She caught me with a lamp, but a few stitches put that right."

"Oh Sam, I'm so sorry," I say sincerely.

I picture Sam cold and tired standing in a phone booth in the middle of the night. "Where are you going to stay?"

"I don't know yet. It's too late to call anyone and the hotels are full because of some festival going on in town. I think I'll just sleep in my car tonight and figure something out in the morning. She called the police and said I'd hit her."

"Did you Sam?" I ask wearily.

"No, of course not. But she did have them escort me out of my own dang house!"

I feel bad for doubting him. "But why did they throw you out if you were the one injured?"

He laughs. "She said she had to hit me to protect herself. What was I going to do? I sure wish you were here."

"Is there anything I can do?"

His voice is thick. "No. Just tell me you love me."

"I do, Sam, you know that."

"I'll call you in the morning and let you know what's happening." He rings off.

I didn't sleep anymore that night.

We fast forward our plans for Sam to move to Wisconsin; he'll be here in two weeks. The lawyers are already in on the marital game of splitting assets and placing blame. Sam seems eager for us to start our new life. It's time to tell Jack; I dread his response. When Jack comes to pick up Carly on Saturday, I tell her to play outside while I talk with her father. Jack is immediately on the alert.

"Jack, Sam, and I have decided to move in together." I hurry on before he can stop me. "I know it's sudden, but we just can't wait any longer."

Jack's body tightens. "Wait a minute, you just started seeing this guy a couple of months ago and now you're going to move in together? What about Carly? How's she going to take all this? She's barely gotten used to the divorce and now you're going to bring in someone new. Christ, Hannah, what are you thinking with, your twat?" His voice gains volume.

"Jack, I don't appreciate your tone, you're not being fair."

His hands curl into fists at his sides. "Fair has nothing to do with this. You just can't wait to get your hands in this guy's pants and now you're letting your middle-aged, oversexed hormones dictate your life and perhaps harm my daughter. I won't allow this Hannah."

My good intentions fly out the window. "What the hell do you mean your daughter and you won't allow?"

Jack jabs his index finger at my chest. "If you insist on acting like an idiot, I think maybe Carly should come live with me," he threatens.

I grab his finger and wrench it back seeing the pain in his face, but he's too proud to say anything. "Don't screw with me, Jack. This can go easy and be a smooth transition for Carly or this can go painfully, and she will get the worst of it, and you know it." I roughly let go of his finger.

Jack's voice softens as he tries a different tact. "Hannah, this is wrong. What you're doing is going to hurt Carly. Can't he stay at a motel or get an apartment and you two gradually ease into this thing? I'm thinking of you too you know."

"I don't want to ease into it. I want him here with me," I say stubbornly.

"Why aren't you two getting married then?" He challenges me.

"I don't want to get married again. Once was enough to cure me for life." I assure him wanting to hurt him and scared he'd figure out the truth about Sam.

"Or maybe he doesn't want to marry you. Maybe he hasn't even asked you. Why buy the cow when you can get the milk for free?" He gives as good as he gets.

"You really think that way, don't you?" I marvel at his zipper intellect.

Carly comes in and interrupts us. "Are you two fighting again?" She asks innocently, the uncanny perception of a small child.

"Of course not sweetheart." Jack lies to reassure her. I give him a dirty look. I don't like him lying to Carly; it sets a bad example. Besides, he always underestimates her. She knows we're fighting and now she's even more confused because Daddy's saying it isn't true.

"We were having a loud discussion." I hug her tightly. "Can you give Daddy and me a few more minutes to finish up? I'll call you when we're done."

"But I'm tired of waiting. There's nothing to do and you guys always talk when daddy comes over and you don't pay any attention to me." She puts her little hands defiantly on her hips.

"Carly," his voice warns.

"All right!" she pouts and loudly stomps off and slams the back door on her way out.

"Let's get back to the problem at hand," I say, "Given this is inevitable, how do you want to handle it with Carly?"

"Let me think about it OK?" Jack asks resigned but still angry. "I'll talk with you on Sunday when I bring her back. But please think about what you're doing, Hannah, this is going to affect her for the rest of her life." He pushes all my guilt buttons at once.

"I know that Jack, I don't want to hurt her, but I can't stop having a life to protect her either. Did you think when you dumped me, I would curl up and die? Did you think I wouldn't carry on with my life and find someone else? Is that what's really bugging you Jack that I found someone else?"

Jack abruptly walks away, gathers up Carly and her overnight things and they're gone; the inflow of silence depresses me.

My loyalties tear me in two. Jack's right: Sam's sudden arrival is going to be hard on Carly. But on the other hand, I don't want to ask Sam to wait. In truth I'm worried that if I ask, I might lose him; a chance I'm not willing to take. I go out to dinner and a movie and then revisit the nightclub that Sam and I went to so I can feel closer to him - he feels so far away right now. I drink too much and worry about getting home. I take a taxi and when I do arrive it's late and I cry myself to sleep.

The next morning my head throbs and my stomach aches; nothing I don't deserve for being an immature idiot. When Jack drops Carly off he wonders what's wrong and asks where my car is. His great detective mind puts it all together and offers me a ride back to my car. I'm embarrassed and feel stupid under his scrutiny. When we return, Carly goes next door to play and Jack and I sit down to talk.

We finally settled the arrangements. Although Jack still expresses his outrage at the whole idea, he's quieted down enough to be civil in front of Carly when she comes home. Sam will be here in one week.

Jack comes by the house unexpectedly one evening after Carly is in bed. He seems agitated, pacing around the room and rejecting my offers of coffee or a drink.

"Jack, why don't you tell me what's on your mind," I say prepared to do battle over Sam one more time.

"Hannah, I don't know how to tell you this."

The hair on the back of my neck instantly comes to attention.

"I hired a private detective to check out this Sam character."

I'm stunned. "You did what?" Then angry, "What the hell did you think you were doing?"

 "Keep your voice down. I don't want Carly to hear us."

I take a deep breath, and with my voice in a near whisper, I launch my words through gritted teeth. "Why did you hire a detective?"

"Hey, this guy's going to live with my daughter, and you don't think I have a right to check him out? I don't know this guy, and your head's stuck in the clouds."

"I can't believe you went behind my back. For God's sake, Jack, you need to get a life and leave us alone."

Jack closes the gap between us, grabs me by the shoulders, and looks me straight in the eyes. "Hannah, he's married."

I stand frozen. I don't know whether to deny it or not. Before I can make up my mind, Jack pounces. "You don't look surprised," he says as the truth sinks in. "You already knew, didn't you?"

I don't disagree. "My God!" He begins to pace around the room again. "Did you also know that his wife filed spousal abuse charges against the son of a gun? Did you know that he beats his wife?" Jack hurls the information at me like a javelin.

"He doesn't beat his wife," I say calmly, "She only said that to get him out of the house."

Jack stops and faces me. "Listen to yourself, Hannah. There you stand quoting the party line. How do you know it isn't true? Because he told you it wasn't true? And he's such a reliable source." The sarcasm drips from his tongue. "Let's see," he continues, "the man is an adulterer, a liar, and a wife-beater. Yeah, I'd say that makes him an impeccable specimen."

"He doesn't beat his wife!" I hiss. I don't even believe me, and I know it's true.

Jack puts his hands on his hips, "OK, let's say you're right and the poor slob has been falsely accused. That still leaves two out of three major character flaws."

I'm tired of defending Sam. "Jack, back off. You don't understand."

Jack closes in for the kill. "What'd he tell you, Hannah; that his wife doesn't understand him, that he isn't getting any at home."

"Shut up, Jack!" I shout, forgetting about Carly. "We're not married anymore so this is none of your business. Now I want you to leave!"

Jack ignores my arm pointed at the front door. "This is my business, Hannah, because Carly's my business."

My arm floats back down to my side "Is that some kind of threat?" I ask with more bluster than I feel.

His voice is deceptively calm. "No, I'm not threatening you, Hannah. I never make threats - just promises."

"What's that supposed to mean," I ask, caught between sudden fear at the thought of such a loss and my anger that he would use Carly against me.

"Nothing." He calms down and takes a seat on the sofa.

I sit across from Jack and catch my breath.

Jack leans forward and puts his elbows on his knees, clears his throat. "One of the reasons I came by to talk with you tonight is to tell you that I'm accepting a new position with another practice. I'll be moving to Virginia at the end of the month."

He catches me completely by surprise. I never expected this. On the one hand, I'll be glad to have Jack out of my hair, especially with Sam arriving. I was worried about how sticky it would be between them. But on the other hand, I feel deep sadness for Carly because she's used to having her Daddy around. Now she'll only see him sporadically. Perhaps there is even more reason to be glad that Sam is coming because Carly needs a full-time male influence in her life.

"Hannah? Are you there?" Jack calls me back to the present.

"I'm sorry. I wasn't expecting this," I explain.

"I know it's kind of sudden but it's a great position and as you know, my family lives on the East Coast."

"Why didn't you tell me sooner?"

He leans back on the sofa. "I interviewed for the job a couple of months ago, but I didn't think I'd get it, especially when I didn't hear back from them. I didn't tell anyone because I didn't want to jinx my chances by talking about it and I didn't want the office to know I was looking around." He explains. "Then, almost out of the blue, they called me back and made me an offer, a very generous offer. I think you'll be impressed."

"I'm sure I would be Jack, but right now I think you better go. We've both got a lot to think about." My head begins to pound. "Why don't you call me later."

Jack leaves. My mind is in overdrive. I call Sam at the hotel he's staying at and tell him everything. He doesn't seem concerned and assures me everything will work out for the best and tells me not to worry. I hardly slept again that night.

Sam is supposed to arrive Friday night; I can't wait anymore. Friday evening, I find myself holding my breath praying that he'll walk off the plane. Then suddenly he's there standing before me. He does look worse for the wear but he's finally here and I swear I hear angels sing my joy is so great. He sees me and breaks into a big grin. He rushes to me and hugs me hard.

"You didn't think I was coming, did you?" he asks. I shake my head. "You've got to learn to have more faith, Hannah," he whispers holding me tighter and kissing me.

If I could forget for a minute that I'm an adulteress, I would believe his being here with me was a miracle.

It's late and Sam and I head back to the house. Carly is staying at her dad's until Sunday to give Sam and me a little time to adjust before we deal with her needs. I keep pinching myself that he's really here. The weekend was wonderful. Sam seems relaxed but a bit pensive. He's much calmer and happier than I expected. On Saturday we go to the library where he browses through want ads and telephone directories looking for lumber mills, looking for work.

We go for a walk in the park by the river. The air is crisp with the first hints of fall. He holds me close, and we talk about our life together.

"Hannah, I have something I want to talk with you about," he says seating us both on a secluded bench under some trees.

"What is it, Sam?" I wonder if something is wrong.

"I want to marry you, Hannah." He surprises me.

I stop dead in my tracks "You do?" I ask stupidly.

"Yes, I do. What do you say, Hannah, will you marry me?"

"Don't you think we ought to wait, at least until your divorce is final before we discuss this?" I say worried he's hurrying things, yet not wanting to hurt his feelings. "I don't want to get married again, Sam. Can't we just live together and be happy." I see his hurt and try to soften the blow. "You know I love you. I didn't like being married, Sam, it wasn't any fun."

"Being married to me will be different, Hannah. I'll take care of you, love you, make love to you." He gives me a mischievous grin. "I'll always be there when you need me; I'll never let you down." He reaches out and pushes my hair back off my face. "And I promise, being married to me will never be boring."

"I know you love me, Sam, I know you'll never let me down and God knows life with you is never boring, but why don't we wait a little while and see how everything goes? Maybe you won't like being an instant parent," I smile at his hurt face.

"How could I not love Carly? This is a second chance for me. I never got to be a part of my son's life and now, thanks to you and Carly, I get a second chance to be a dad. I don't mean to take Jack's place or anything, but to be there if she needs me, you know," he says flustered.

I hug Sam for loving me and for loving Carly. When I got divorced, I thought having custody of Carly meant never getting another chance to fall in love because most men don't want instant families. But Sam views Carly's existence as one of my better selling points.

I pick up Carly from Jack's apartment late Sunday afternoon. I'm apprehensive. Even though Carly knows Sam's coming and Jack and I have both talked with her about it, I am nervous about her reaction. She seems to take Sam's arrival in stride, and we have an almost picture-perfect evening as

I lay in the hammock and Carly and Sam play kickball. I have trouble getting her to go to bed, but she eventually settles down and drifts off.

Monday arrives and reality makes a crash landing. I get breakfast ready. Carly seems subdued and a bit wary of Sam this morning; a predictable response, I suppose, but it's upsetting to Sam who so desperately wants her to accept him. I feel guilty leaving Sam alone all day. I take Carly to school and come back to the house to get my things together and to head off for work. While I'm collecting my papers, Sam keeps me company by telling me about his plans for the day. There is a knock on the front door. I look through the peephole and see a deputy sheriff standing outside. I quickly open the door. "Can I help you?" I wonder if the neighbors are watching the house. I feel guilty and embarrassed, and I don't even know what for.

"Are you Hannah Emily Wheeler?" he asks, his voice monotone and his face impassive.

"Yes, I am. Is there something I can do for you?" My anxiety level rises by the second.

He hands me a piece of paper all folded up nice and neat.

I take the paper from his outstretched hand. "What's this?"

"It's a subpoena, Ms. Wheeler."

"A subpoena for what?" My mind races a hundred miles an hour looking for something to latch onto that will help make some sense of this.

"You're being sued for the custody of your daughter." He says so politely I have an urge to leap on him and mash his face until it's flat. He turns and heads calmly back to his cruiser. I stand stupidly in the doorway, not moving, my mouth hanging open with the piece of paper still clutched tightly in my hand. I hear Sam behind me whisper: "Oh my God."

CHAPTER FOURTEEN

I practically run Sam over, getting to the phone to call Jack. I don't hear anything but the angry blood pounding past my ears as I stab in the digits to Jack's office. His nurse says he's out. I growl at her asking her when he'll be back. She says he just stepped out for a minute. What the hell does that mean? I slam down the phone and grab my purse heading for the car.

Sam grabs my sleeve. "Hannah, wait a minute."

I turn to face him almost surprised to see him there and a moment of unreality flashes before my eyes.

"What?" I bark at him as I tug loose from his grip.

"Hannah, you can't go down there like this. You're only going to make it worse!" He shouts after me.

I don't even slow down as I head towards the door. "If you think I'm going to let this creep have my daughter you're wrong! I'll kill that son of a gun before he gets his dang hands on my kid!"

He follows on my heels. "Hannah, I'm not the enemy. You need to calm down and think of a plan or you're going to lose Carly. You can't go off half-cocked like this. Please, listen to me!"

I slip past him and get in my car. "Not now, Sam. I know you're trying to help but this is between me and Jack."

The closer I get to Jack's office the angrier I become. I slide my car around corners as the tires squeal distantly in my ears while I think about what I'm going to do to Jack once I find that cowardly bum. I flagrantly park in the handicapped spot in front of Jack's office. I swoop into the reception area pushing past the gawking receptionist. I turn right and then left passing examination rooms and nurses sitting on stools with their ears glued to their phones while assistants fill out charts and other paperwork that is the lifeblood and first defensive line in any medical practice. I come to Jack's office at the end of the hall; it's empty.

His nurse is hot on my heels. "Can I help you, Ms. Wheeler?" She asks in that cloying you-have-no-power-here tone of voice.

"Where's Jack?" I spit out at her.

"I'm afraid Dr. Hoskins isn't available right now. Is there something I can do to help you?" She sounds very territorial. I've never liked this woman; her breasts are too perky, and I suspect she was spreading her legs for good old Jack before we were divorced.

I turn to face her relishing an opportunity to unleash some of my pent-up rage. "Yeah, there's something you can do for me, Nurse Smithfield. You can find my unfaithful ex-husband and tell him I'm here!"

"There's no need to use that kind of language, Ms. Wheeler." A small crack shows in her veneer.

I walk around Jack's desk. "That's Dr. Wheeler to you. Now run along and go find Jack or I'll have to do some house cleaning." When she doesn't move, I use my right arm to sweep off Jack's desk, successfully clearing everything off in one pass. I admire my handiwork for a moment and then turn back to Nurse Smithfield. She's gone; no doubt to fetch Dr. Jack.

By the time Jack shows up I have made myself comfortable in his swanky office chair and have my feet up on his newly organized desk.

He stops in the doorway. "Hannah, what are you doing here?" he asks pointedly leaving the door open.

The look of surprise on his face makes me bold and dangerous. "What do you think I'm doing here Jack? I got the most interesting piece of news this morning, hand-delivered by the city's finest. I roughly pull the subpoena out of my purse and wave it in the air. "Do you want to explain this to me, Jack?"

He is immediately on the defensive. "Listen, Hannah, I felt I had to do something before you destroyed Carly with all your carrying on."

I nearly explode out of the chair and am rewarded to see him back up a step. "Carrying on, Jack? What do you mean, carrying on?" I come around the desk. "Why don't you close the door so we can have some privacy while we discuss this little matter." He hesitates. "Don't be a wuss Jack, go on, close the door."

He closes the door. "Hannah, before you go flying off the handle, I want you to know I'm only doing what I think is best for Carly," he whines. "Now why don't you calm down and we can talk about this rationally."

I can see nothing but his stupid silly face before me as I come at him full force. I catch him by surprise and hit him with both hands in the chest shoving him back against the door, knocking the wind out of him. He grabs me by the shoulders, but I start pounding his chest and then try to get a clear swing at his pudgy little self-righteous face. He manages to slip away from me and puts his two patient chairs between us.

I'm out of control but can't help myself. "You can't run from me, Jack. I told you not to screw with me, but you didn't listen!"

He edges himself closer to the phone resting on the floor. "Hannah you're acting like an animal. If you don't calm down, I'm going to have to call security."

"If you touch that phone, I'll have to hurt you, Jack."

He hesitates wavering between his fears. "Hannah, I think we should let the lawyers handle this. You obviously can't talk about this in a civil manner."

"A civil manner! How dare you!" I scream. "You send over a piece of paper saying you're going to take my daughter and you want to know why I can't be civil?"

There's a knock and then a deep voice calls through the door. "Is everything all right, Dr. Wheeler?"

I back away and Jack approaches the door never taking his eyes off me. He grabs the knob still watching me and opens the door. Outside are two security men.

Jack turns and says: "Dr. Wheeler is a bit upset and she's just leaving. Perhaps you could walk Dr. Wheeler out to her car?" He stands out of the way.

I start toward the door. "You haven't heard the last of this!" I threaten. I take a menacing step toward him, and he jumps back out of harm's way. "You always were a scaredy cat, Jack. I guess some things never change."

I angrily try to shake off the security guards' hold on my arms, but they are rather insistent. Everyone seems frozen watching the lunatic being escorted through the building. The patients in the reception area are silent and staring at me like deer caught in headlights. The receptionist has a contemptuous scowl plastered on her face. Jack's partner glares at me disapprovingly. "Go screw yourself," I say to his face. He at least gives me the satisfaction of looking horrified before my new friends roughly escort me out the double glass doors and stuff me into my car with a very unchivalrous warning not to return.

Sam was right, I shouldn't have gone. I only made things worse even if it did feel good to unload both barrels on Jack and watch him squirm. That despicable worm, he's just envious of my happiness, jealous I have a better lover, and this is how he plans to punish me.

When I get home, Sam is waiting. No lecture, no 'I told you so,' and for that I'm grateful. I'm also grateful he didn't see my awful display at Jack's office. That's a side of me I don't want Sam to ever see. I called the school and canceled my class; I certainly shouldn't be loose among the young and impressionable today. I flop on the sofa exhausted.

Sam sits down next to me. "What are you going to do now?"

I close my eyes. "I don't know. I guess I need to get a lawyer and after the stunt that I just pulled I better see what I can do about a miracle as well."

My divorce lawyer, Cheryl Brown, works in an appointment for me late that afternoon. Her office is in a downtown high-rise where she shares office space and a receptionist with several other lawyers. The first thing she tells me after lecturing me about antagonizing Jack is to get rid of Sam. She makes some calls and finds that the custody hearing is scheduled for one week from today.

I arrive home from the lawyer's office to find Sam upstairs packing his bags. "What are you doing?"

"You can't afford to have me here, Hannah. You'll lose Carly over this once Jack finds out I'm still legally married." Sam plops a few more of his shirts on top of the growing pile in his suitcase.

I sit wearily on the bed. "He already knows."

Sam stops his packing and faces me. "He knows? Why didn't you tell me, Hannah?"

"What was there to tell you? I didn't think it was any of his business."

"How'd he find out? Did you tell him?" Sam absently tosses socks into his bag.

"He hired a private detective to have you checked out," I confess.

"Damn." That's all Sam says as he goes to the bathroom to collect his personal belongings. I hear him clearing out the medicine cabinet. I lie down on the bed and cry.

Sam comes back into the bedroom and lies down on the bed next to me and holds me in his arms.

"Hannah, it isn't over between us, we had bad timing that's all. Soon my divorce will be final, and you'll get this straightened out with Jack and then we can get married and be a happy family. You must be patient. Right now, though I need to get out of here before I cause you any more trouble." He kisses my cheek and resumes his packing.

"Do you have to leave right away?" I already know the answer.

Sam closes his suitcase and zips it shut. "I have a seven o'clock flight. Carly's next door playing with her little friend. I hope that's all right?" Sam asks.

"Oh my God! I forgot about Carly! Can you believe that? I forgot about my own daughter. Maybe Jack's right. Maybe I don't deserve to have her." My tears start anew.

"That's ridiculous, Hannah. You're a good mother. Jack is angry because of me. As soon as I'm out of the picture, he'll calm down and this whole thing will blow over. I promise." He says reassuringly.

I'm too tired to argue anymore. Carly comes home and plays quietly in her room. I go up to explain about Sam leaving. She is docile and accepting, which of course worries me.

We take Sam to the airport, and I try to put on a brave front for him and Carly. I don't go in with him but merely help him unload at the curb because I know I won't hold together for anything else. He kisses me but doesn't seem to have his heart in it. He makes his way through the thickening crowd and slips through the sliding doors. One minute he's here, the next he's gone. A cold wind passes over my heart as I stand on the curb holding Carly's hand in mine watching the other half of my life walk away.

The court battle begins on a Tuesday. The only people present are the judge, both lawyers, and Jack and me. We sit on either side of the courtroom facing the judge. The judge is a man, which I consider to be a strike against me, although my lawyer disagrees.

Jack's lawyer presents his case for seeking temporary custody of Carly. They are well prepared. They begin by pointing out that I am living with a married man and the bad influence this will have on Carly. Surprisingly, and unfortunately, Jack's detective has also dug up the fact that I was named correspondent in Sam's first divorce - making me look like a habitual adulteress. Nurse Smithfield testified I made threats and generally made me look like the maniac I was that day. They have a witness that saw me drunk at the night club and they recount how poor, put-upon Jack had to take me to pick up my car because I was too drunk to drive it home. They claim that the recent death of my mother and the news of my mother's rape and father's suicide and my history of being molested makes me inherently unstable. They contend that my public drunkenness and my poor judgment of having Sam live with me are evidence of my instability.

We fight back saying Sam has returned home and was only a house guest. We argue that my taxi ride home showed good judgment and that Nurse Smithfield has a personal ax to grind. My lawyer maintains that a parent's childhood traumas shouldn't have any bearing on her current ability to be a good mother. It all falls on deaf ears.

The judge awards Jack temporary custody with another hearing to determine permanent custody set for six months later.

The devastation is complete. How could Jack do this to me? How could he do this to Carly? I foolishly trusted him and told him my secrets. How could I have been so stupid? He was plotting against me all along, taking me to lunch, being so solicitous, coaxing out the details. He even feigned concern for my happiness as he reeled me in like a professional con artist and I fell for it.

While Carly's at school, Jack comes to the house with a sheriff to collect her things. He's won but doesn't gloat. I'm too destroyed to even spit my venom at him. I climb into bed and don't come out for nearly a week except to go to the bathroom and call in sick. The days inch by, measured with the agony of losing my child.

The days metamorphosize into weeks and I must face work again. Sam calls, but I hardly have the strength to talk to him and, according to my lawyer, I can't afford to be seen with him until his divorce is final. Of course, there are inevitable problems and delays as property debates get lengthy and loud. Sam seems to call less often but says he's very busy. I don't blame him. I'm not exactly thrilling to talk to anymore.

My career turns into a job; the days merely tick by until they're over. Bills to pay and lawyer fees hemorrhaging from a severed vein give me the incentive to continue. Given my proven instability the judge curbs visitation and I won't be able to see Carly until Christmas. I talked with her on the phone. She seems adjusted but misses her mom. I don't let on how miserable I am without her. Trying to be cheerful with her on the phone exhausts me. The weeks now transform themselves into months.

Three months later and I am looking forward to seeing Carly in a few weeks. Sam calls in the afternoon and we have a good talk. I feel the worst is over and time has healed some of my more gaping wounds. I feel hope again and my courage is returning. At the end of the week, Sam calls early in the morning waking me up.

"What's wrong Sam?" I know he wouldn't call so early unless it was important.

He sounds guilty. "I saw Jamie yesterday afternoon."

"You did? What did she want?" I ask the first knot in my stomach already tied up tight.

"She wants to get back together," he announces. "She misses me. I told her it wouldn't work unless she's willing to forgive everything."

"Sam, what are you saying?" I already know the answer.

Sam hesitates. "I miss her, Hannah. I know our marriage wasn't perfect, but we understood each other, and we're comfortable with each other."

"That's not a reason to stay married." I try to undo the inevitable.

"I'm sorry, Hannah. I wish things had turned out differently. I pray you get Carly back. I hope you have a good life."

"Wait! You mean you're saying goodbye? You're saying we're through? Why, Sam?" I ask desperately.

"I still love her, Hannah," he says, his voice nearly a whisper. "I wouldn't fit into your world. I need to stay here where I belong with my friends and where I'm comfortable. I'm sorry if I hurt you. I never should have toyed with your emotions." He pauses. "I guess I've always loved you Hannah and I know I always will, but I have to get on with my life and my life is here,"

I feel him slip from my grasp. "I love you, Sam." That is all I can manage to say. "I'll always love you."

"Goodbye, Hannah." And with that, he's gone and the vacuum he leaves behind is cold and silent.

It's been three years now since I lost Carly and Sam. I lost the permanent custody hearing. After another year I ran out of money and didn't pursue it any further. In the end, I let it go because it seemed like just punishment for being so stupid and naive about Jack and Sam. I have looked at my love for Sam from every angle and the pain is all I ever see. Sometimes though, for a moment, I catch glimpses of the love he felt for me and feel reassured it wasn't all my imagination. In the next fleeting moment, however, I see Carly's face and know the price was too high.

I find my life has a predictable, if not tolerable, pattern. I often go downtown to window shop during the late summer days to pass the time. On this particular Sunday afternoon, standing on the sidewalk outside an upscale department store, I see a beautiful crystal elephant displayed in the window. It turns slowly on a motorized pedestal and catches the sun's reflection until it almost seems alive. I stand mesmerized by the sight. Someone behind me calls my name. There is no mistaking the voice, it's Sam.